NANCY DREW

girl detective ®

P9-BYY-105

P9-DOE-133

PAPERCUT Z™

0 45395481

CA

NANCY DREW
girl detective®

Graphic Novels
Available from Papercutz

#1 The Demon of River Heights
#2 Writ In Stone
#3 The Haunted Dollhouse
#4 The Girl Who Wasn't There
#5 The Fake Heir
#6 Mr. Cheeters Is Missing (coming August 2006)

$7.95 each in paperback
$12.95 each in hardcover

Please add $3.00 for postage and handling for the first book, add $1.00 for each additional book.

Send for our catalog:
Papercutz
555 Eighth Avenue, Suite 1202
New York, NY 10018
www.papercutz.com

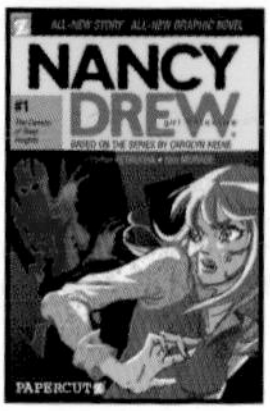
NANCY
DREW

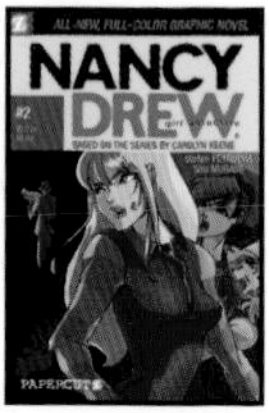
NANCY
DREW

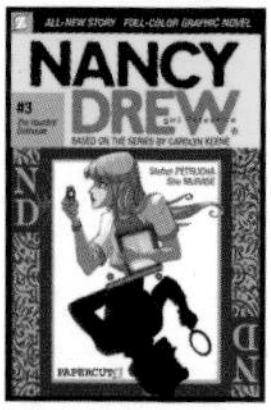
NANCY
DREW

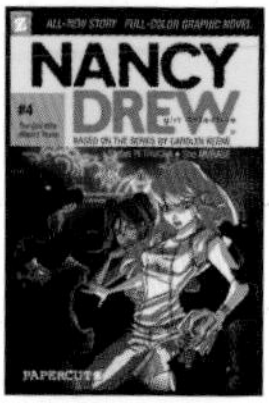
NANCY
DREW

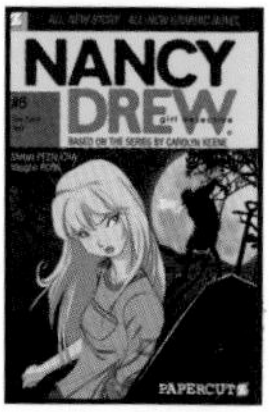
NANCY
DREW

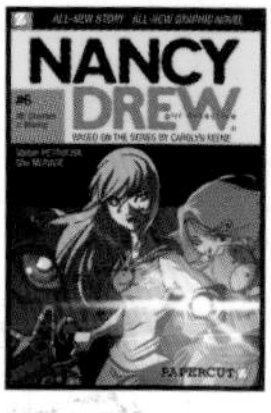
NANCY
DREW

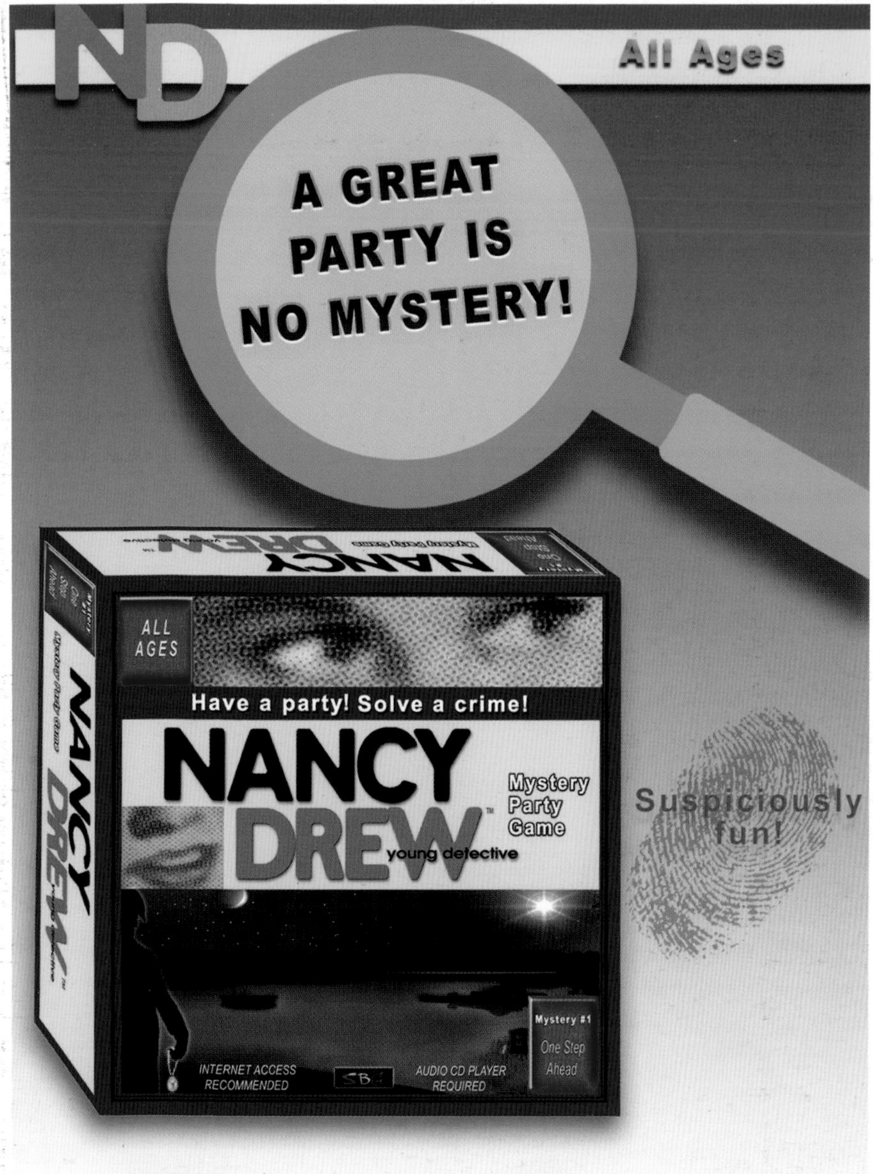
ND
All Ages
A GREAT PARTY IS NO MYSTERY!
ALL AGES
Have a party! Solve a crime!
NANCY DREW™ young detective
Mystery Party Game
Mystery #1 One Step Ahead
INTERNET ACCESS RECOMMENDED
SBG
AUDIO CD PLAYER REQUIRED
Suspiciously fun!

NANCY DREW

girl detective

#5

®

The Fake Heir

STEFAN PETRUCHA • Writer
DANIEL VAUGHN ROSS • Artist
with 3D CG elements by LUIS LUNDGREN
Cover, preview pages, and art direction by SHO MURASE
Based on the series by
CAROLYN KEENE

New York

The Fake Heir
STEFAN PETRUCHA – Writer
DANIEL VAUGHN ROSS – Artist
with 3D CG elements by LUIS LUNDGREN
BRYAN SENKA – Letterer
CARLOS JOSE GUZMAN – Colorist
JIM SALICRUP
Editor-in-Chief

project sunshine
bringing sunshine to a cloudy day℠

Nancy Drew volunteers with Project Sunshine.
Project Sunshine is a nonprofit organization that provides free
services to children and families affected by medical challenges.
We send volunteers to hospitals to provide arts and crafts, tutoring
and other special services. For more information on Project
Sunshine please visit www.projectsunshine.org.

ISBN 10: 1-59707-024-6 paperback edition
ISBN 13: 978-1-59707-024-9 paperback edition
ISBN 10: 1-59707-025-4 hardcover edition
ISBN 13: 978-1-59707-025-6 hardcover edition

Printed in China.
Distributed by Holtzbrinck Publishers.

10 9 8 7 6 5 4 3 2 1

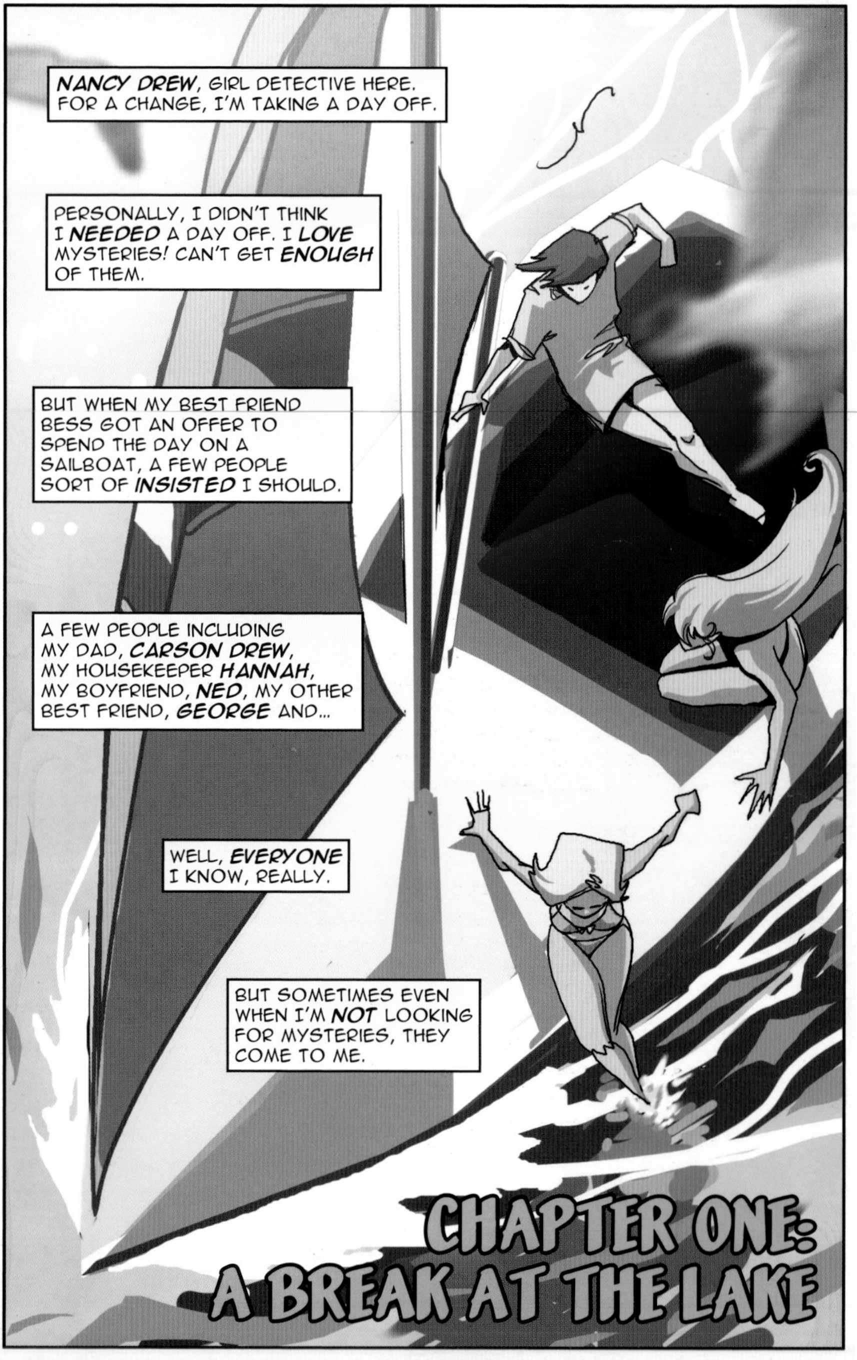
NANCY DREW, GIRL DETECTIVE HERE. FOR A CHANGE, I'M TAKING A DAY OFF.
PERSONALLY, I DIDN'T THINK I NEEDED A DAY OFF. I LOVE MYSTERIES! CAN'T GET ENOUGH OF THEM.
BUT WHEN MY BEST FRIEND BESS GOT AN OFFER TO SPEND THE DAY ON A SAILBOAT, A FEW PEOPLE SORT OF INSISTED I SHOULD.
A FEW PEOPLE INCLUDING MY DAD, CARSON DREW, MY HOUSEKEEPER HANNAH, MY BOYFRIEND, NED, MY OTHER BEST FRIEND, GEORGE AND...
WELL, EVERYONE I KNOW, REALLY.
BUT SOMETIMES EVEN WHEN I'M NOT LOOKING FOR MYSTERIES, THEY COME TO ME.
CHAPTER ONE: A BREAK AT THE LAKE

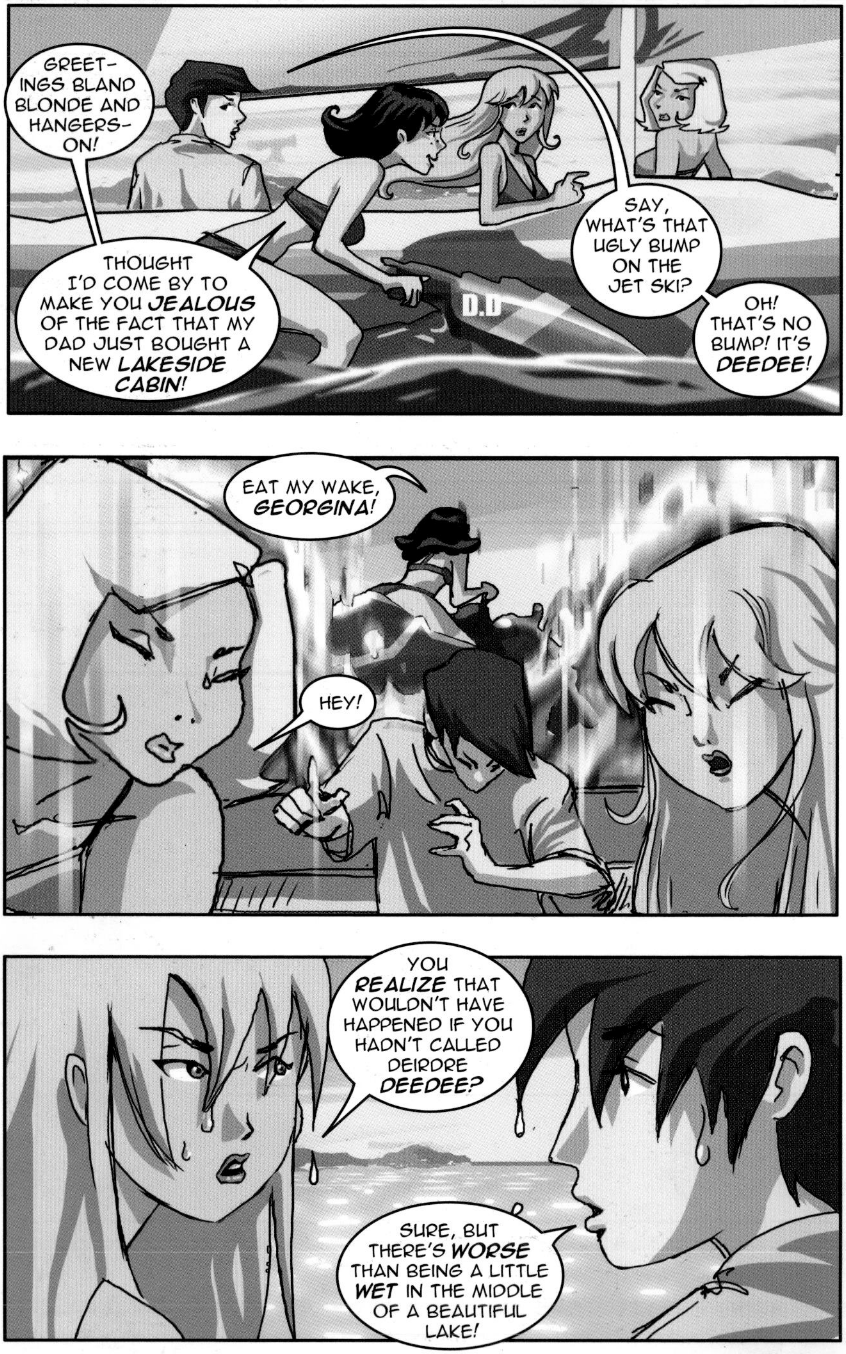
GREETINGS BLAND BLONDE AND HANGERS-ON!
THOUGHT I'D COME BY TO MAKE YOU JEALOUS OF THE FACT THAT MY DAD JUST BOUGHT A NEW LAKESIDE CABIN!
D.D
SAY, WHAT'S THAT UGLY BUMP ON THE JET SKI?
OH! THAT'S NO BUMP! IT'S DEEDEE!
EAT MY WAKE, GEORGINA!
HEY!
YOU REALIZE THAT WOULDN'T HAVE HAPPENED IF YOU HADN'T CALLED DEIRDRE DEEDEE?
SURE, BUT THERE'S WORSE THAN BEING A LITTLE WET IN THE MIDDLE OF A BEAUTIFUL LAKE!

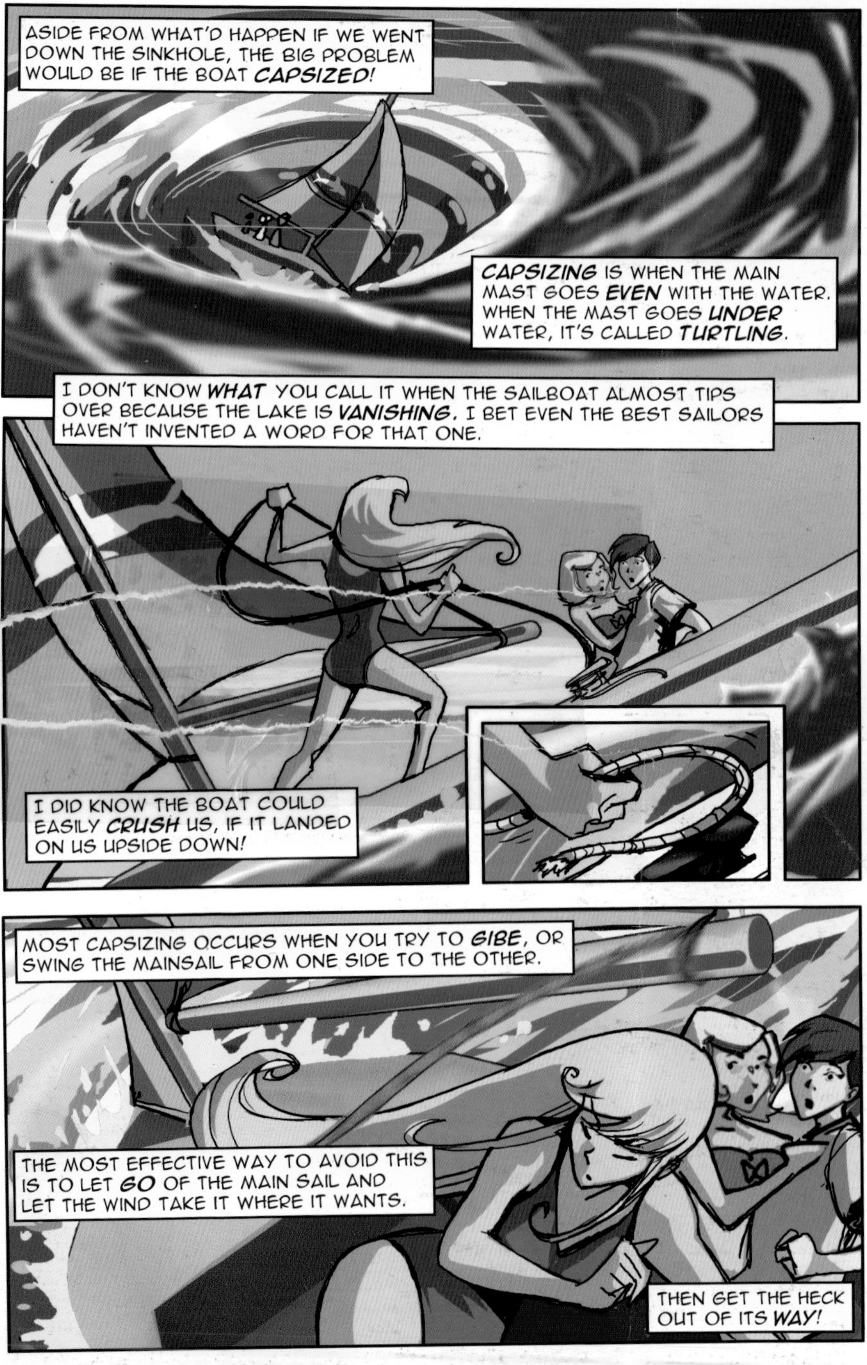
ASIDE FROM WHAT'D HAPPEN IF WE WENT DOWN THE SINKHOLE, THE BIG PROBLEM WOULD BE IF THE BOAT CAPSIZED!
CAPSIZING IS WHEN THE MAIN MAST GOES EVEN WITH THE WATER. WHEN THE MAST GOES UNDER WATER, IT'S CALLED TURTLING.
I DON'T KNOW WHAT YOU CALL IT WHEN THE SAILBOAT ALMOST TIPS OVER BECAUSE THE LAKE IS VANISHING. I BET EVEN THE BEST SAILORS HAVEN'T INVENTED A WORD FOR THAT ONE.
I DID KNOW THE BOAT COULD EASILY CRUSH US, IF IT LANDED ON US UPSIDE DOWN!
MOST CAPSIZING OCCURS WHEN YOU TRY TO GIBE, OR SWING THE MAINSAIL FROM ONE SIDE TO THE OTHER.
THE MOST EFFECTIVE WAY TO AVOID THIS IS TO LET GO OF THE MAIN SAIL AND LET THE WIND TAKE IT WHERE IT WANTS.
THEN GET THE HECK OUT OF ITS WAY!

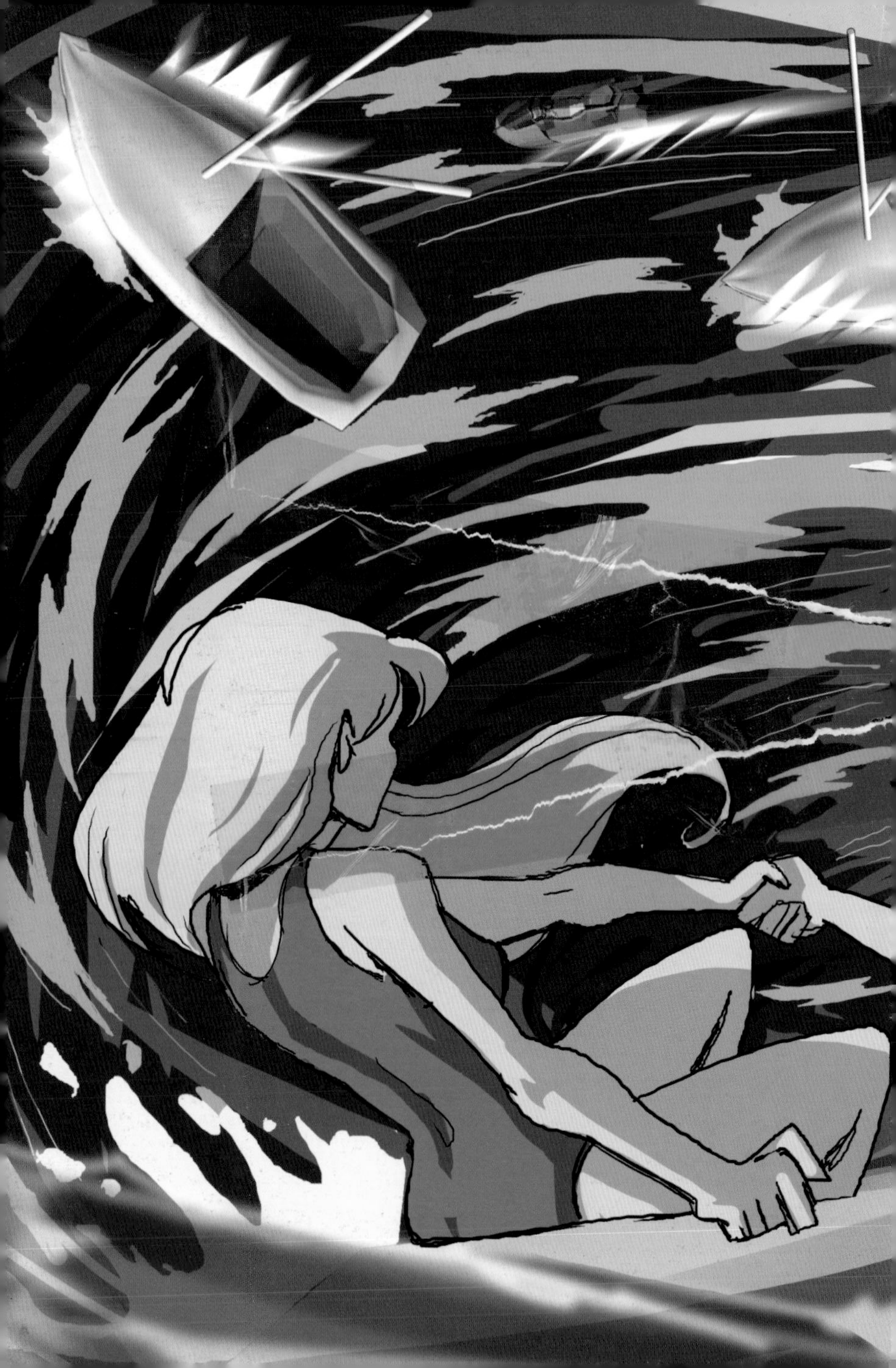

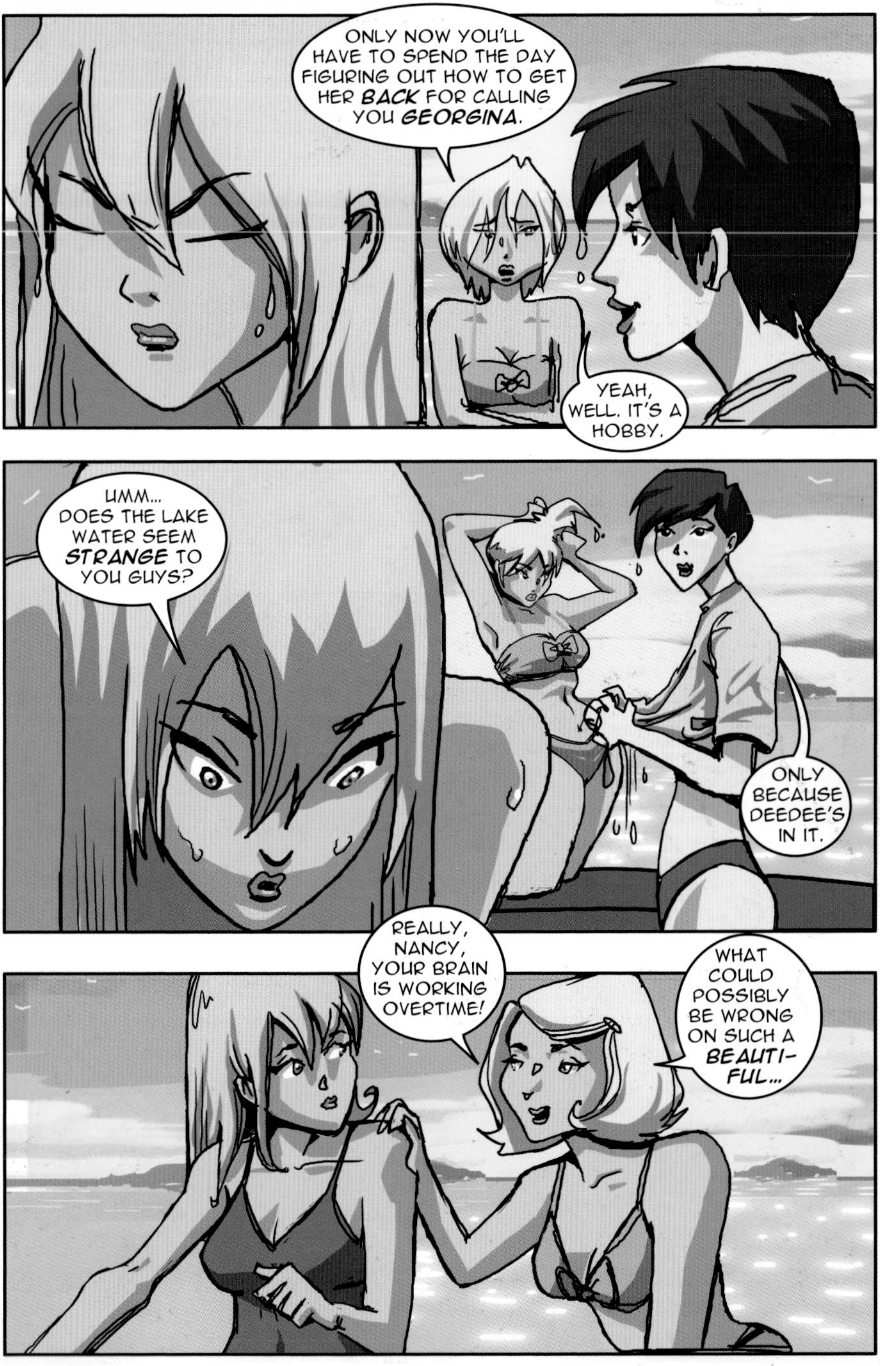
ONLY NOW YOU'LL HAVE TO SPEND THE DAY FIGURING OUT HOW TO GET HER BACK FOR CALLING YOU GEORGINA.
YEAH, WELL. IT'S A HOBBY.
UMM... DOES THE LAKE WATER SEEM STRANGE TO YOU GUYS?
ONLY BECAUSE DEEDEE'S IN IT.
REALLY, NANCY, YOUR BRAIN IS WORKING OVERTIME!
WHAT COULD POSSIBLY BE WRONG ON SUCH A BEAUTI-FUL...

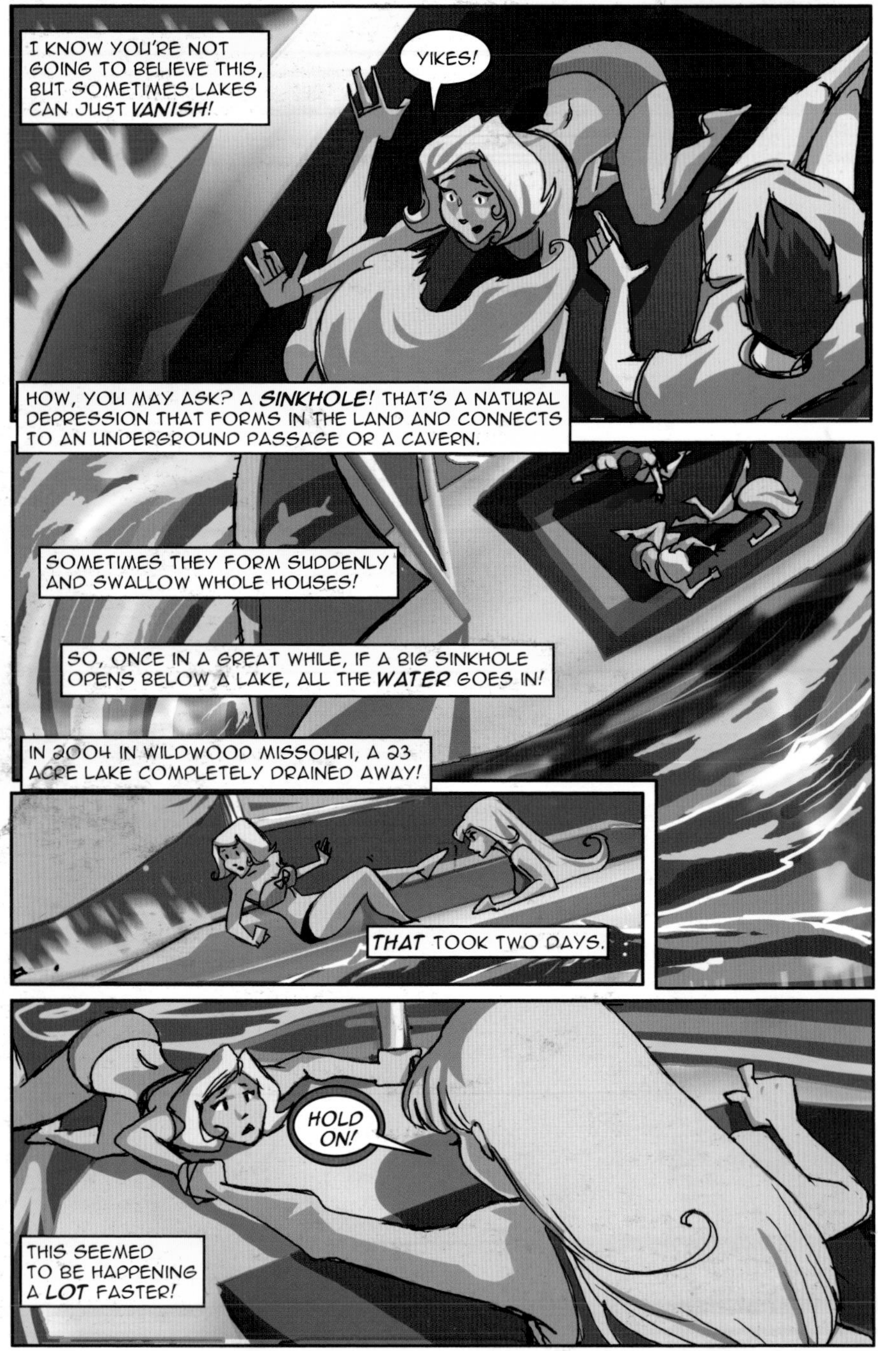
I KNOW YOU'RE NOT GOING TO BELIEVE THIS, BUT SOMETIMES LAKES CAN JUST VANISH!
YIKES!
HOW, YOU MAY ASK? A SINKHOLE! THAT'S A NATURAL DEPRESSION THAT FORMS IN THE LAND AND CONNECTS TO AN UNDERGROUND PASSAGE OR A CAVERN.
SOMETIMES THEY FORM SUDDENLY AND SWALLOW WHOLE HOUSES!
SO, ONCE IN A GREAT WHILE, IF A BIG SINKHOLE OPENS BELOW A LAKE, ALL THE WATER GOES IN!
IN 2004 IN WILDWOOD MISSOURI, A 23 ACRE LAKE COMPLETELY DRAINED AWAY!
THAT TOOK TWO DAYS.
HOLD ON!
THIS SEEMED TO BE HAPPENING A LOT FASTER!

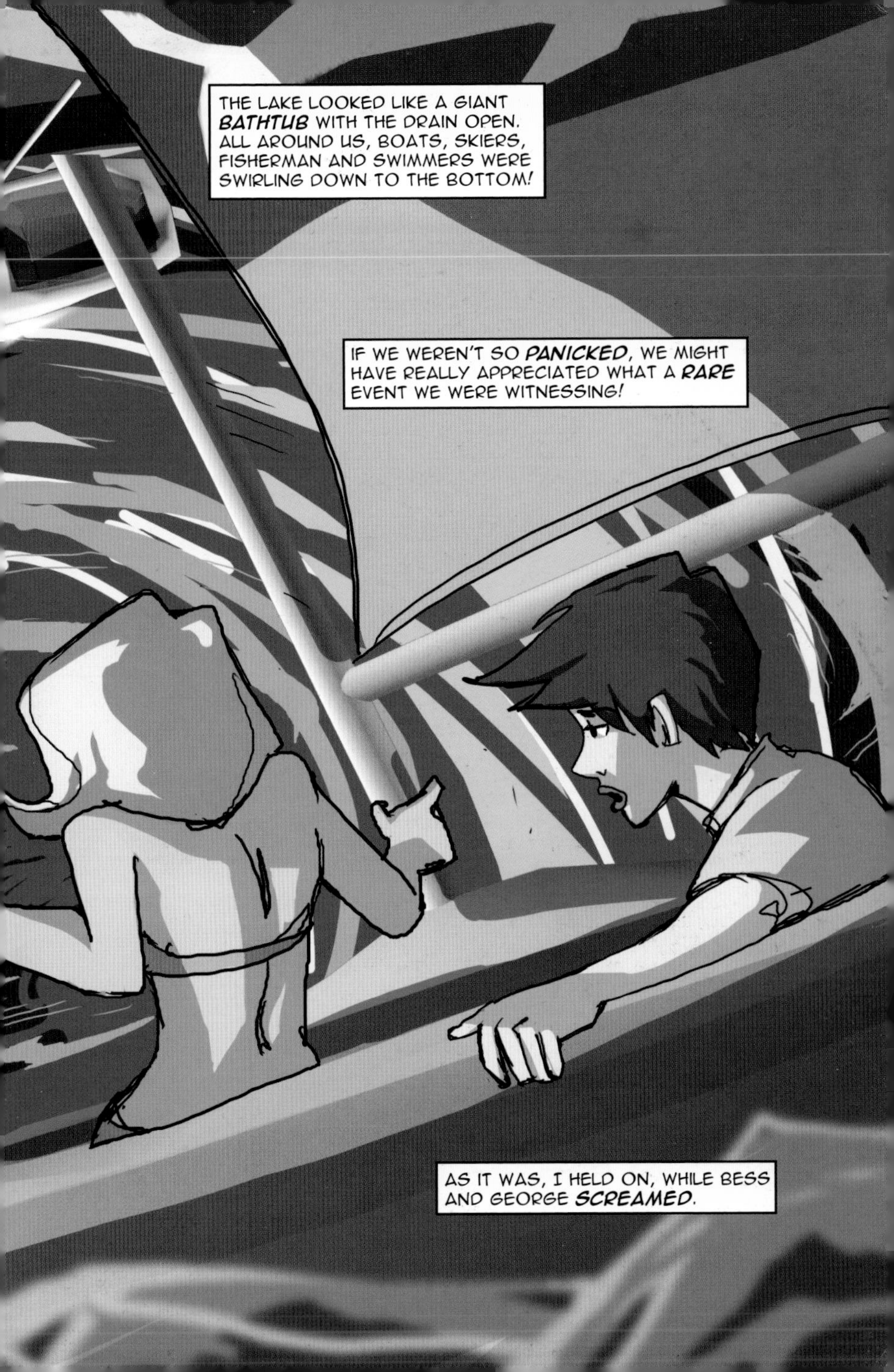
THE LAKE LOOKED LIKE A GIANT BATHTUB WITH THE DRAIN OPEN. ALL AROUND US, BOATS, SKIERS, FISHERMAN AND SWIMMERS WERE SWIRLING DOWN TO THE BOTTOM!
IF WE WEREN'T SO PANICKED, WE MIGHT HAVE REALLY APPRECIATED WHAT A RARE EVENT WE WERE WITNESSING!
AS IT WAS, I HELD ON, WHILE BESS AND GEORGE SCREAMED.

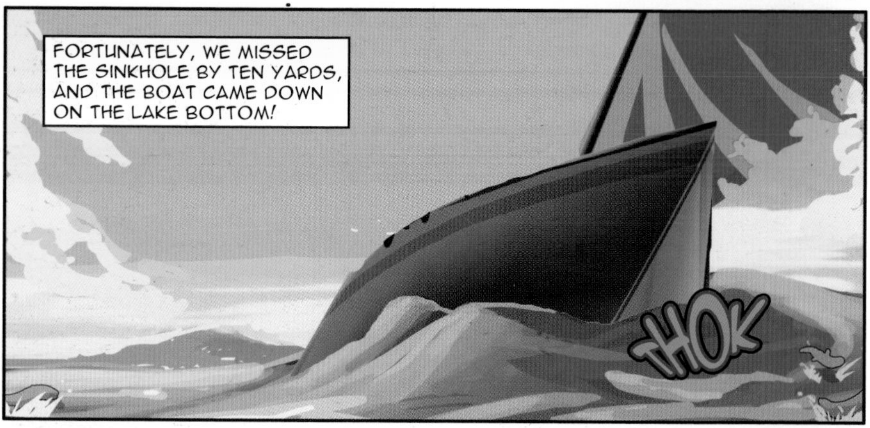
FORTUNATELY, WE MISSED THE SINKHOLE BY TEN YARDS, AND THE BOAT CAME DOWN ON THE LAKE BOTTOM!
THOK

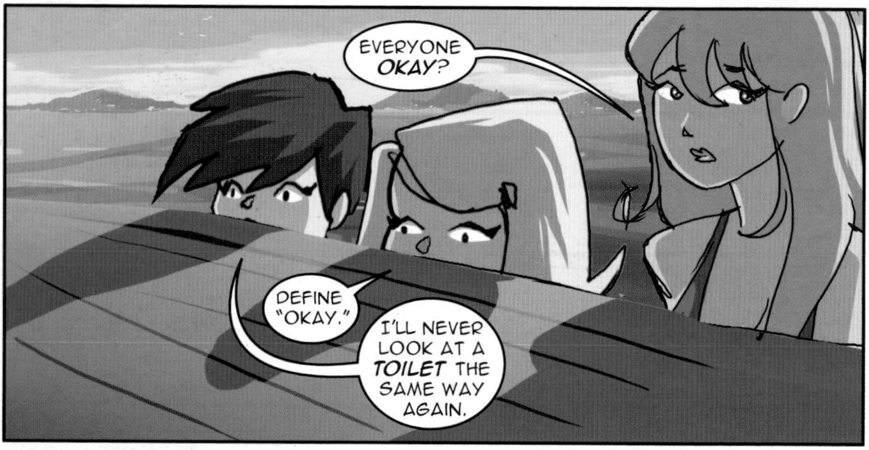
EVERYONE OKAY?
DEFINE "OKAY."
I'LL NEVER LOOK AT A TOILET THE SAME WAY AGAIN.

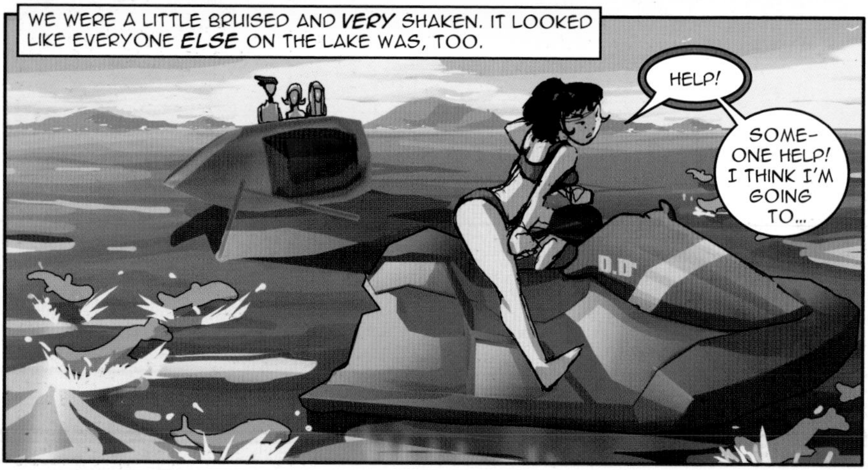
WE WERE A LITTLE BRUISED AND VERY SHAKEN. IT LOOKED LIKE EVERYONE ELSE ON THE LAKE WAS, TOO.
HELP!
SOME-ONE HELP! I THINK I'M GOING TO...
D.D

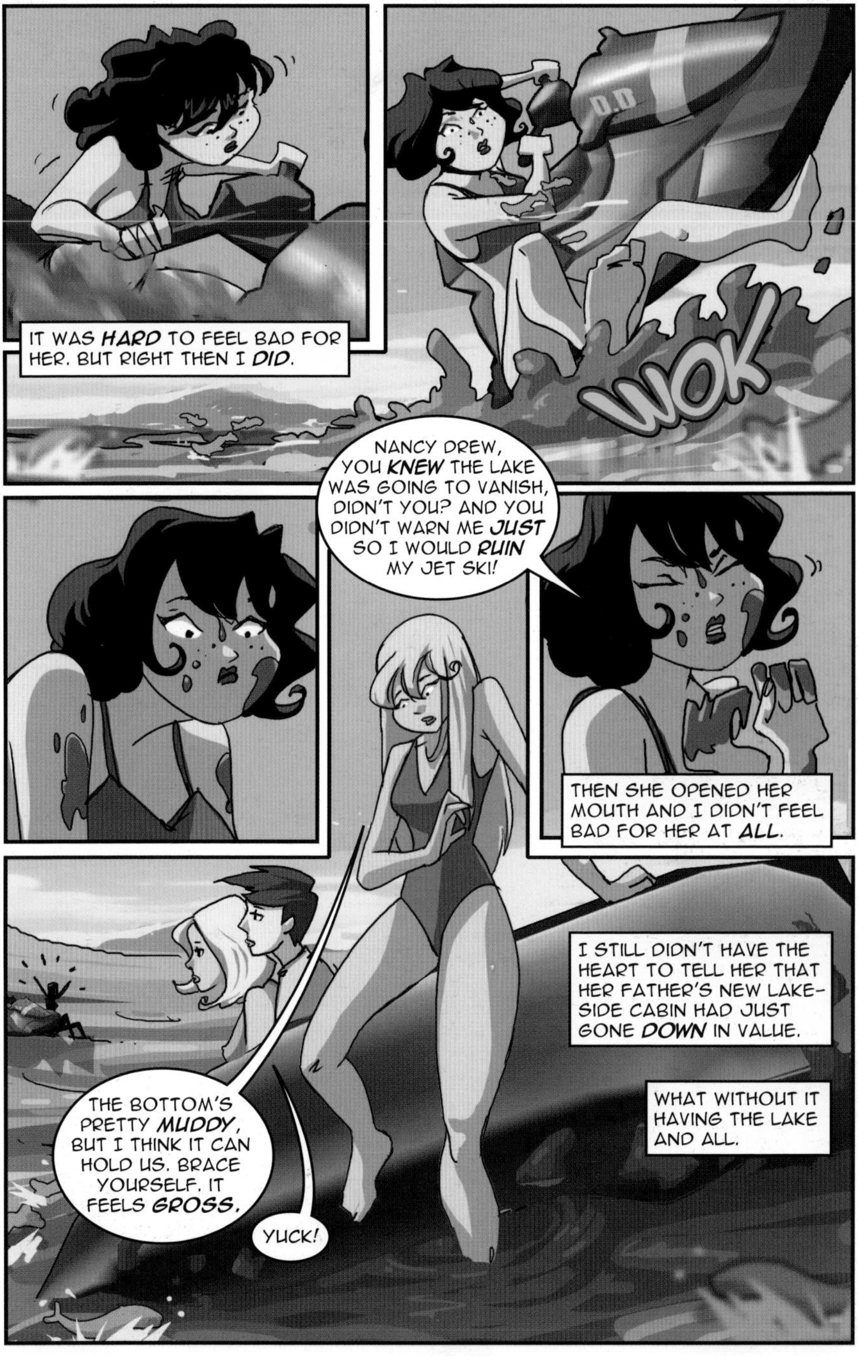
IT WAS HARD TO FEEL BAD FOR HER. BUT RIGHT THEN I DID.
WOK
NANCY DREW, YOU KNEW THE LAKE WAS GOING TO VANISH, DIDN'T YOU? AND YOU DIDN'T WARN ME JUST SO I WOULD RUIN MY JET SKI!
THEN SHE OPENED HER MOUTH AND I DIDN'T FEEL BAD FOR HER AT ALL.
I STILL DIDN'T HAVE THE HEART TO TELL HER THAT HER FATHER'S NEW LAKE-SIDE CABIN HAD JUST GONE DOWN IN VALUE.
WHAT WITHOUT IT HAVING THE LAKE AND ALL.
THE BOTTOM'S PRETTY MUDDY, BUT I THINK IT CAN HOLD US. BRACE YOURSELF. IT FEELS GROSS.
YUCK!

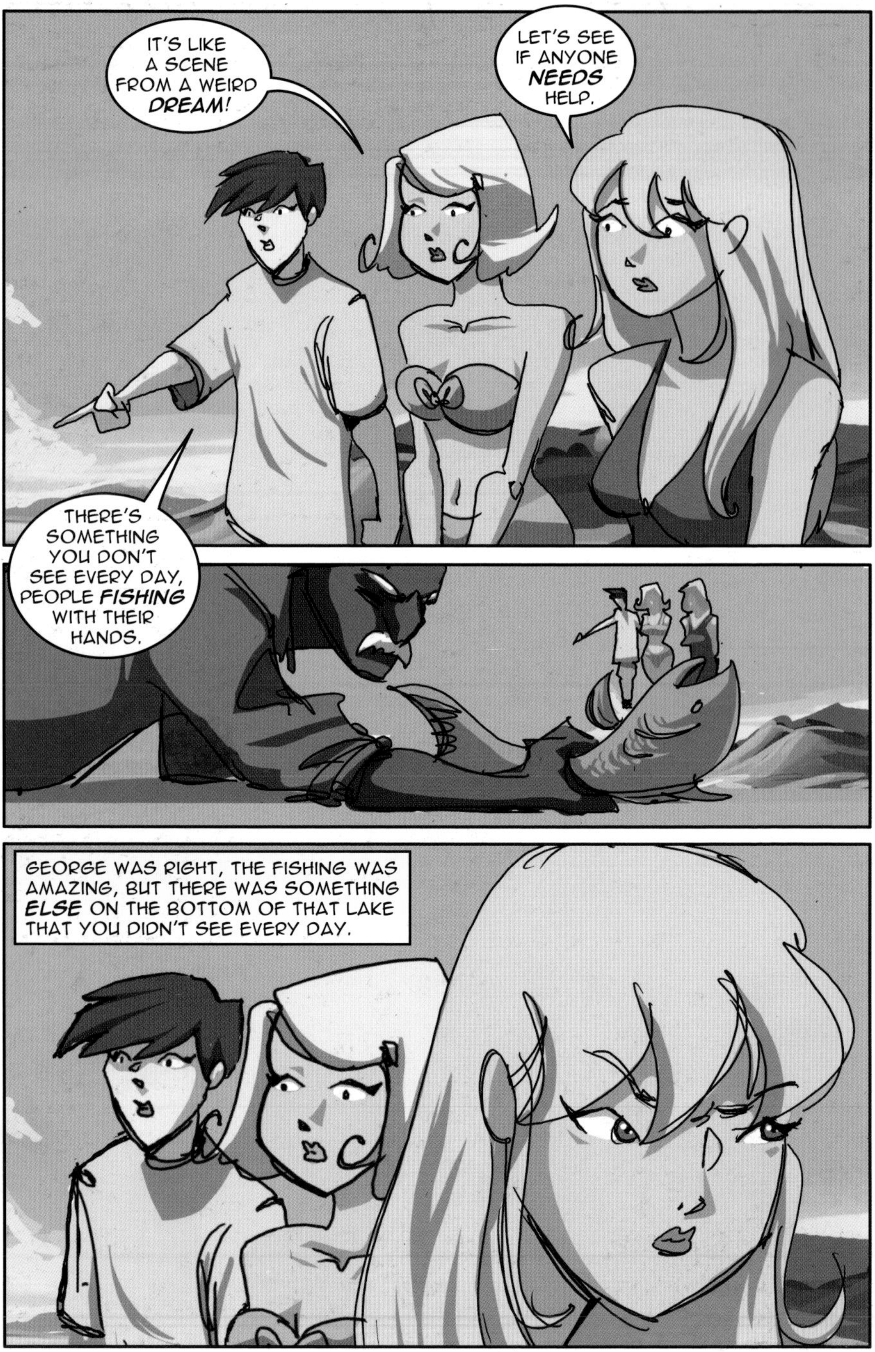
IT'S LIKE A SCENE FROM A WEIRD *DREAM*!
LET'S SEE IF ANYONE ***NEEDS*** HELP.
THERE'S SOMETHING YOU DON'T SEE EVERY DAY, PEOPLE ***FISHING*** WITH THEIR HANDS.
GEORGE WAS RIGHT, THE FISHING WAS AMAZING, BUT THERE WAS SOMETHING ***ELSE*** ON THE BOTTOM OF THAT LAKE THAT YOU DIDN'T SEE EVERY DAY.

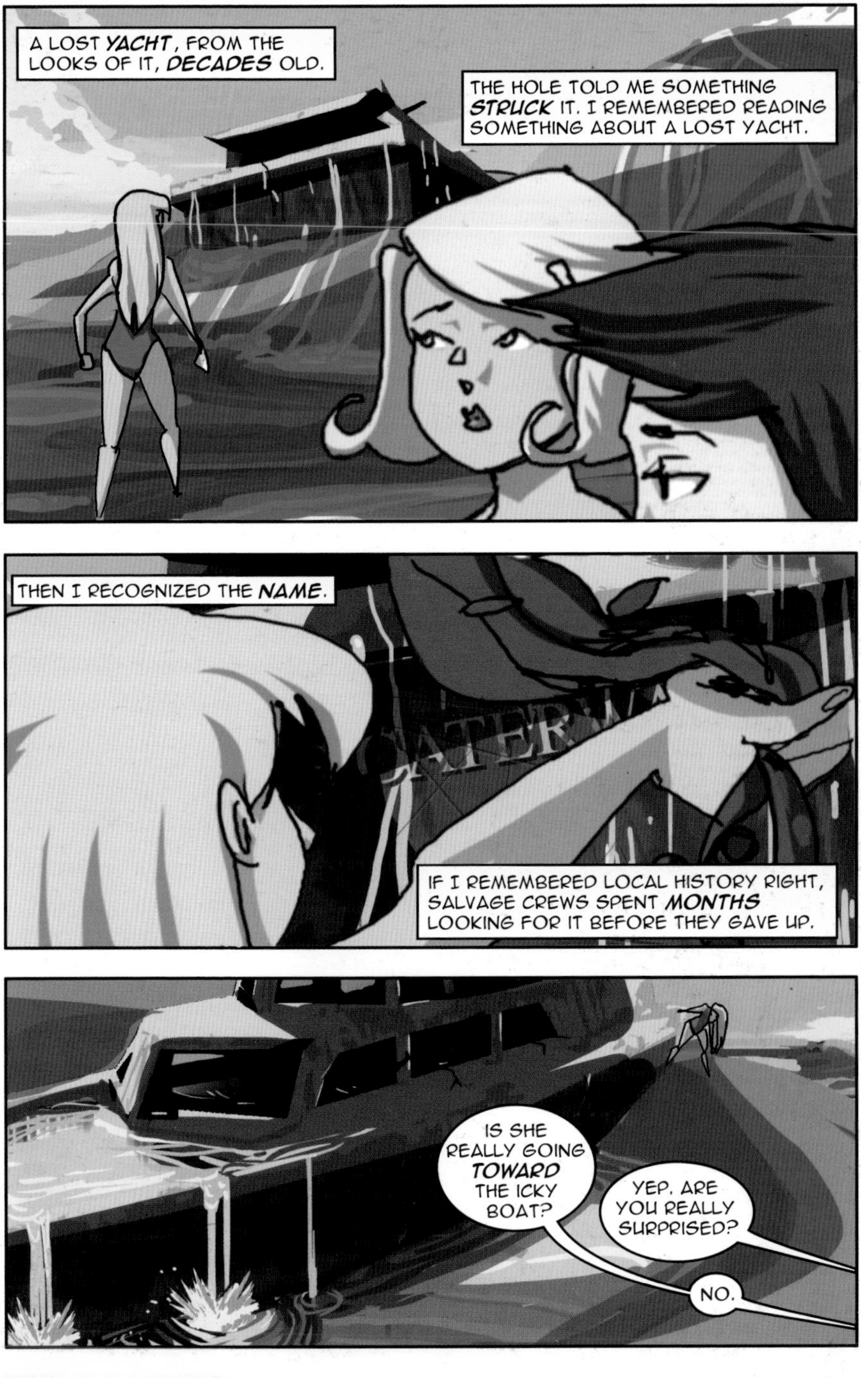
A LOST YACHT, FROM THE LOOKS OF IT, DECADES OLD.
THE HOLE TOLD ME SOMETHING STRUCK IT. I REMEMBERED READING SOMETHING ABOUT A LOST YACHT.
THEN I RECOGNIZED THE NAME.
IF I REMEMBERED LOCAL HISTORY RIGHT, SALVAGE CREWS SPENT MONTHS LOOKING FOR IT BEFORE THEY GAVE UP.
IS SHE REALLY GOING TOWARD THE ICKY BOAT?
YEP. ARE YOU REALLY SURPRISED?
NO.

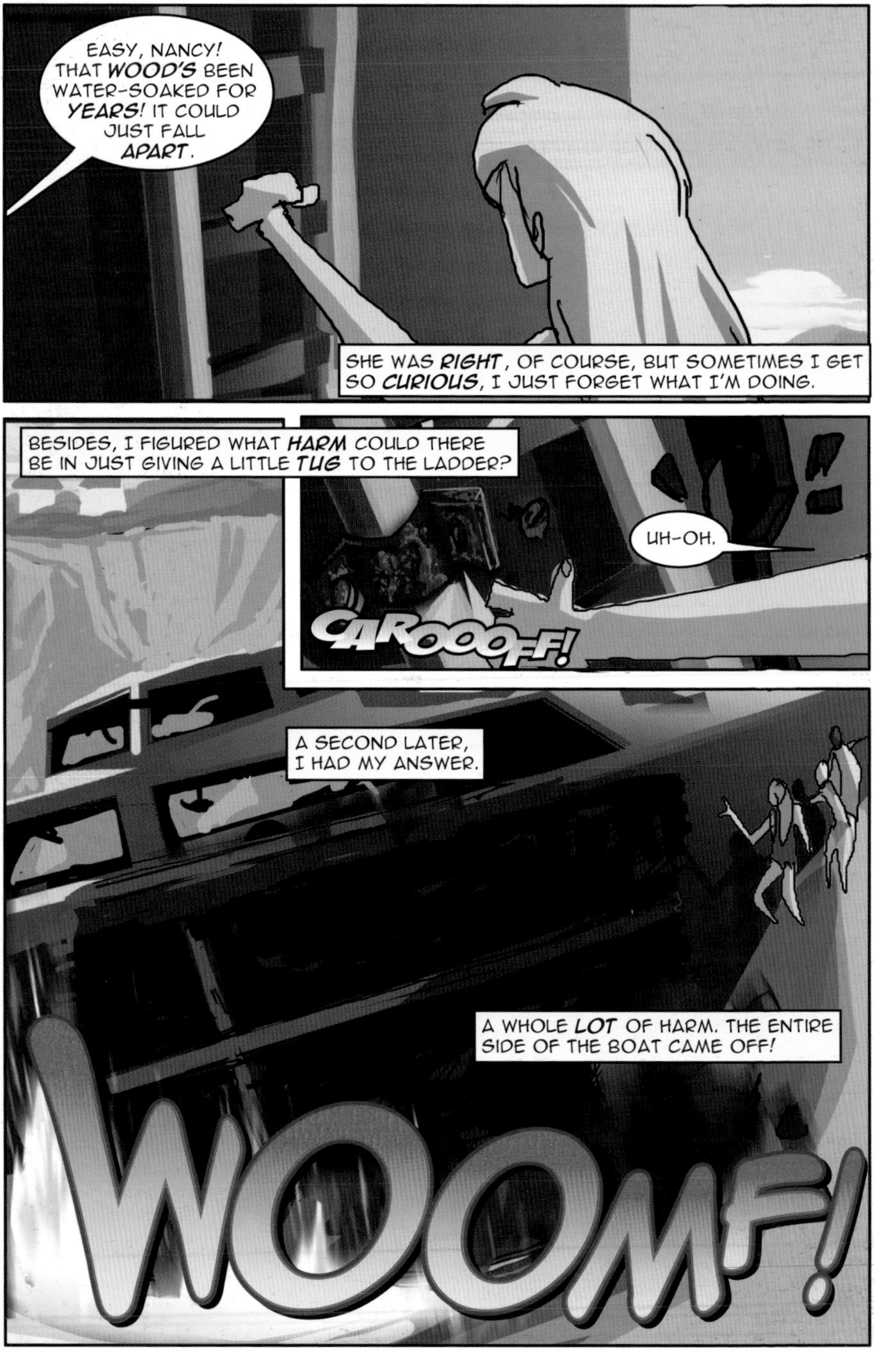
EASY, NANCY! THAT WOOD'S BEEN WATER-SOAKED FOR YEARS! IT COULD JUST FALL APART.
SHE WAS RIGHT, OF COURSE, BUT SOMETIMES I GET SO CURIOUS, I JUST FORGET WHAT I'M DOING.
BESIDES, I FIGURED WHAT HARM COULD THERE BE IN JUST GIVING A LITTLE TUG TO THE LADDER?
UH-OH.
CAROOOFF!
A SECOND LATER, I HAD MY ANSWER.
A WHOLE LOT OF HARM. THE ENTIRE SIDE OF THE BOAT CAME OFF!
WOOMF!

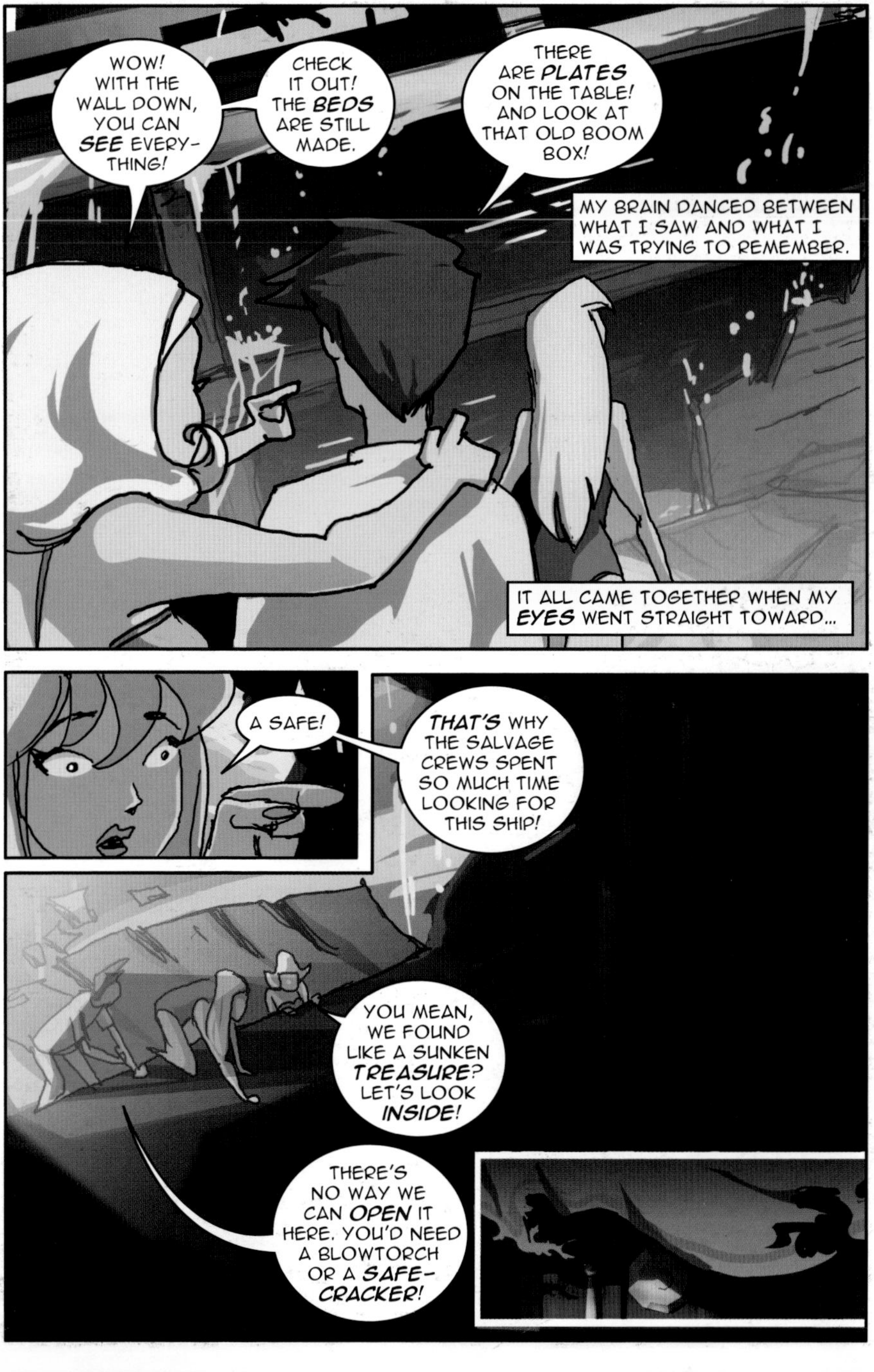
WOW! WITH THE WALL DOWN, YOU CAN SEE EVERY-THING!
CHECK IT OUT! THE BEDS ARE STILL MADE.
THERE ARE PLATES ON THE TABLE! AND LOOK AT THAT OLD BOOM BOX!
MY BRAIN DANCED BETWEEN WHAT I SAW AND WHAT I WAS TRYING TO REMEMBER.
IT ALL CAME TOGETHER WHEN MY EYES WENT STRAIGHT TOWARD...
A SAFE!
THAT'S WHY THE SALVAGE CREWS SPENT SO MUCH TIME LOOKING FOR THIS SHIP!
YOU MEAN, WE FOUND LIKE A SUNKEN TREASURE? LET'S LOOK INSIDE!
THERE'S NO WAY WE CAN OPEN IT HERE. YOU'D NEED A BLOWTORCH OR A SAFE-CRACKER!

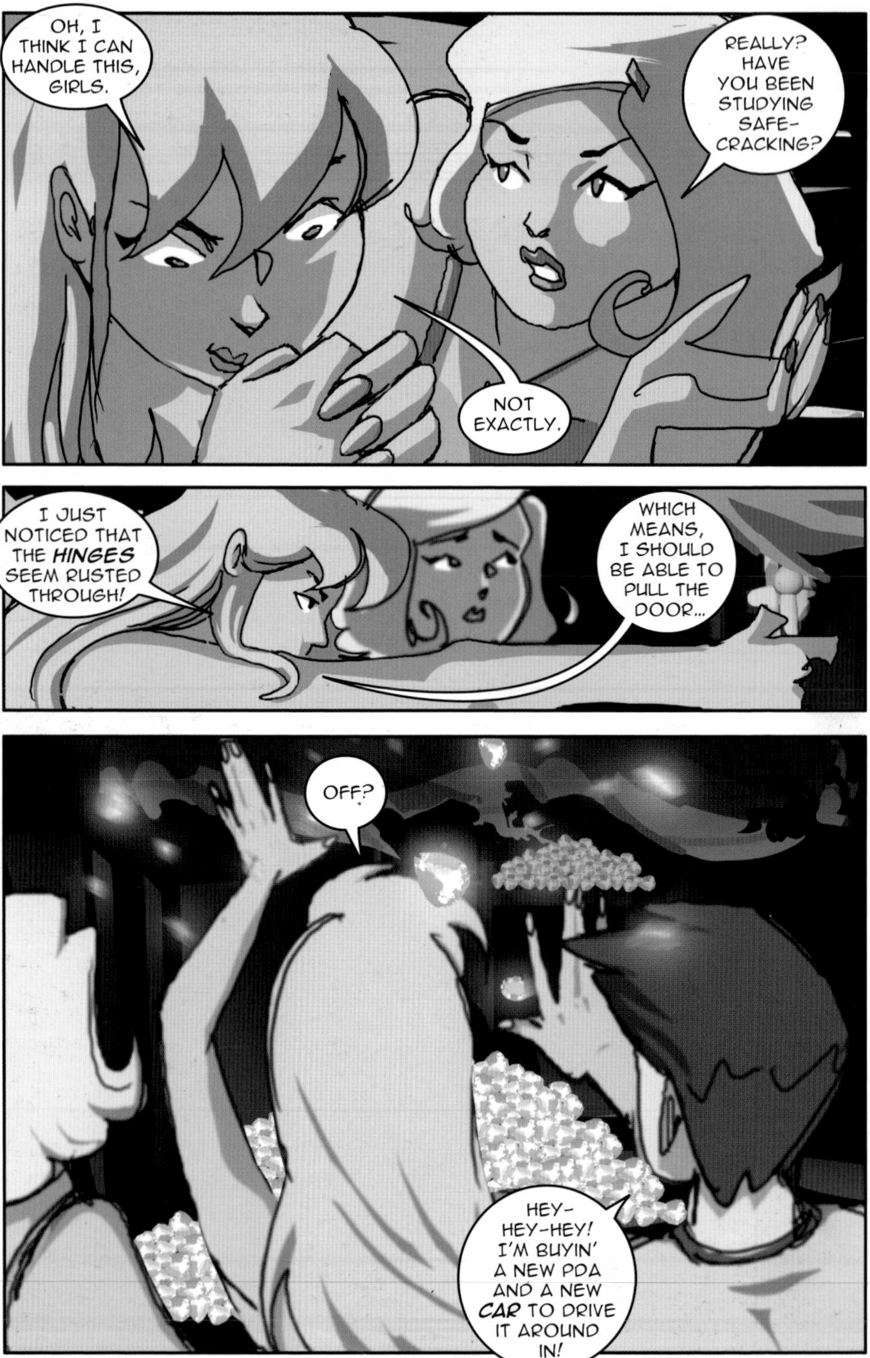

OH, I THINK I CAN HANDLE THIS, GIRLS.
REALLY? HAVE YOU BEEN STUDYING SAFE-CRACKING?
NOT EXACTLY.
I JUST NOTICED THAT THE HINGES SEEM RUSTED THROUGH!
WHICH MEANS, I SHOULD BE ABLE TO PULL THE DOOR...
OFF?
HEY-HEY-HEY! I'M BUYIN' A NEW PDA AND A NEW CAR TO DRIVE IT AROUND IN!

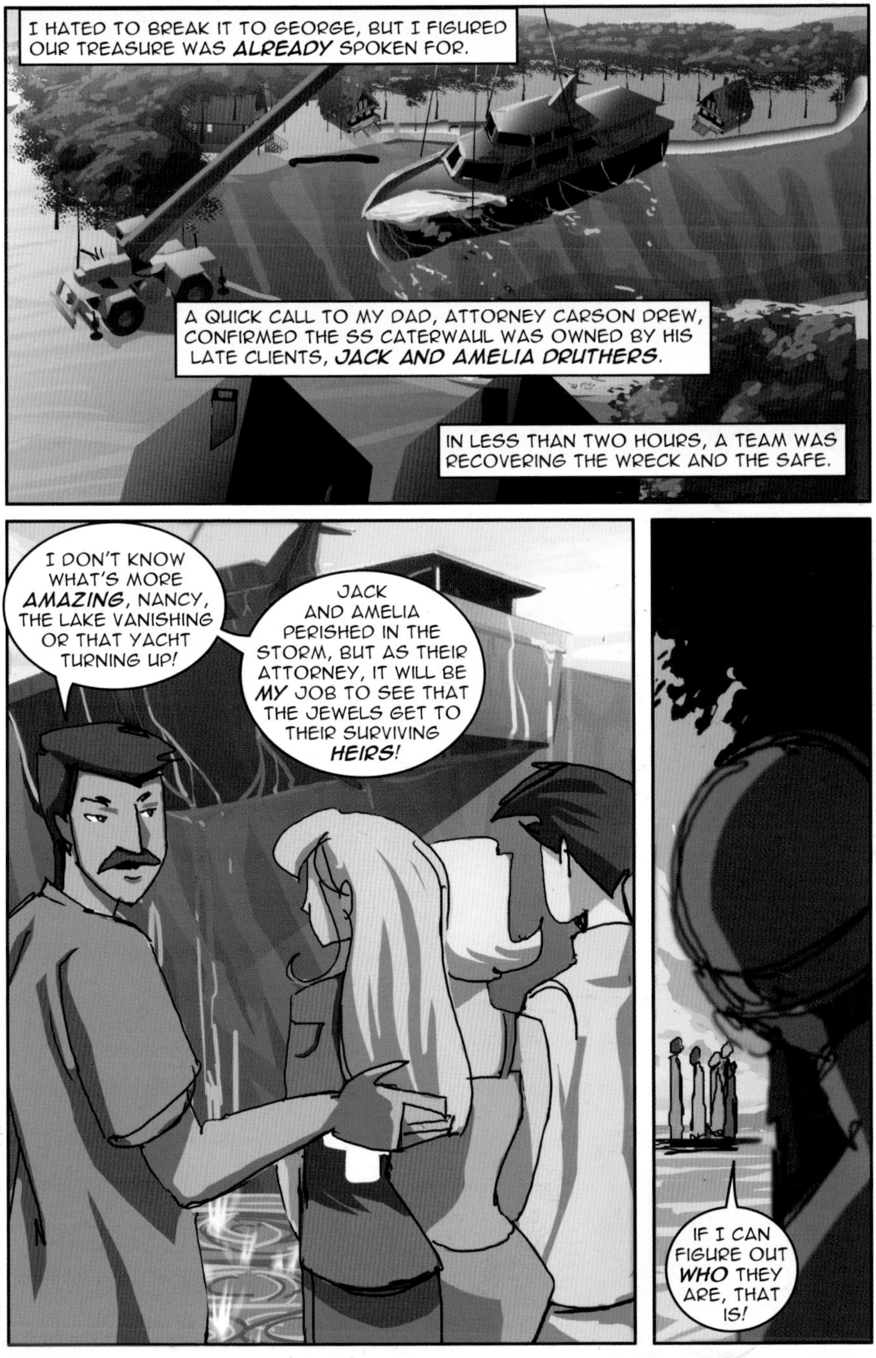
I HATED TO BREAK IT TO GEORGE, BUT I FIGURED OUR TREASURE WAS ALREADY SPOKEN FOR.
A QUICK CALL TO MY DAD, ATTORNEY CARSON DREW, CONFIRMED THE SS CATERWAUL WAS OWNED BY HIS LATE CLIENTS, JACK AND AMELIA DRUTHERS.
IN LESS THAN TWO HOURS, A TEAM WAS RECOVERING THE WRECK AND THE SAFE.
I DON'T KNOW WHAT'S MORE AMAZING, NANCY, THE LAKE VANISHING OR THAT YACHT TURNING UP!
JACK AND AMELIA PERISHED IN THE STORM, BUT AS THEIR ATTORNEY, IT WILL BE MY JOB TO SEE THAT THE JEWELS GET TO THEIR SURVIVING HEIRS!
IF I CAN FIGURE OUT WHO THEY ARE, THAT IS!

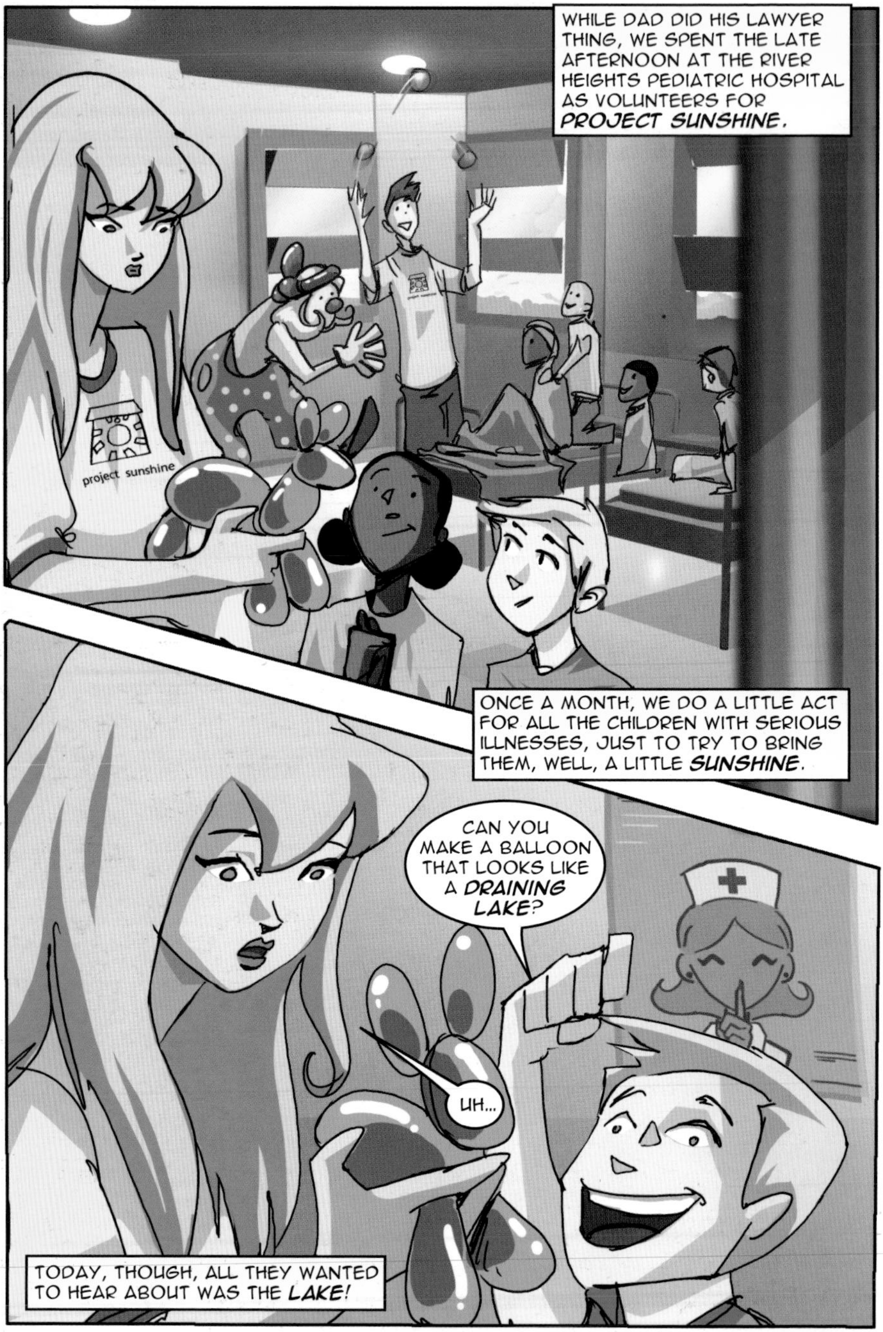
WHILE DAD DID HIS LAWYER THING, WE SPENT THE LATE AFTERNOON AT THE RIVER HEIGHTS PEDIATRIC HOSPITAL AS VOLUNTEERS FOR PROJECT SUNSHINE.
project sunshine
ONCE A MONTH, WE DO A LITTLE ACT FOR ALL THE CHILDREN WITH SERIOUS ILLNESSES, JUST TO TRY TO BRING THEM, WELL, A LITTLE SUNSHINE.
CAN YOU MAKE A BALLOON THAT LOOKS LIKE A DRAINING LAKE?
UH...
TODAY, THOUGH, ALL THEY WANTED TO HEAR ABOUT WAS THE LAKE!

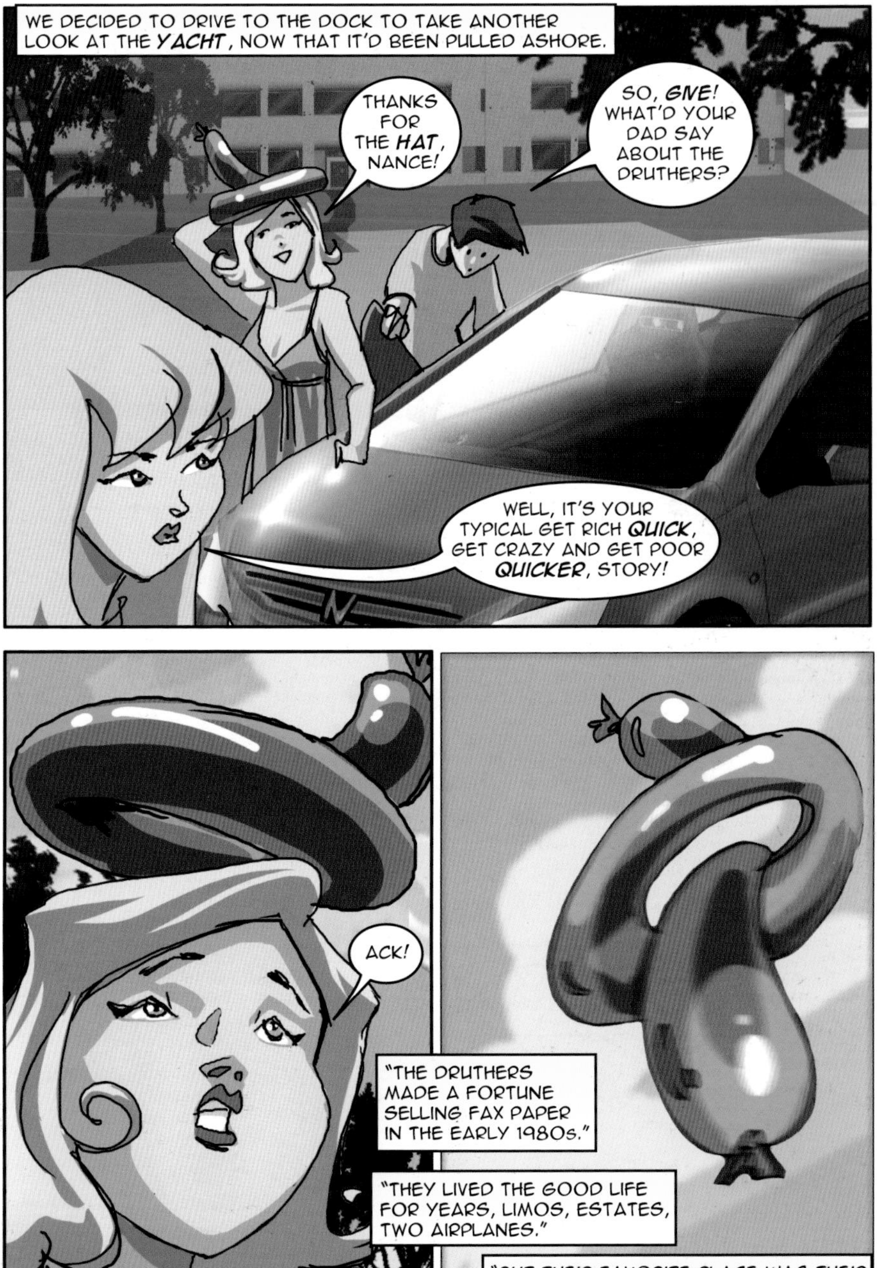
WE DECIDED TO DRIVE TO THE DOCK TO TAKE ANOTHER LOOK AT THE *YACHT*, NOW THAT IT'D BEEN PULLED ASHORE.
THANKS FOR THE **HAT**, NANCE!
SO, **GIVE**! WHAT'D YOUR DAD SAY ABOUT THE DRUTHERS?
WELL, IT'S YOUR TYPICAL GET RICH **QUICK**, GET CRAZY AND GET POOR **QUICKER**, STORY!
ACK!
"THE DRUTHERS MADE A FORTUNE SELLING FAX PAPER IN THE EARLY 1980s."
"THEY LIVED THE GOOD LIFE FOR YEARS, LIMOS, ESTATES, TWO AIRPLANES."
"BUT THEIR FAVORITE PLACE WAS THEIR YACHT, THE **CATERWAUL**. THEY WERE ON IT NEARLY EVERY DAY, MOVING IT FROM LAKE TO LAKE."

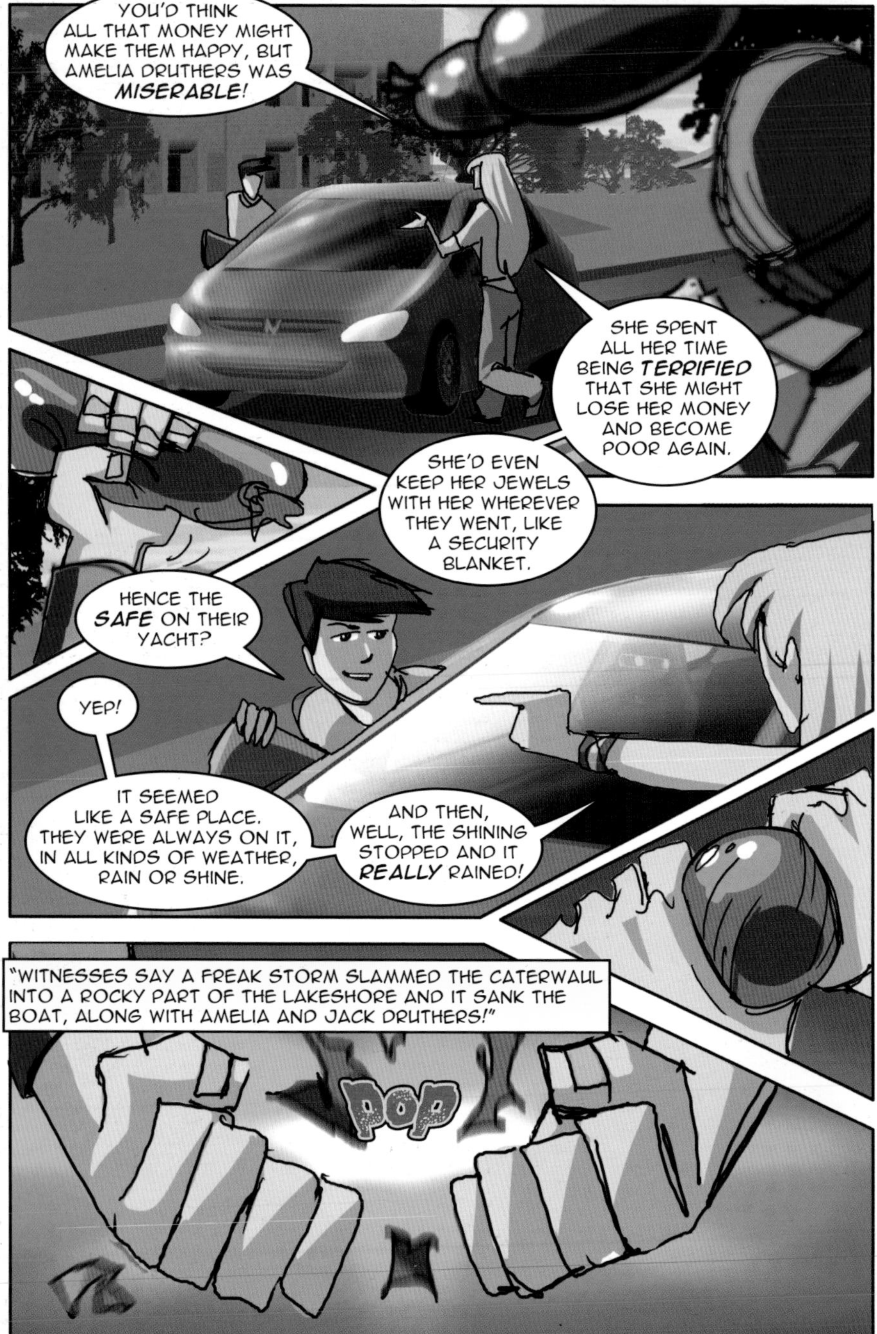
YOU'D THINK ALL THAT MONEY MIGHT MAKE THEM HAPPY, BUT AMELIA DRUTHERS WAS MISERABLE!
SHE SPENT ALL HER TIME BEING TERRIFIED THAT SHE MIGHT LOSE HER MONEY AND BECOME POOR AGAIN.
SHE'D EVEN KEEP HER JEWELS WITH HER WHEREVER THEY WENT, LIKE A SECURITY BLANKET.
HENCE THE SAFE ON THEIR YACHT?
YEP!
IT SEEMED LIKE A SAFE PLACE. THEY WERE ALWAYS ON IT, IN ALL KINDS OF WEATHER, RAIN OR SHINE.
AND THEN, WELL, THE SHINING STOPPED AND IT REALLY RAINED!
"WITNESSES SAY A FREAK STORM SLAMMED THE CATERWAUL INTO A ROCKY PART OF THE LAKESHORE AND IT SANK THE BOAT, ALONG WITH AMELIA AND JACK DRUTHERS!"
POP

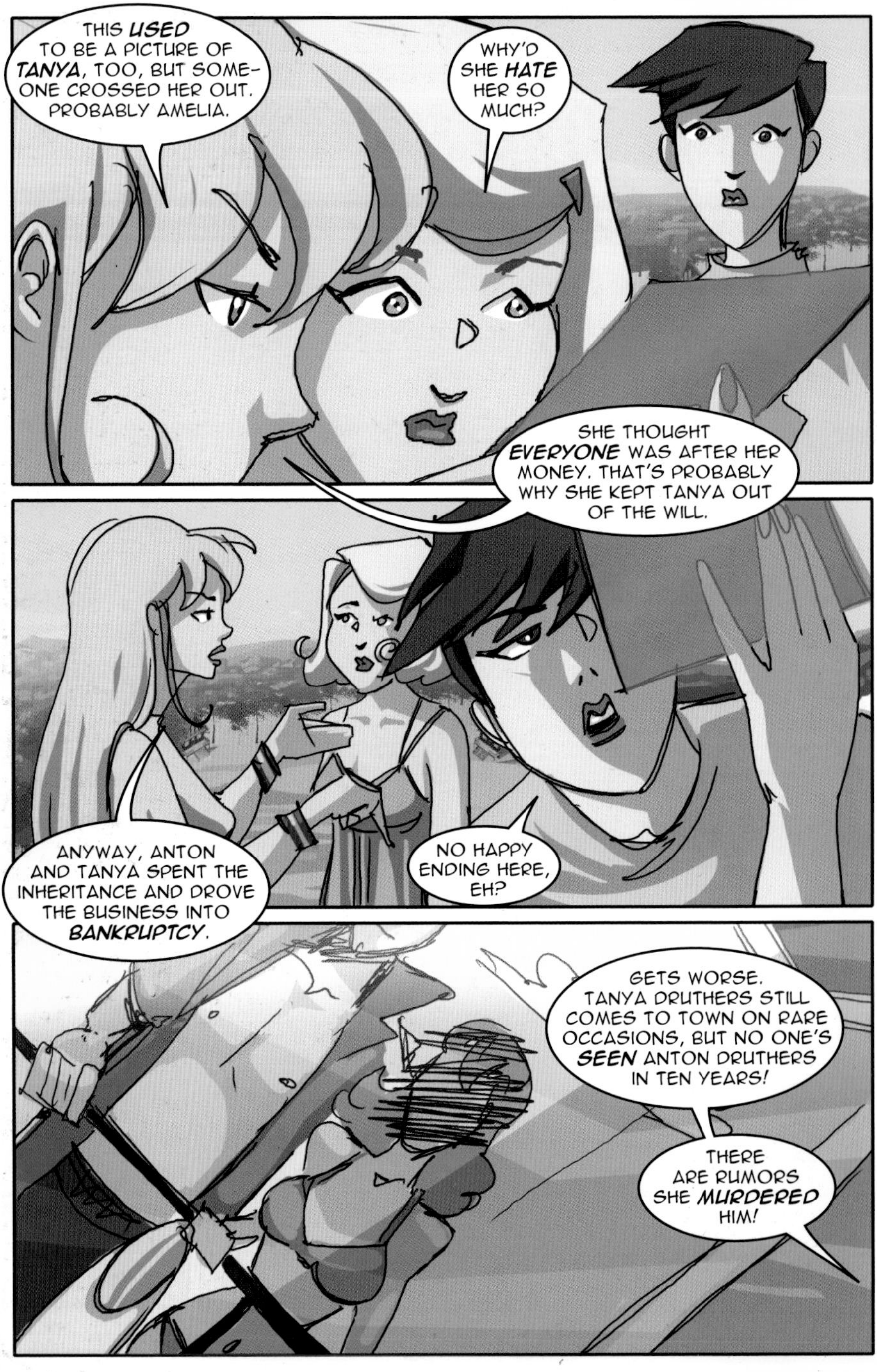
THIS USED TO BE A PICTURE OF TANYA, TOO, BUT SOME-ONE CROSSED HER OUT. PROBABLY AMELIA.
WHY'D SHE HATE HER SO MUCH?
SHE THOUGHT EVERYONE WAS AFTER HER MONEY. THAT'S PROBABLY WHY SHE KEPT TANYA OUT OF THE WILL.
ANYWAY, ANTON AND TANYA SPENT THE INHERITANCE AND DROVE THE BUSINESS INTO BANKRUPTCY.
NO HAPPY ENDING HERE, EH?
GETS WORSE. TANYA DRUTHERS STILL COMES TO TOWN ON RARE OCCASIONS, BUT NO ONE'S SEEN ANTON DRUTHERS IN TEN YEARS!
THERE ARE RUMORS SHE MURDERED HIM!

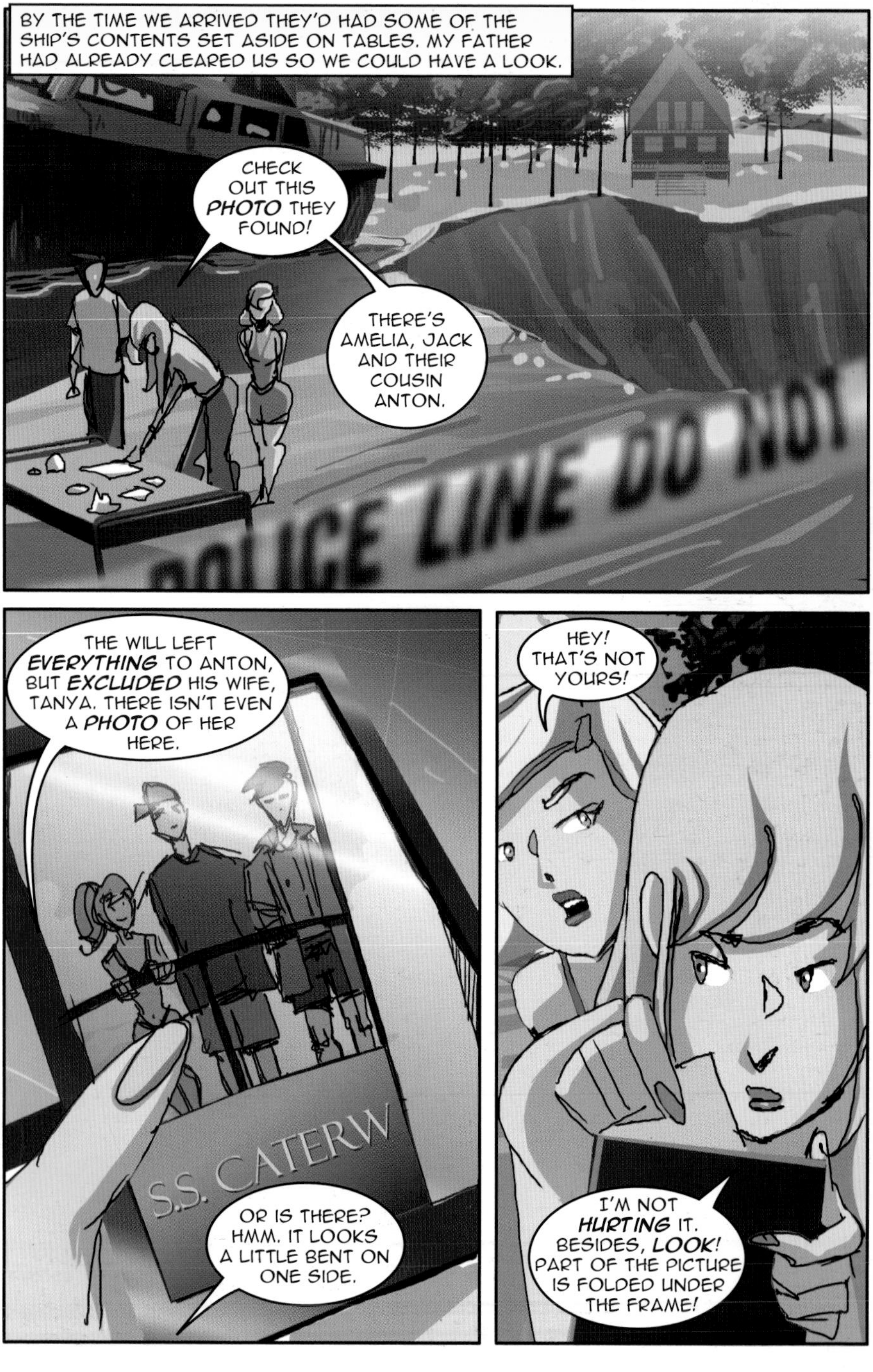
BY THE TIME WE ARRIVED THEY'D HAD SOME OF THE SHIP'S CONTENTS SET ASIDE ON TABLES. MY FATHER HAD ALREADY CLEARED US SO WE COULD HAVE A LOOK.
CHECK OUT THIS *PHOTO* THEY FOUND!
THERE'S AMELIA, JACK AND THEIR COUSIN ANTON.
THE WILL LEFT *EVERYTHING* TO ANTON, BUT *EXCLUDED* HIS WIFE, TANYA. THERE ISN'T EVEN A *PHOTO* OF HER HERE.
S.S. CATERW
OR IS THERE? HMM. IT LOOKS A LITTLE BENT ON ONE SIDE.
HEY! THAT'S NOT YOURS!
I'M NOT *HURTING* IT. BESIDES, *LOOK*! PART OF THE PICTURE IS FOLDED UNDER THE FRAME!

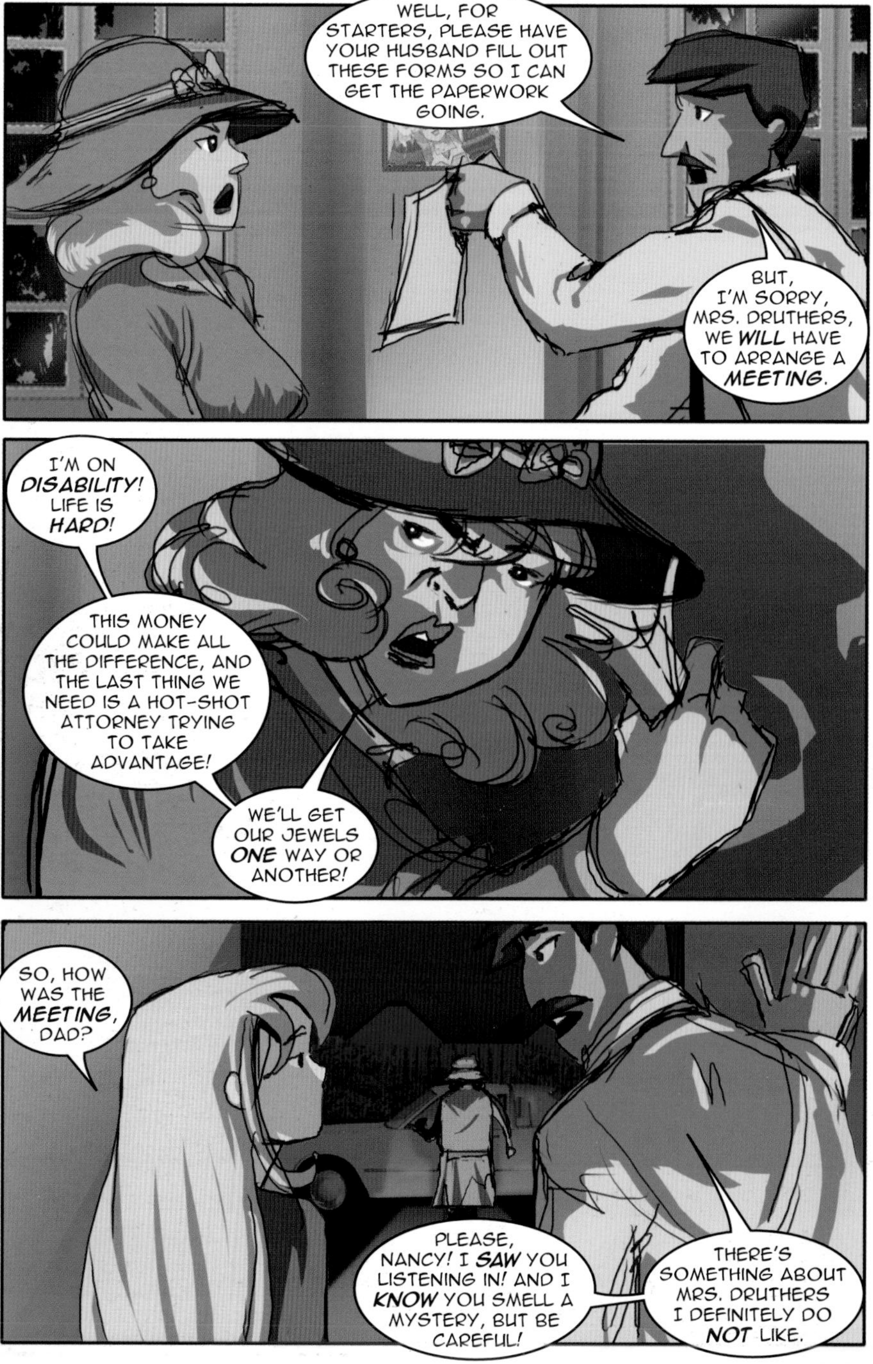
WELL, FOR STARTERS, PLEASE HAVE YOUR HUSBAND FILL OUT THESE FORMS SO I CAN GET THE PAPERWORK GOING.
BUT, I'M SORRY, MRS. DRUTHERS, WE **WILL** HAVE TO ARRANGE A **MEETING**.
I'M ON **DISABILITY**! LIFE IS **HARD**!
THIS MONEY COULD MAKE ALL THE DIFFERENCE, AND THE LAST THING WE NEED IS A HOT-SHOT ATTORNEY TRYING TO TAKE ADVANTAGE!
WE'LL GET OUR JEWELS **ONE** WAY OR ANOTHER!
SO, HOW WAS THE **MEETING**, DAD?
PLEASE, NANCY! I **SAW** YOU LISTENING IN! AND I **KNOW** YOU SMELL A MYSTERY, BUT BE CAREFUL!
THERE'S SOMETHING ABOUT MRS. DRUTHERS I DEFINITELY DO **NOT** LIKE.

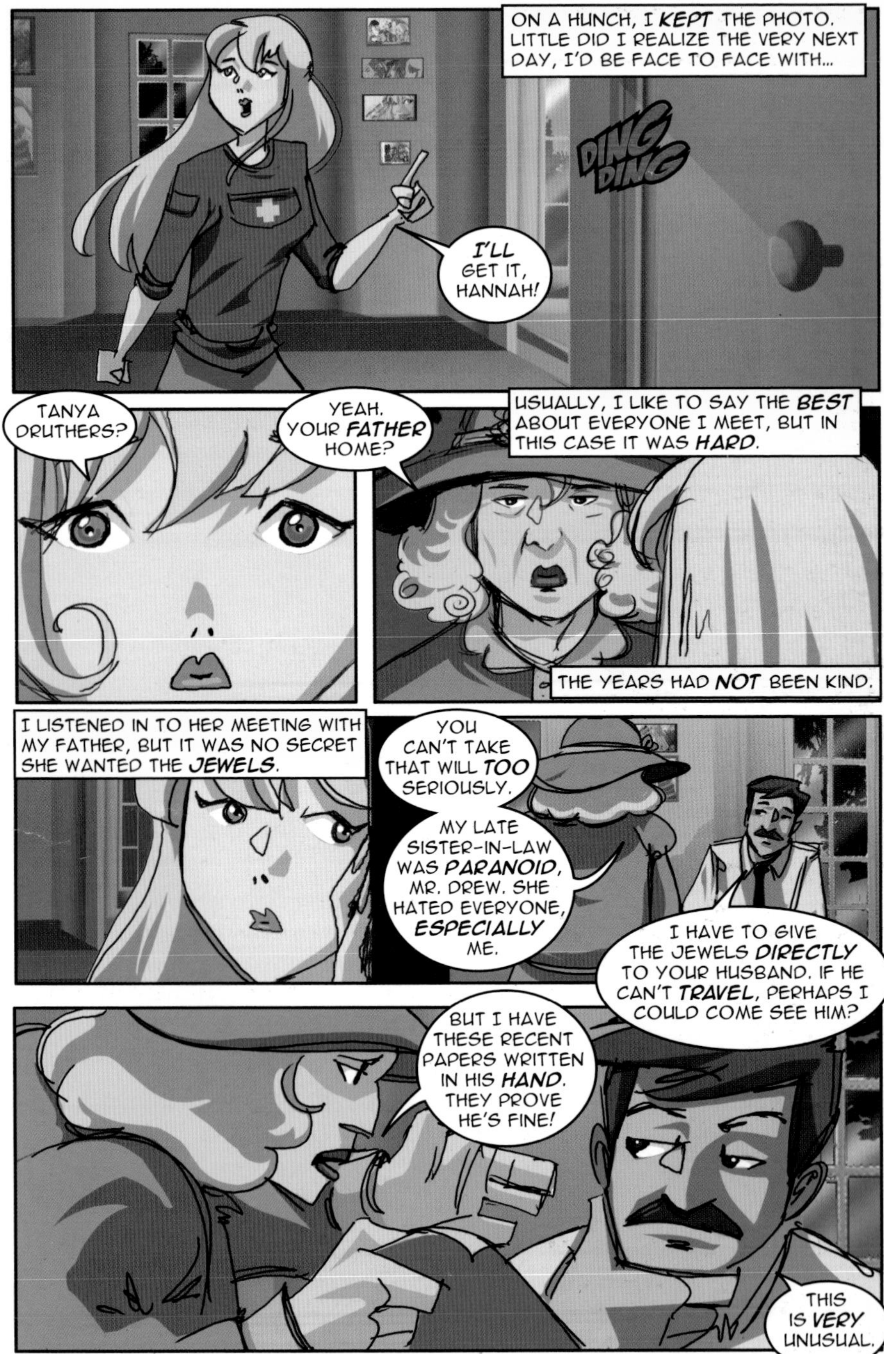
ON A HUNCH, I KEPT THE PHOTO. LITTLE DID I REALIZE THE VERY NEXT DAY, I'D BE FACE TO FACE WITH...
DING DING
I'LL GET IT, HANNAH!
TANYA DRUTHERS?
YEAH. YOUR FATHER HOME?
USUALLY, I LIKE TO SAY THE BEST ABOUT EVERYONE I MEET, BUT IN THIS CASE IT WAS HARD.
THE YEARS HAD NOT BEEN KIND.
I LISTENED IN TO HER MEETING WITH MY FATHER, BUT IT WAS NO SECRET SHE WANTED THE JEWELS.
YOU CAN'T TAKE THAT WILL TOO SERIOUSLY.
MY LATE SISTER-IN-LAW WAS PARANOID, MR. DREW. SHE HATED EVERYONE, ESPECIALLY ME.
I HAVE TO GIVE THE JEWELS DIRECTLY TO YOUR HUSBAND. IF HE CAN'T TRAVEL, PERHAPS I COULD COME SEE HIM?
BUT I HAVE THESE RECENT PAPERS WRITTEN IN HIS HAND. THEY PROVE HE'S FINE!
THIS IS VERY UNUSUAL.

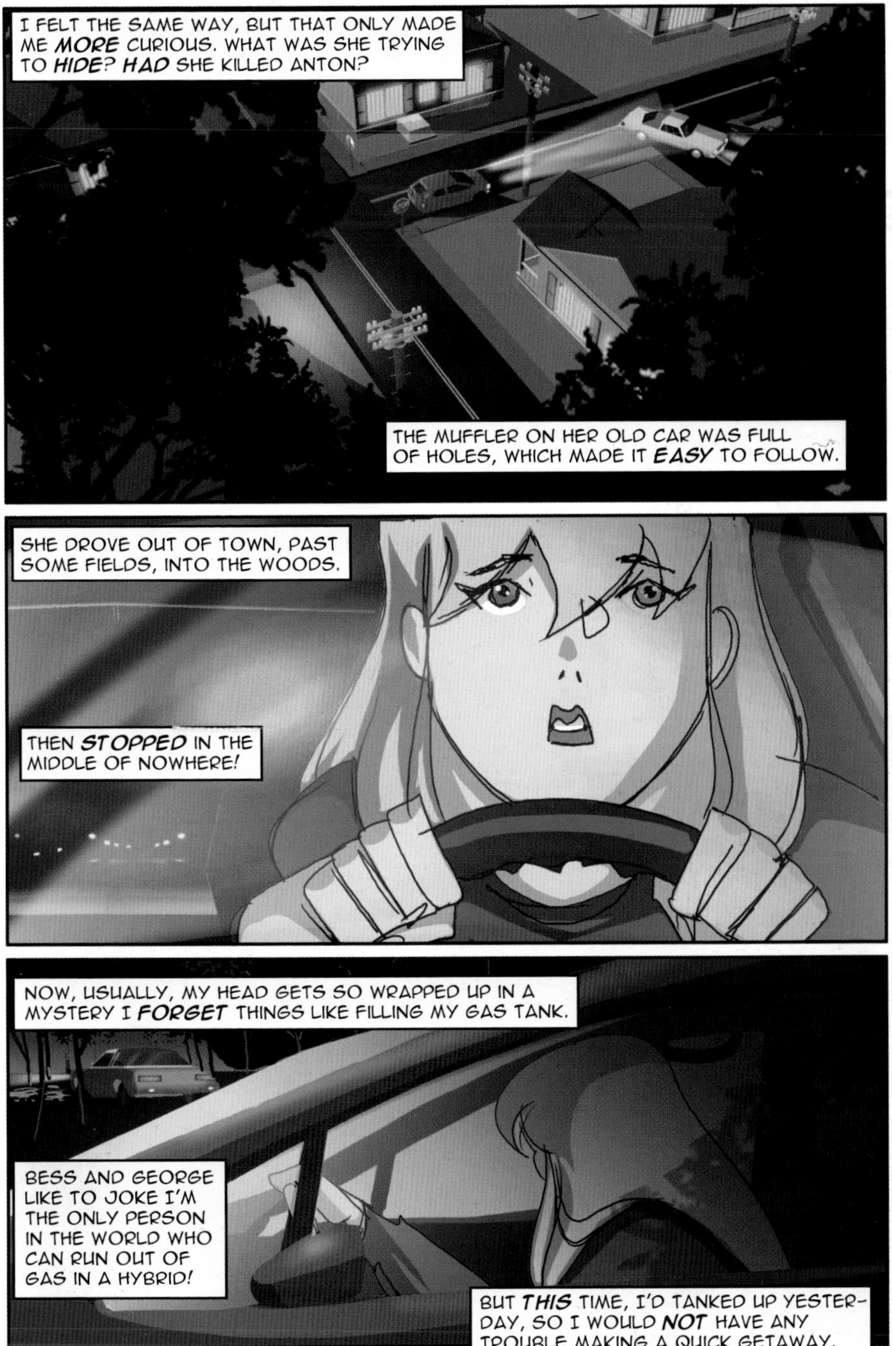
I FELT THE SAME WAY, BUT THAT ONLY MADE ME MORE CURIOUS. WHAT WAS SHE TRYING TO HIDE? HAD SHE KILLED ANTON?
THE MUFFLER ON HER OLD CAR WAS FULL OF HOLES, WHICH MADE IT EASY TO FOLLOW.
SHE DROVE OUT OF TOWN, PAST SOME FIELDS, INTO THE WOODS.
THEN STOPPED IN THE MIDDLE OF NOWHERE!
NOW, USUALLY, MY HEAD GETS SO WRAPPED UP IN A MYSTERY I FORGET THINGS LIKE FILLING MY GAS TANK.
BESS AND GEORGE LIKE TO JOKE I'M THE ONLY PERSON IN THE WORLD WHO CAN RUN OUT OF GAS IN A HYBRID!
BUT THIS TIME, I'D TANKED UP YESTERDAY, SO I WOULD NOT HAVE ANY TROUBLE MAKING A QUICK GETAWAY.

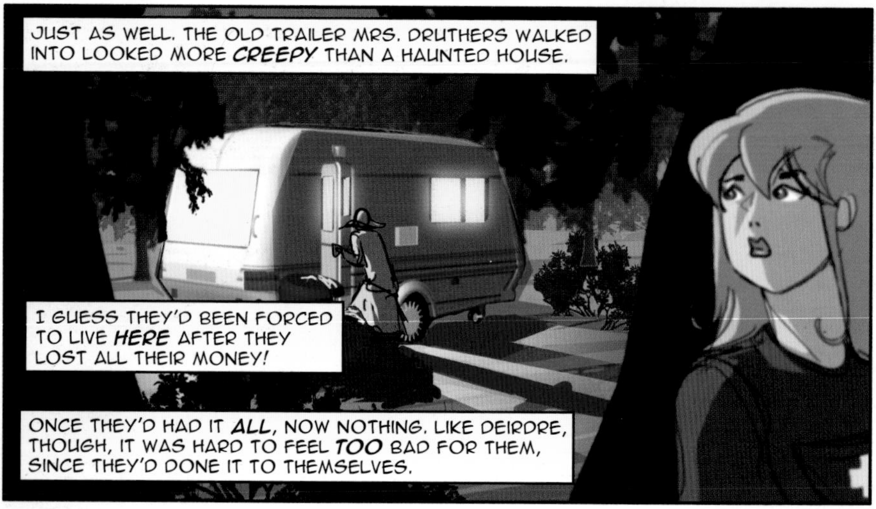
JUST AS WELL. THE OLD TRAILER MRS. DRUTHERS WALKED INTO LOOKED MORE CREEPY THAN A HAUNTED HOUSE.
I GUESS THEY'D BEEN FORCED TO LIVE HERE AFTER THEY LOST ALL THEIR MONEY!
ONCE THEY'D HAD IT ALL, NOW NOTHING. LIKE DEIRDRE, THOUGH, IT WAS HARD TO FEEL TOO BAD FOR THEM, SINCE THEY'D DONE IT TO THEMSELVES.

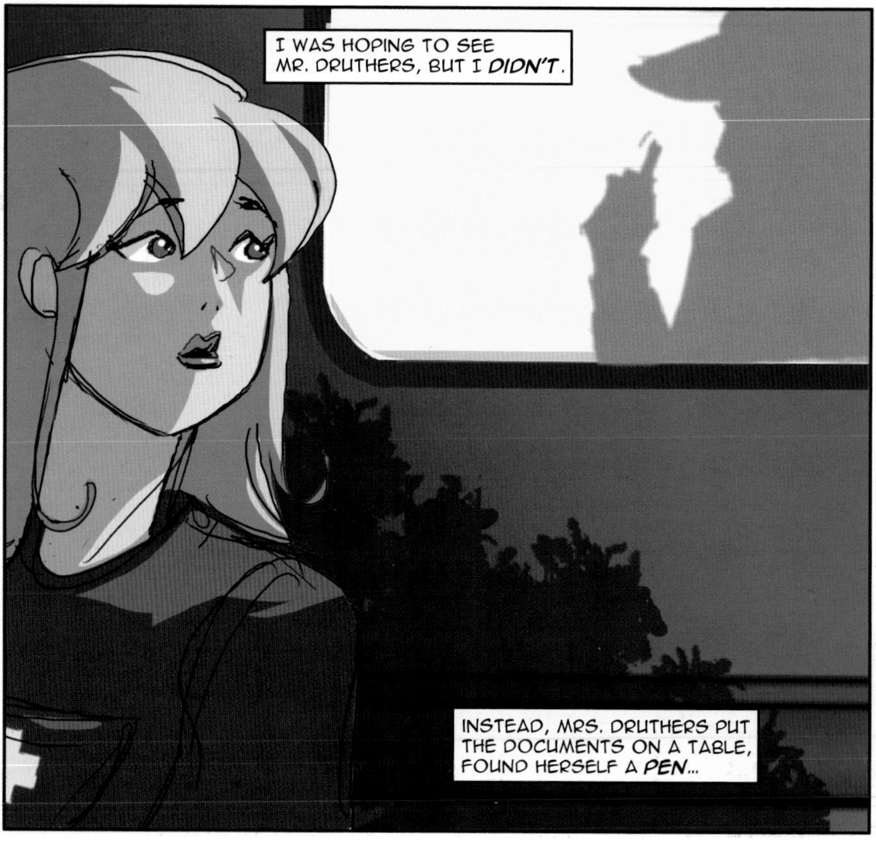
I WAS HOPING TO SEE MR. DRUTHERS, BUT I DIDN'T.
INSTEAD, MRS. DRUTHERS PUT THE DOCUMENTS ON A TABLE, FOUND HERSELF A PEN...

AND STARTED *FORGING* HER HUSBAND'S HAND-WRITING ON THE FORMS MY FATHER GAVE HER!

NOW WHY WOULD SHE DO *THAT*, UNLESS HER HUSBAND WAS *DEAD*?

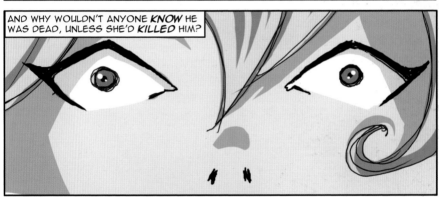

AND WHY WOULDN'T ANYONE *KNOW* HE WAS DEAD, UNLESS SHE'D *KILLED* HIM?

THE FIRST THING I THOUGHT OF WAS CALLING MY *DAD*.

UNFORTUNATELY, THOUGH I'D REMEMBERED THE *GAS*, THIS TIME, I FORGOT TO CHARGE MY CELL PHONE. IT WAS *DEAD*.

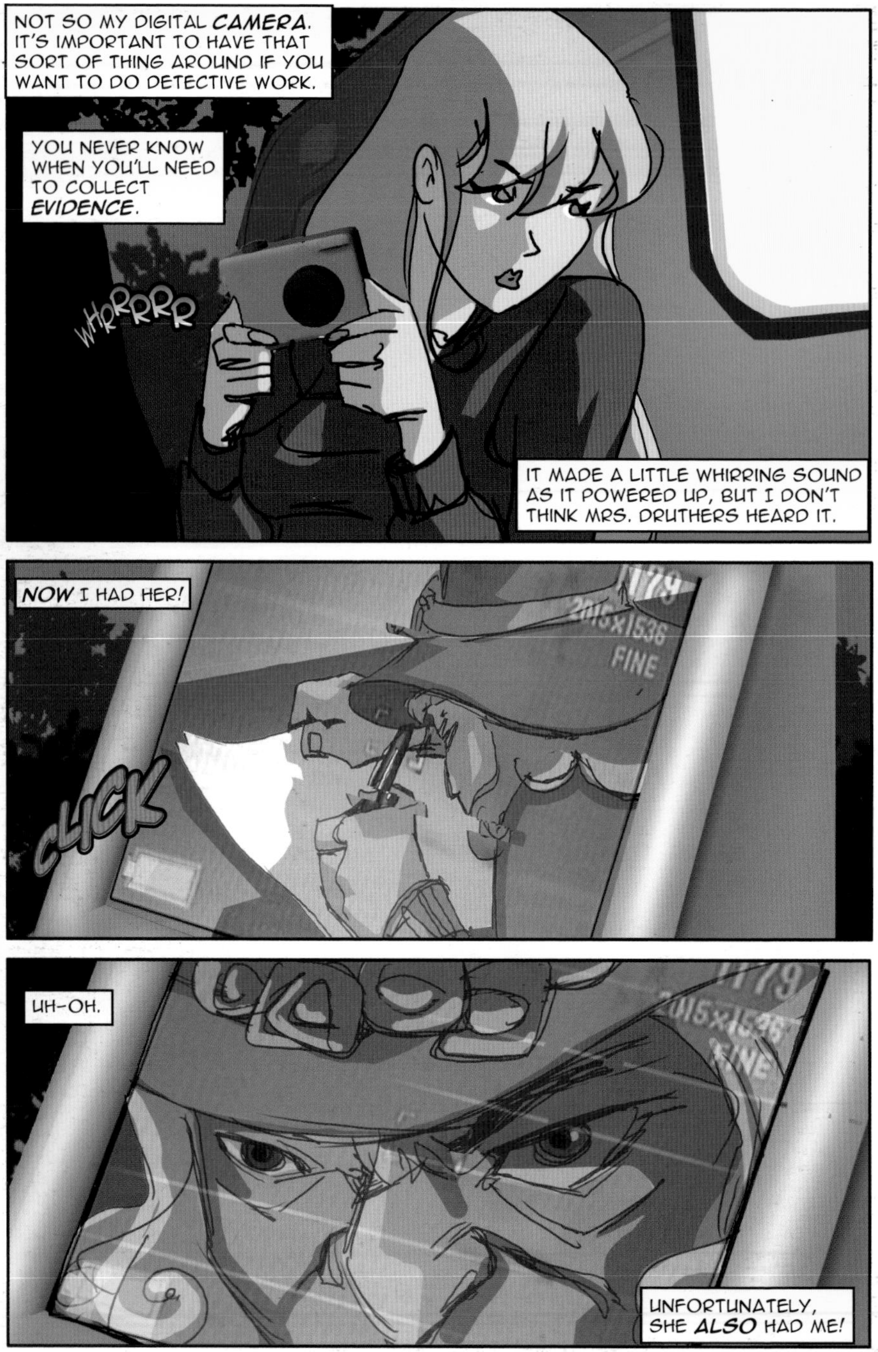
NOT SO MY DIGITAL *CAMERA*. IT'S IMPORTANT TO HAVE THAT SORT OF THING AROUND IF YOU WANT TO DO DETECTIVE WORK.
YOU NEVER KNOW WHEN YOU'LL NEED TO COLLECT *EVIDENCE*.
WHRRRRR
IT MADE A LITTLE WHIRRING SOUND AS IT POWERED UP, BUT I DON'T THINK MRS. DRUTHERS HEARD IT.
NOW I HAD HER!
1179
2015x1536
FINE
CLICK
UH-OH.
1179
2015x1536
FINE
UNFORTUNATELY, SHE *ALSO* HAD ME!

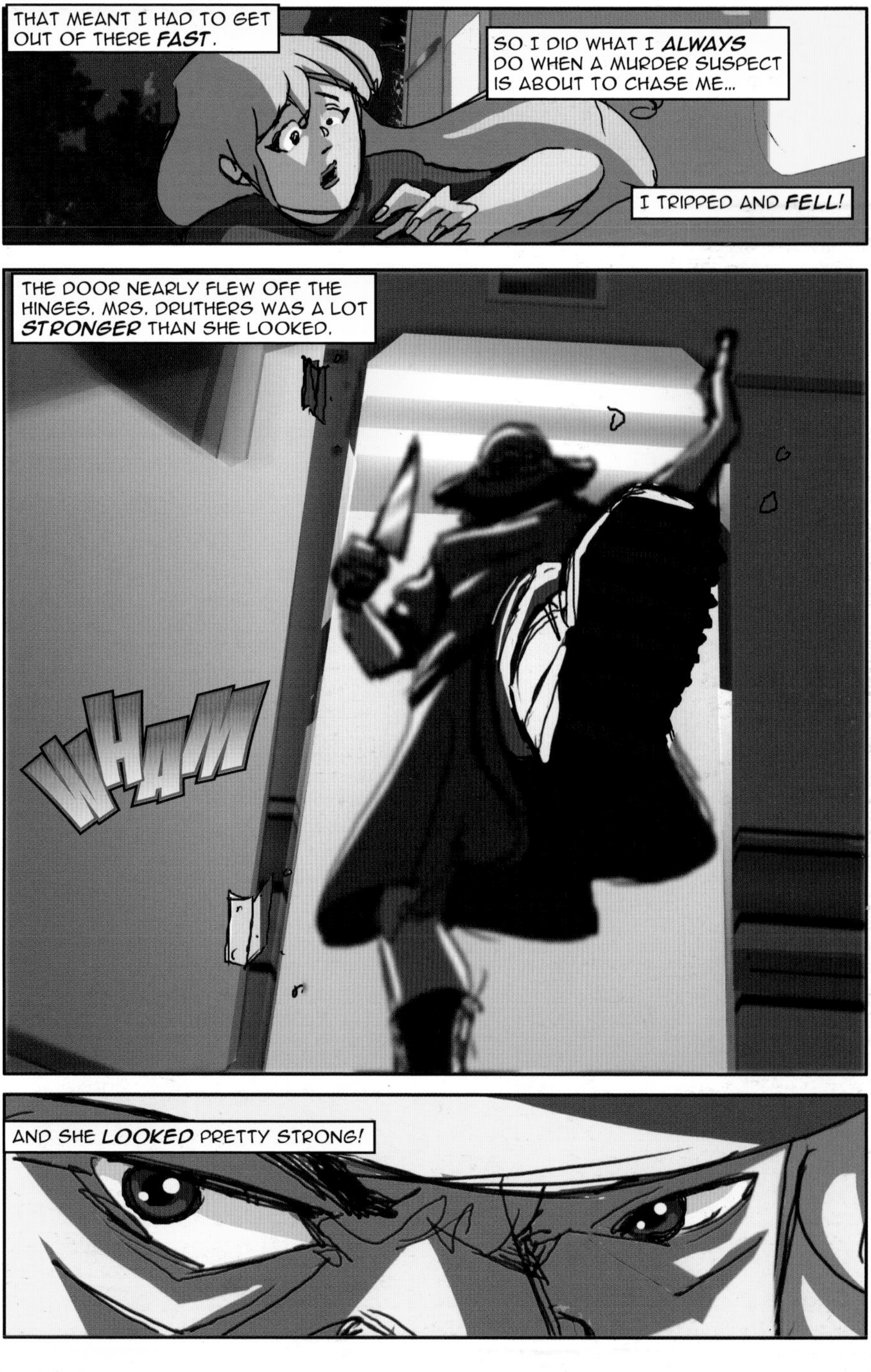
THAT MEANT I HAD TO GET OUT OF THERE FAST.
SO I DID WHAT I ALWAYS DO WHEN A MURDER SUSPECT IS ABOUT TO CHASE ME...
I TRIPPED AND FELL!
THE DOOR NEARLY FLEW OFF THE HINGES. MRS. DRUTHERS WAS A LOT STRONGER THAN SHE LOOKED.
WHAM
AND SHE LOOKED PRETTY STRONG!

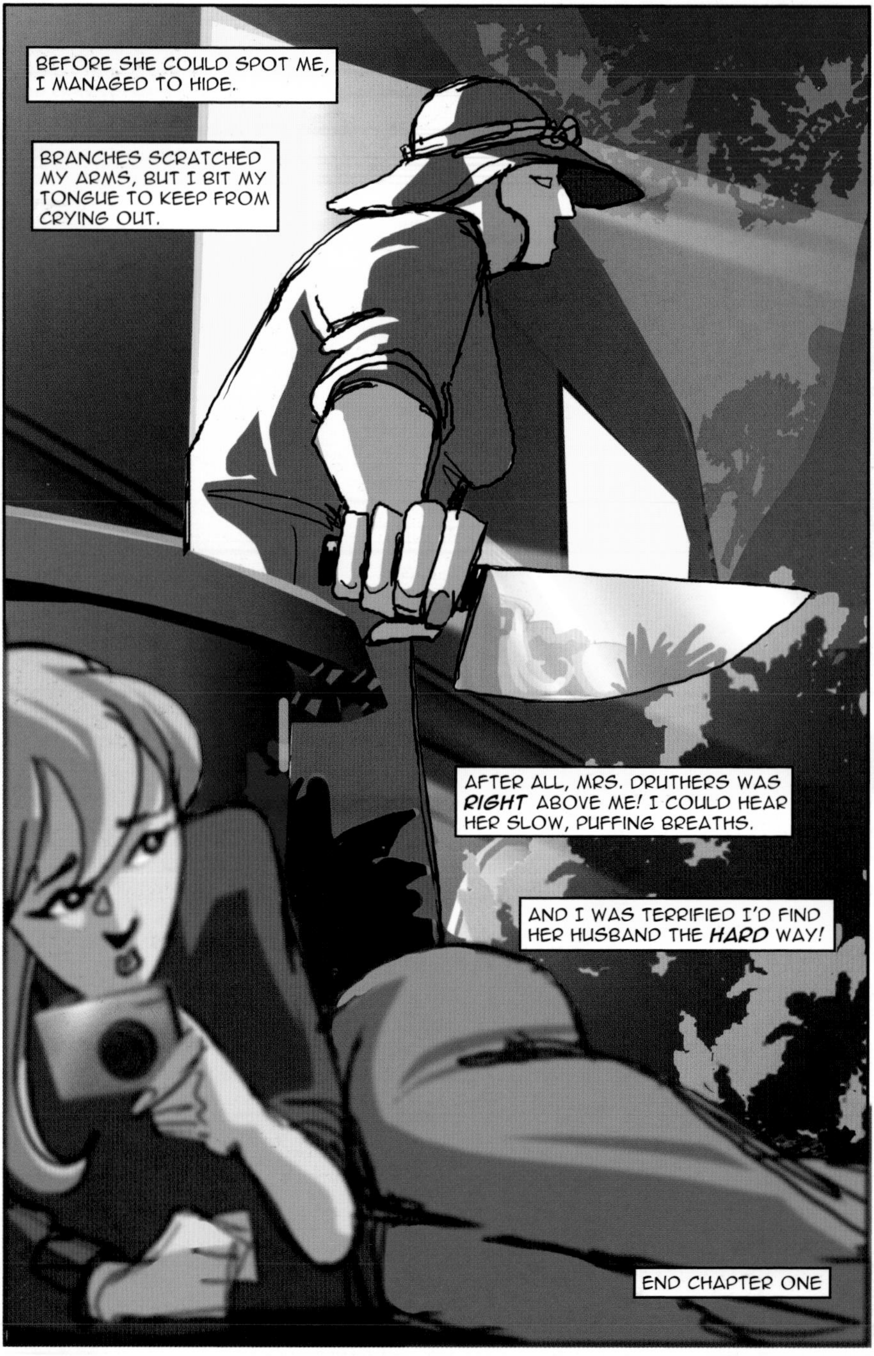
BEFORE SHE COULD SPOT ME, I MANAGED TO HIDE.
BRANCHES SCRATCHED MY ARMS, BUT I BIT MY TONGUE TO KEEP FROM CRYING OUT.
AFTER ALL, MRS. DRUTHERS WAS RIGHT ABOVE ME! I COULD HEAR HER SLOW, PUFFING BREATHS.
AND I WAS TERRIFIED I'D FIND HER HUSBAND THE HARD WAY!
END CHAPTER ONE

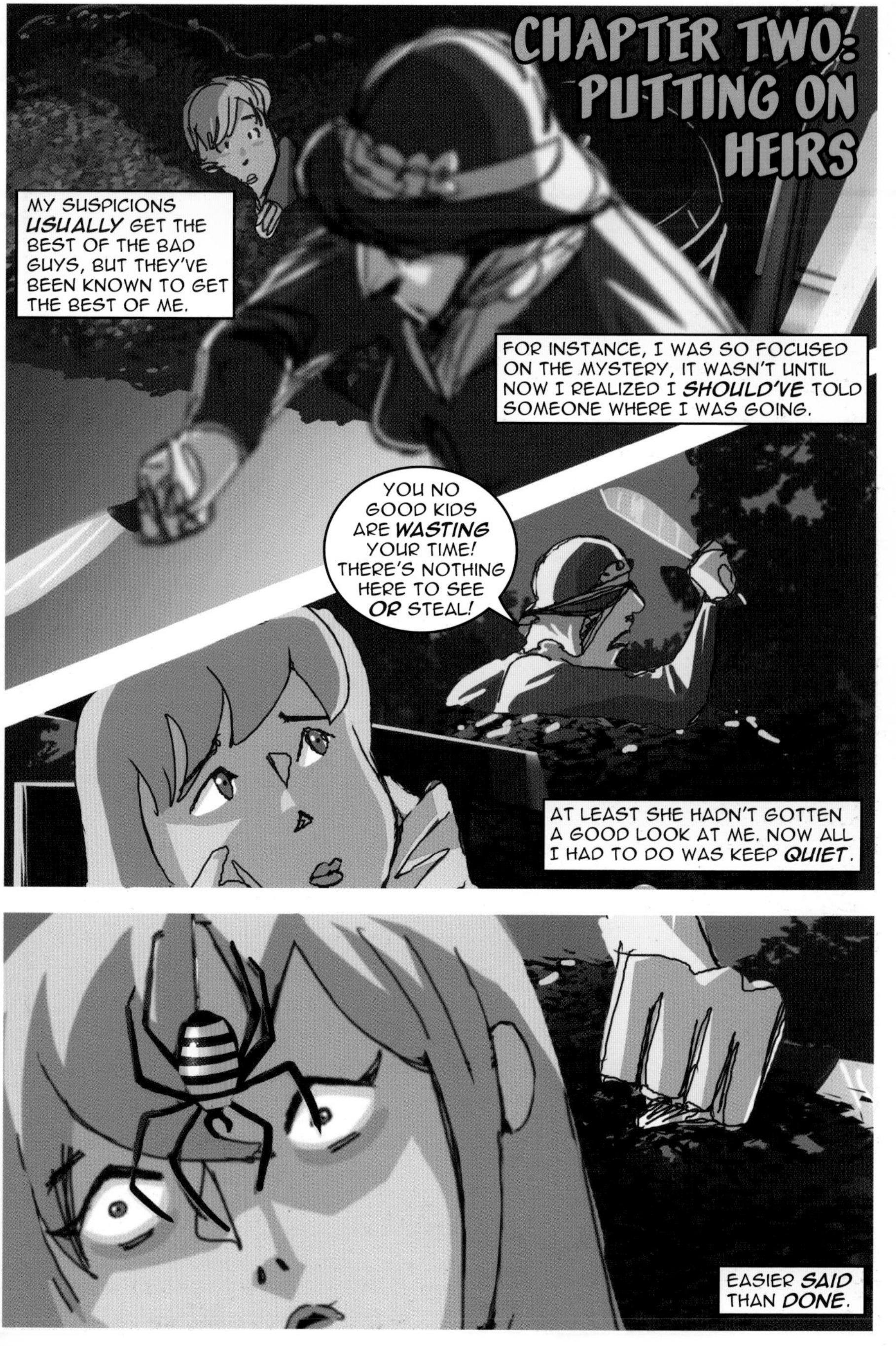
CHAPTER TWO: PUTTING ON HEIRS
MY SUSPICIONS USUALLY GET THE BEST OF THE BAD GUYS, BUT THEY'VE BEEN KNOWN TO GET THE BEST OF ME.
FOR INSTANCE, I WAS SO FOCUSED ON THE MYSTERY, IT WASN'T UNTIL NOW I REALIZED I SHOULD'VE TOLD SOMEONE WHERE I WAS GOING.
YOU NO GOOD KIDS ARE WASTING YOUR TIME! THERE'S NOTHING HERE TO SEE OR STEAL!
AT LEAST SHE HADN'T GOTTEN A GOOD LOOK AT ME. NOW ALL I HAD TO DO WAS KEEP QUIET.
EASIER SAID THAN DONE.

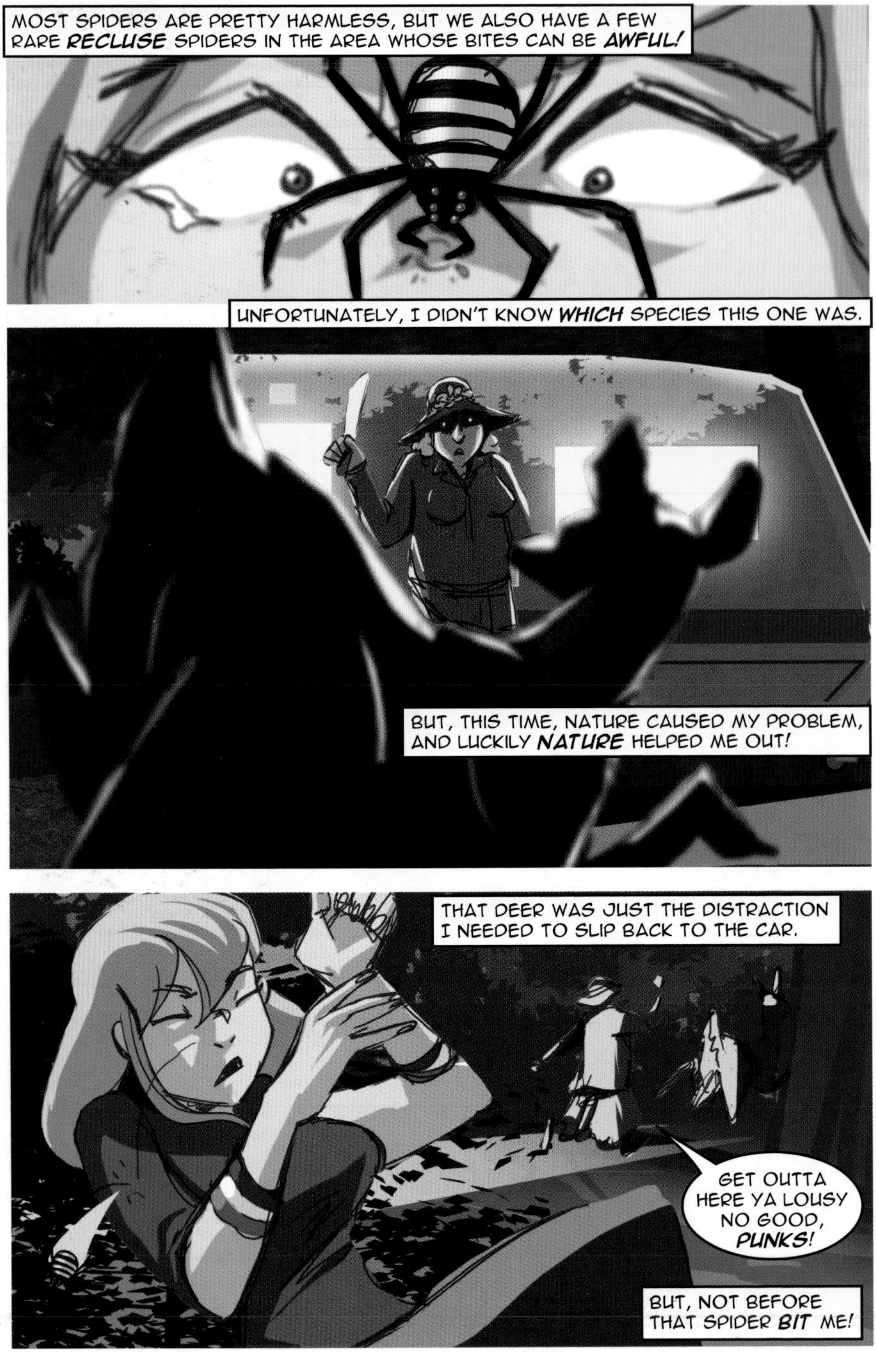
MOST SPIDERS ARE PRETTY HARMLESS, BUT WE ALSO HAVE A FEW RARE RECLUSE SPIDERS IN THE AREA WHOSE BITES CAN BE AWFUL!
UNFORTUNATELY, I DIDN'T KNOW WHICH SPECIES THIS ONE WAS.
BUT, THIS TIME, NATURE CAUSED MY PROBLEM, AND LUCKILY NATURE HELPED ME OUT!
THAT DEER WAS JUST THE DISTRACTION I NEEDED TO SLIP BACK TO THE CAR.
GET OUTTA HERE YA LOUSY NO GOOD, PUNKS!
BUT, NOT BEFORE THAT SPIDER BIT ME!

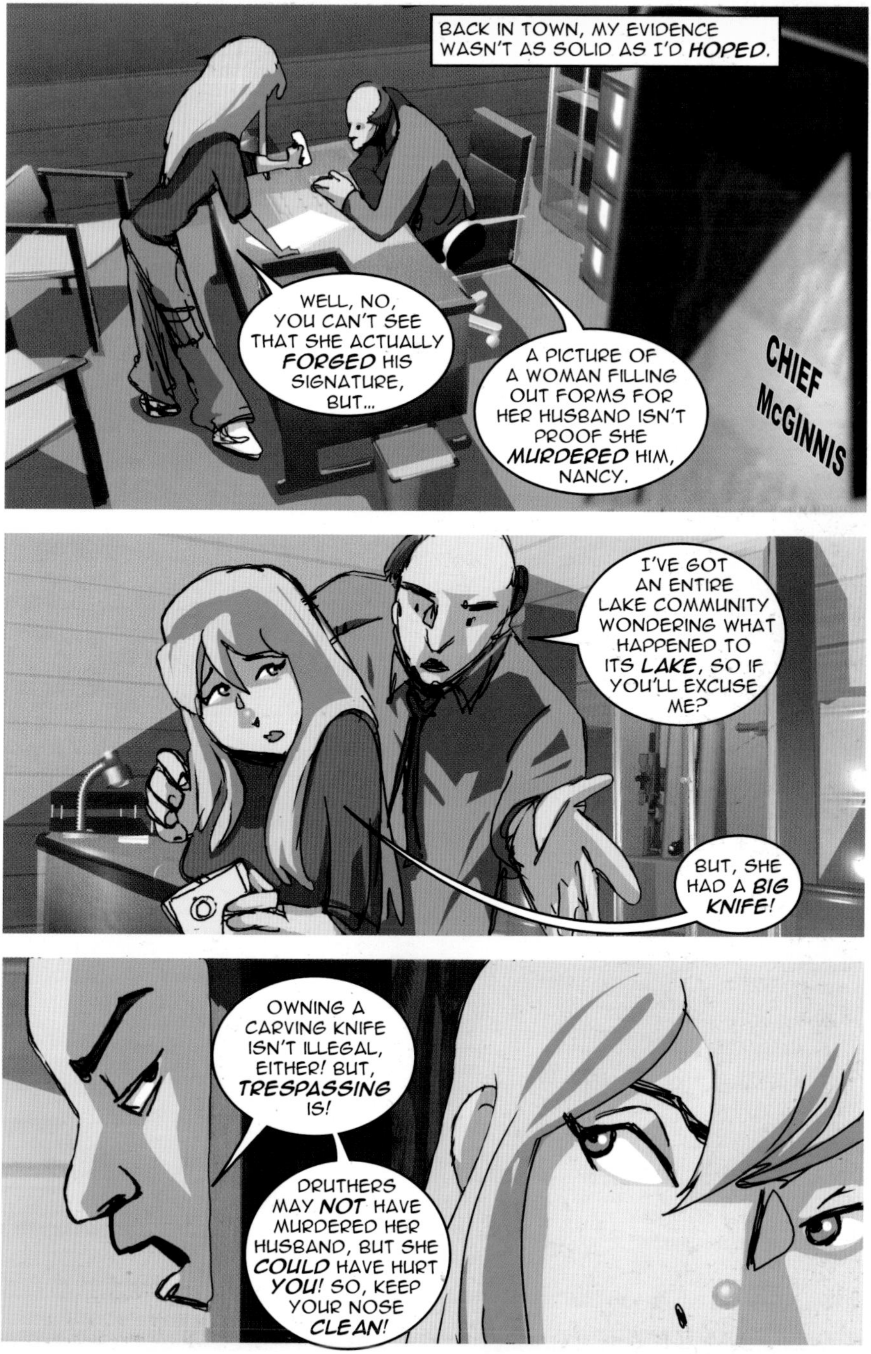
BACK IN TOWN, MY EVIDENCE WASN'T AS SOLID AS I'D HOPED.
WELL, NO, YOU CAN'T SEE THAT SHE ACTUALLY FORGED HIS SIGNATURE, BUT...
A PICTURE OF A WOMAN FILLING OUT FORMS FOR HER HUSBAND ISN'T PROOF SHE MURDERED HIM, NANCY.
CHIEF McGINNIS
I'VE GOT AN ENTIRE LAKE COMMUNITY WONDERING WHAT HAPPENED TO ITS LAKE, SO IF YOU'LL EXCUSE ME?
BUT, SHE HAD A BIG KNIFE!
OWNING A CARVING KNIFE ISN'T ILLEGAL, EITHER! BUT, TRESPASSING IS!
DRUTHERS MAY NOT HAVE MURDERED HER HUSBAND, BUT SHE COULD HAVE HURT YOU! SO, KEEP YOUR NOSE CLEAN!

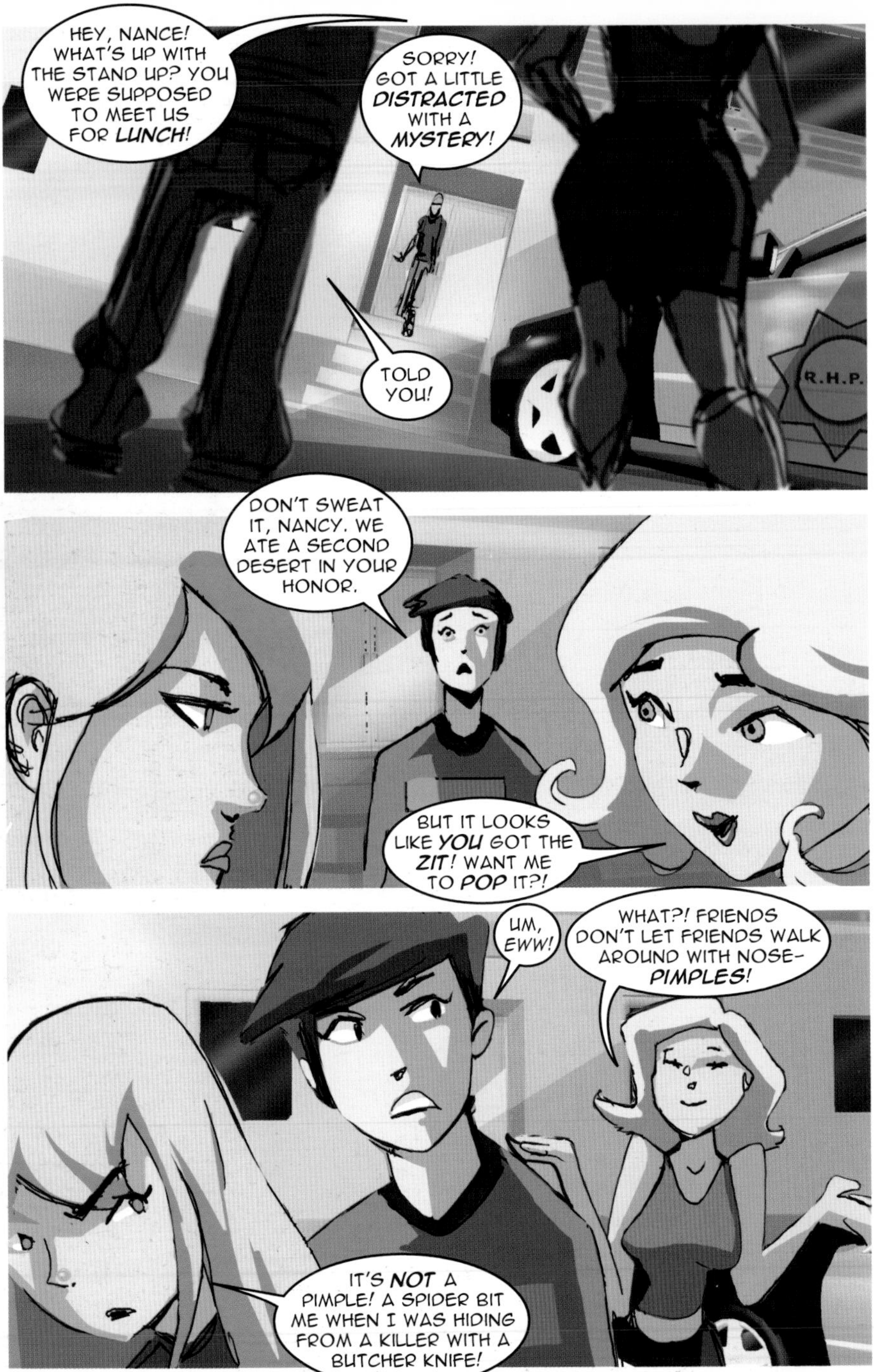
HEY, NANCE! WHAT'S UP WITH THE STAND UP? YOU WERE SUPPOSED TO MEET US FOR LUNCH!
SORRY! GOT A LITTLE DISTRACTED WITH A MYSTERY!
TOLD YOU!
R.H.P.
DON'T SWEAT IT, NANCY. WE ATE A SECOND DESERT IN YOUR HONOR.
BUT IT LOOKS LIKE YOU GOT THE ZIT! WANT ME TO POP IT?!
UM, EWW!
WHAT?! FRIENDS DON'T LET FRIENDS WALK AROUND WITH NOSE-PIMPLES!
IT'S NOT A PIMPLE! A SPIDER BIT ME WHEN I WAS HIDING FROM A KILLER WITH A BUTCHER KNIFE!

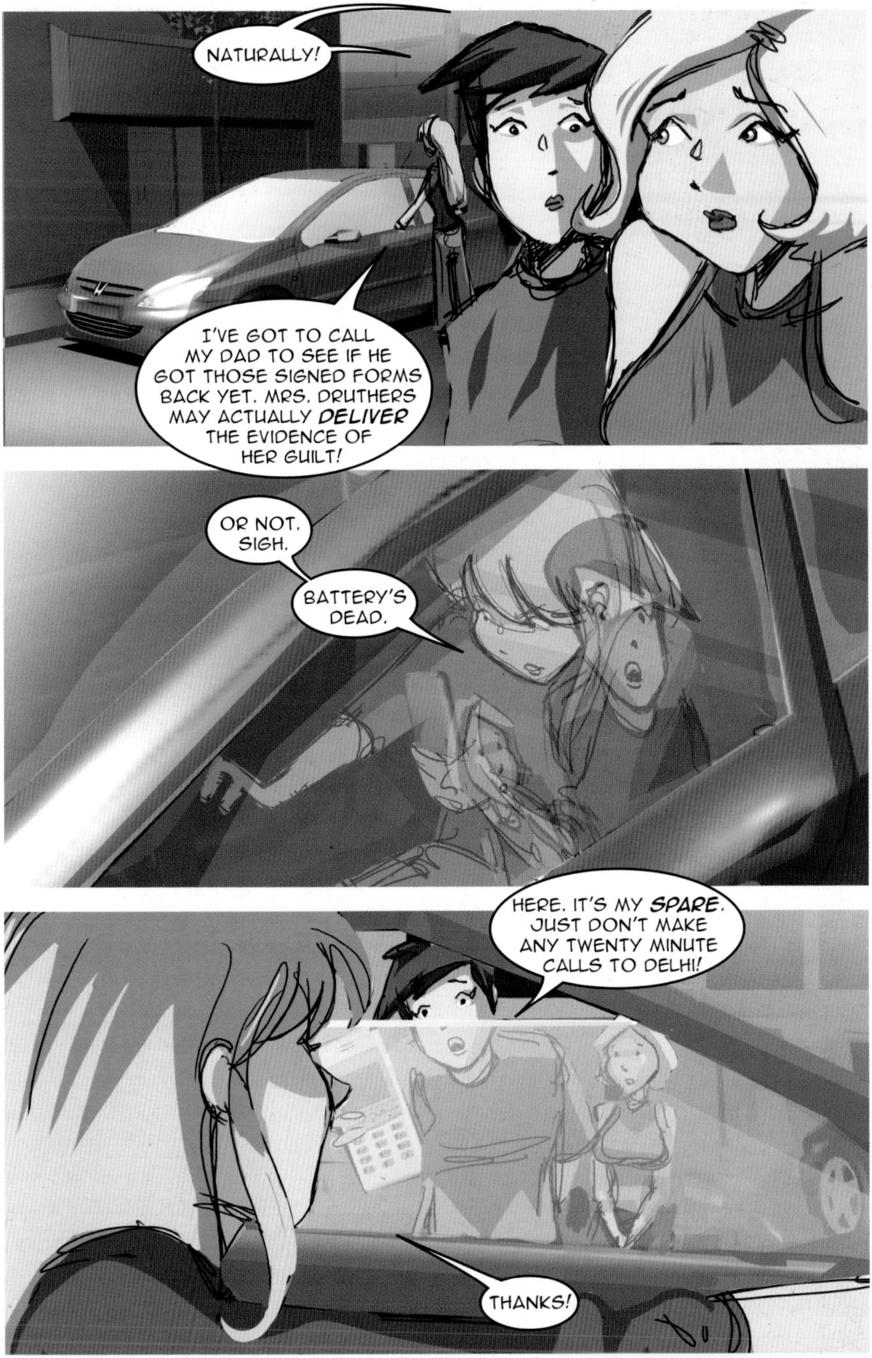
NATURALLY!
I'VE GOT TO CALL MY DAD TO SEE IF HE GOT THOSE SIGNED FORMS BACK YET. MRS. DRUTHERS MAY ACTUALLY DELIVER THE EVIDENCE OF HER GUILT!
OR NOT. SIGH.
BATTERY'S DEAD.
HERE. IT'S MY SPARE. JUST DON'T MAKE ANY TWENTY MINUTE CALLS TO DELHI!
THANKS!

AFTER I EXPLAINED WHAT HAPPENED, DAD CALLED ON *HANDWRITING* EXPERT BILL DALE.

ALL MR. DALE HAD TO DO WAS *CONFIRM* THAT THE HANDWRITING ON THAT FORM DID *NOT* BELONG TO MR. DRUTHERS! IT WAS A SLAM DUNK!

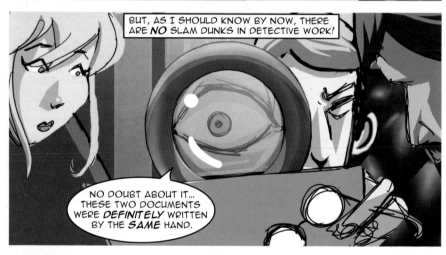

BUT, AS I SHOULD KNOW BY NOW, THERE ARE *NO* SLAM DUNKS IN DETECTIVE WORK!

NO DOUBT ABOUT IT... THESE TWO DOCUMENTS WERE *DEFINITELY* WRITTEN BY THE *SAME* HAND.

THAT'S *IMPOSSIBLE!* I SAW *MRS.* DRUTHERS FILLING OUT *THAT* FORM. AND MY FATHER SAW *MR.* DRUTHERS SIGN THE *OTHER* TEN YEARS AGO!

NOT TO BOAST, BUT I'M PRETTY *GOOD* AT SPOTTING FORGERIES!

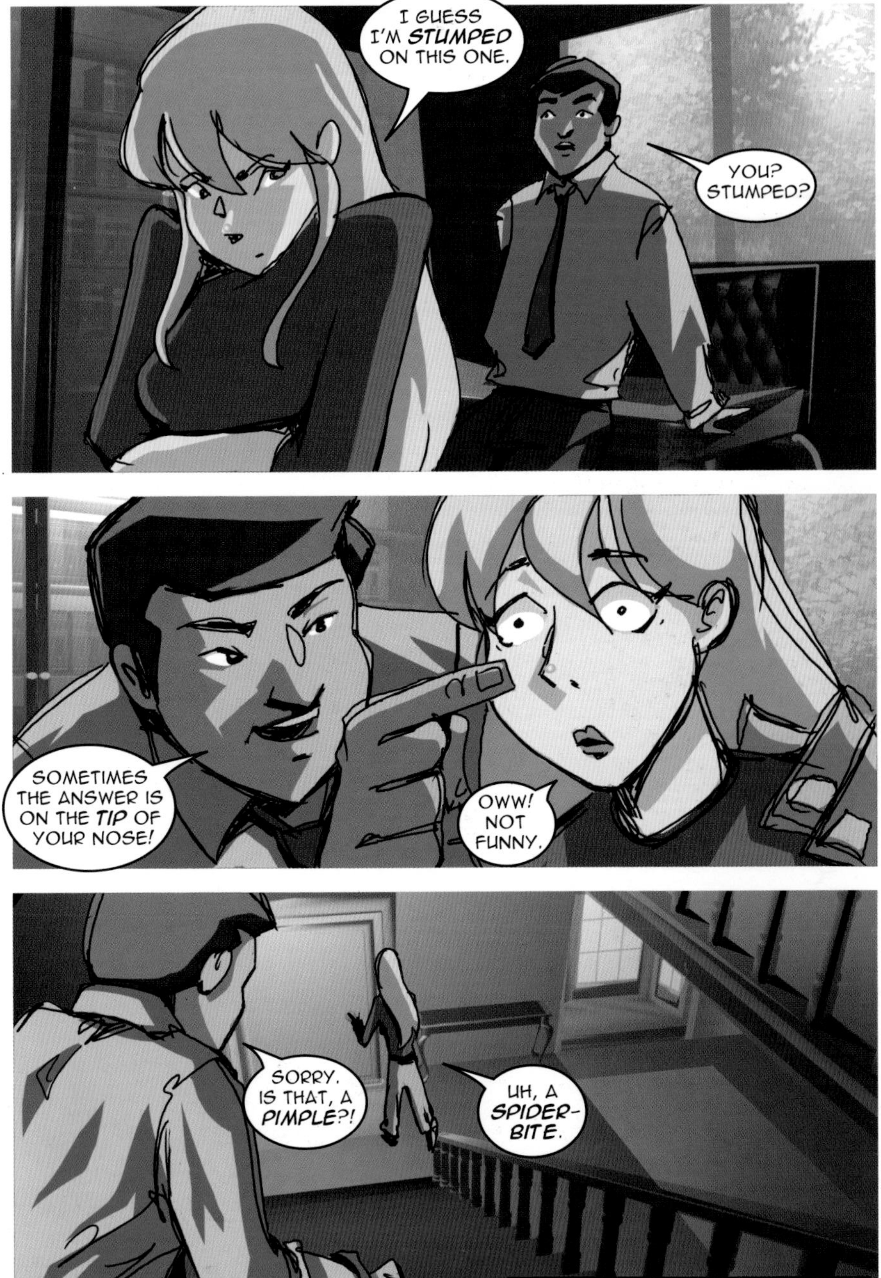
I GUESS I'M STUMPED ON THIS ONE.
YOU? STUMPED?
SOMETIMES THE ANSWER IS ON THE TIP OF YOUR NOSE!
OWW! NOT FUNNY.
SORRY. IS THAT, A PIMPLE?!
UH, A SPIDER-BITE.
I DOUBTED DAD WOULD ENJOY THE STORY OF MY HIDING IN THE BUSH, SO I LEFT OUT THE DETAILS.

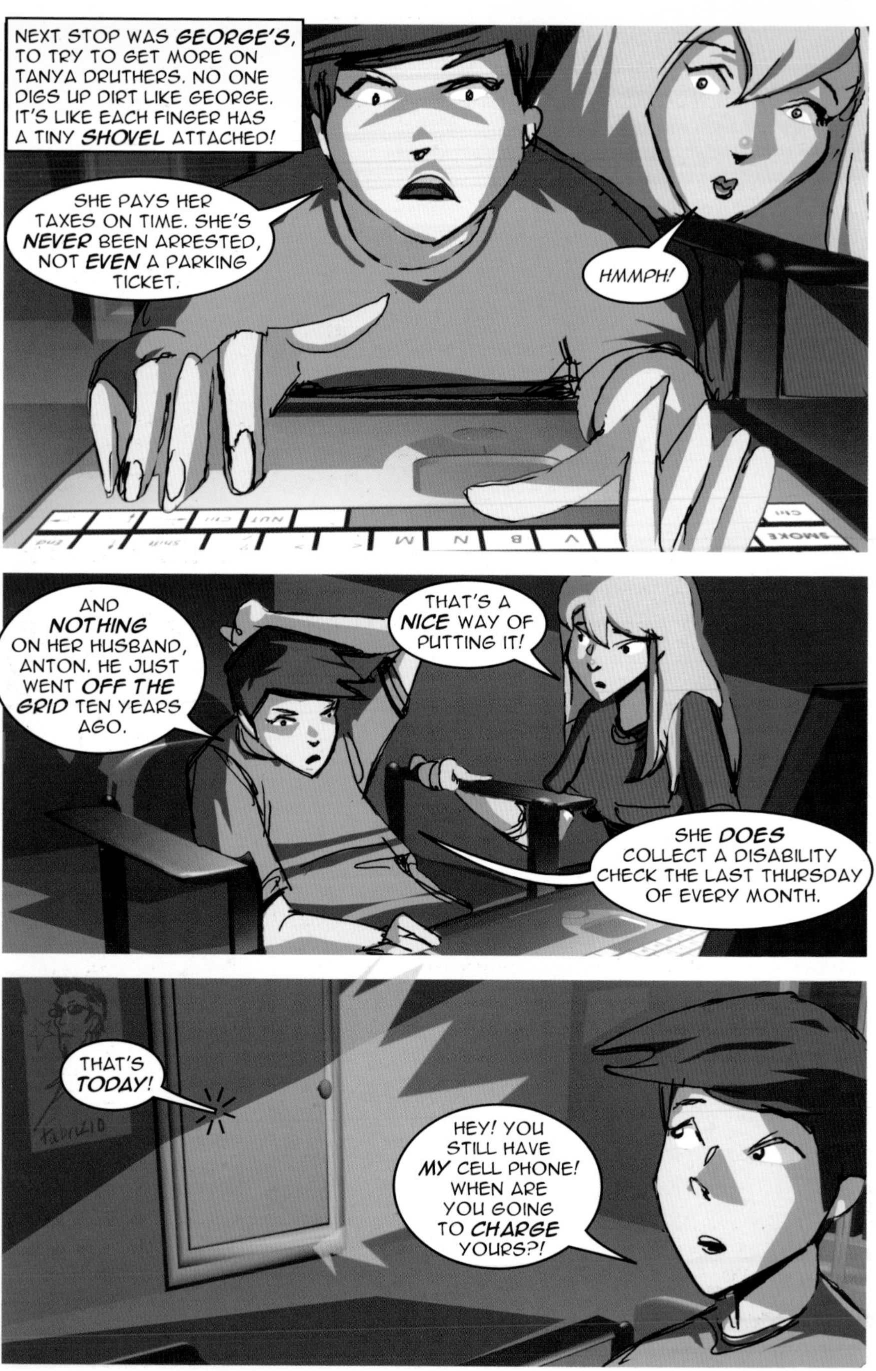
NEXT STOP WAS GEORGE'S, TO TRY TO GET MORE ON TANYA DRUTHERS. NO ONE DIGS UP DIRT LIKE GEORGE. IT'S LIKE EACH FINGER HAS A TINY SHOVEL ATTACHED!
SHE PAYS HER TAXES ON TIME. SHE'S NEVER BEEN ARRESTED, NOT EVEN A PARKING TICKET.
HMMPH!
AND NOTHING ON HER HUSBAND, ANTON. HE JUST WENT OFF THE GRID TEN YEARS AGO.
THAT'S A NICE WAY OF PUTTING IT!
SHE DOES COLLECT A DISABILITY CHECK THE LAST THURSDAY OF EVERY MONTH.
THAT'S TODAY!
HEY! YOU STILL HAVE MY CELL PHONE! WHEN ARE YOU GOING TO CHARGE YOURS?!

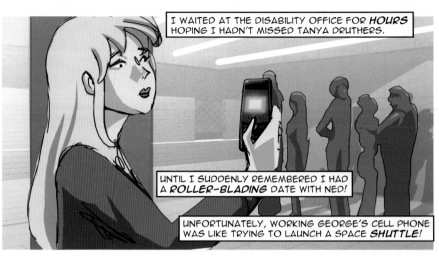

I WAITED AT THE DISABILITY OFFICE FOR *HOURS* HOPING I HADN'T MISSED TANYA DRUTHERS.

UNTIL I SUDDENLY REMEMBERED I HAD A *ROLLER-BLADING* DATE WITH NED!

UNFORTUNATELY, WORKING GEORGE'S CELL PHONE WAS LIKE TRYING TO LAUNCH A SPACE *SHUTTLE!*

NED'S PRETTY PATIENT ABOUT MY MISSING DATES WHEN I'M ON A CASE, BUT HE *DOES* PREFER I CALL.

ONLY, IT TOOK ME FOREVER TO FIGURE OUT THERE WAS NO *SIGNAL.*

SO, I HAD TO GO *OUTSIDE*, WHEREUPON I QUICKLY LEARNED THERE ARE WORSE THINGS THAN WAITING BOYFRIENDS...

WHY, *NANCY DREW,* COMING OUT OF THE *UNEMPLOYMENT* OFFICE! THIS IS JUST *TOO* GOOD!

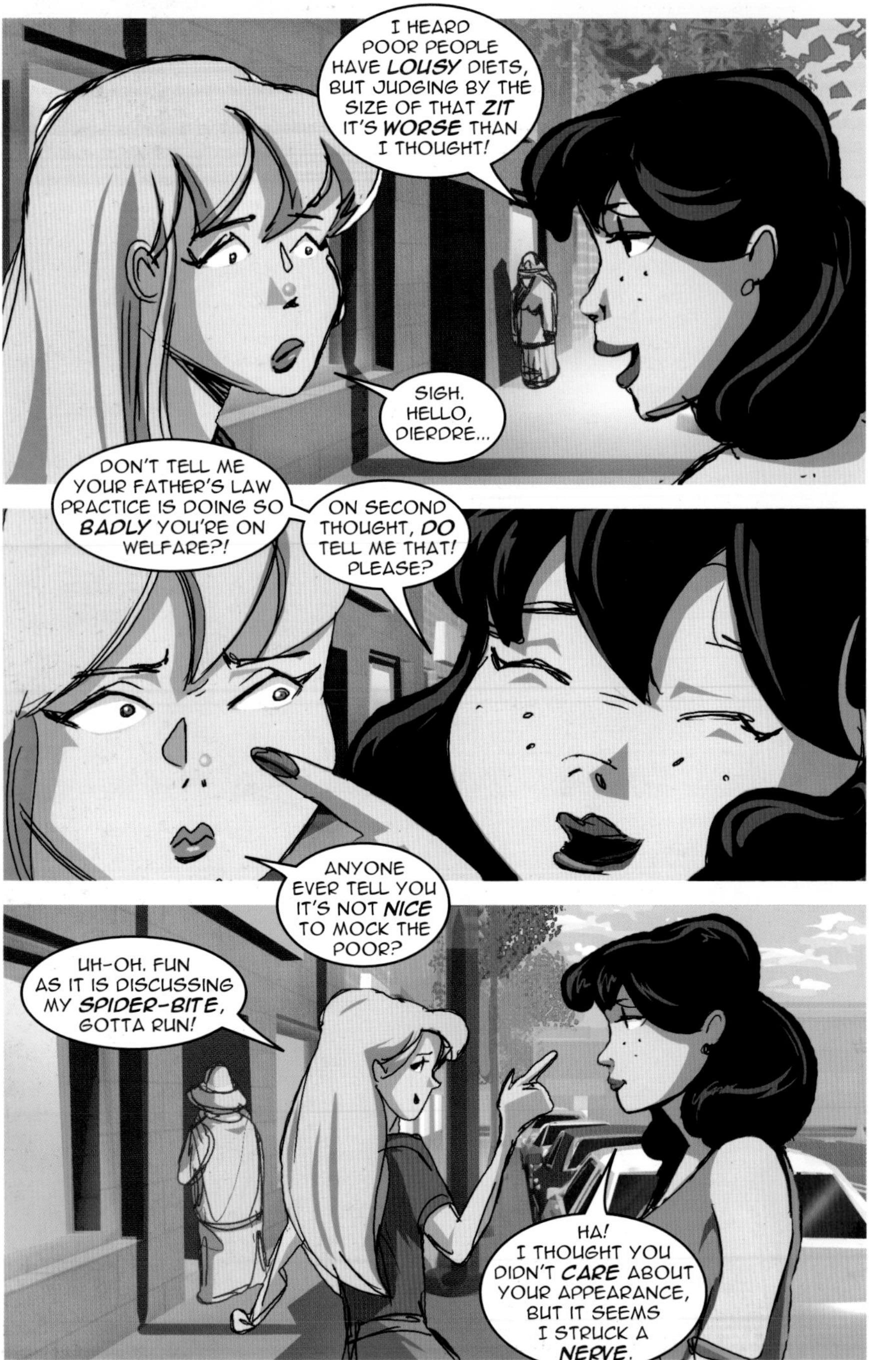
I HEARD POOR PEOPLE HAVE LOUSY DIETS, BUT JUDGING BY THE SIZE OF THAT ZIT IT'S WORSE THAN I THOUGHT!
SIGH. HELLO, DIERDRE...
DON'T TELL ME YOUR FATHER'S LAW PRACTICE IS DOING SO BADLY YOU'RE ON WELFARE?!
ON SECOND THOUGHT, DO TELL ME THAT! PLEASE?
ANYONE EVER TELL YOU IT'S NOT NICE TO MOCK THE POOR?
UH-OH. FUN AS IT IS DISCUSSING MY SPIDER-BITE, GOTTA RUN!
HA! I THOUGHT YOU DIDN'T CARE ABOUT YOUR APPEARANCE, BUT IT SEEMS I STRUCK A NERVE.

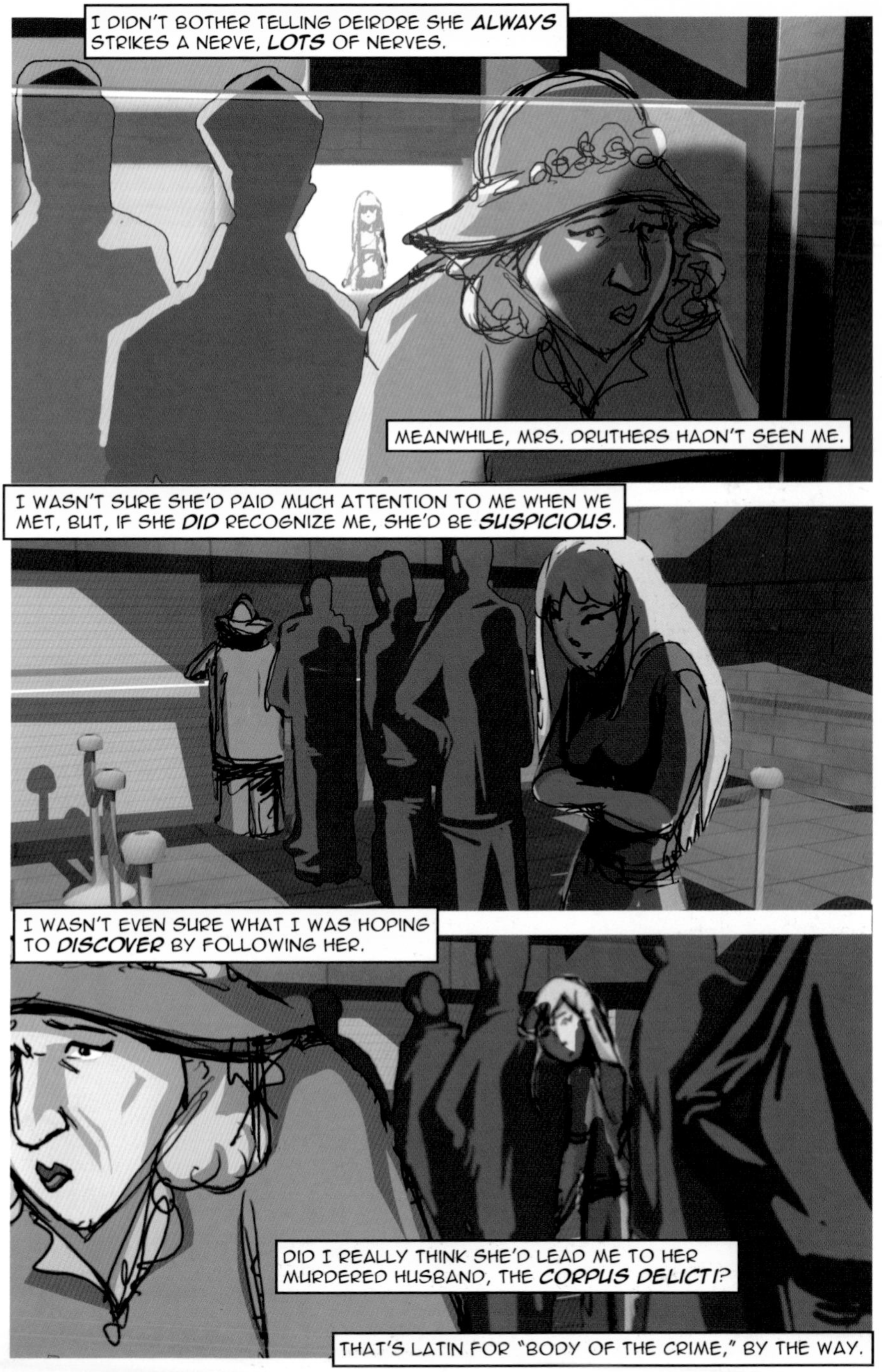
I DIDN'T BOTHER TELLING DEIRDRE SHE ALWAYS STRIKES A NERVE, LOTS OF NERVES.
MEANWHILE, MRS. DRUTHERS HADN'T SEEN ME.
I WASN'T SURE SHE'D PAID MUCH ATTENTION TO ME WHEN WE MET, BUT, IF SHE DID RECOGNIZE ME, SHE'D BE SUSPICIOUS.
I WASN'T EVEN SURE WHAT I WAS HOPING TO DISCOVER BY FOLLOWING HER.
DID I REALLY THINK SHE'D LEAD ME TO HER MURDERED HUSBAND, THE CORPUS DELICTI?
THAT'S LATIN FOR "BODY OF THE CRIME," BY THE WAY.

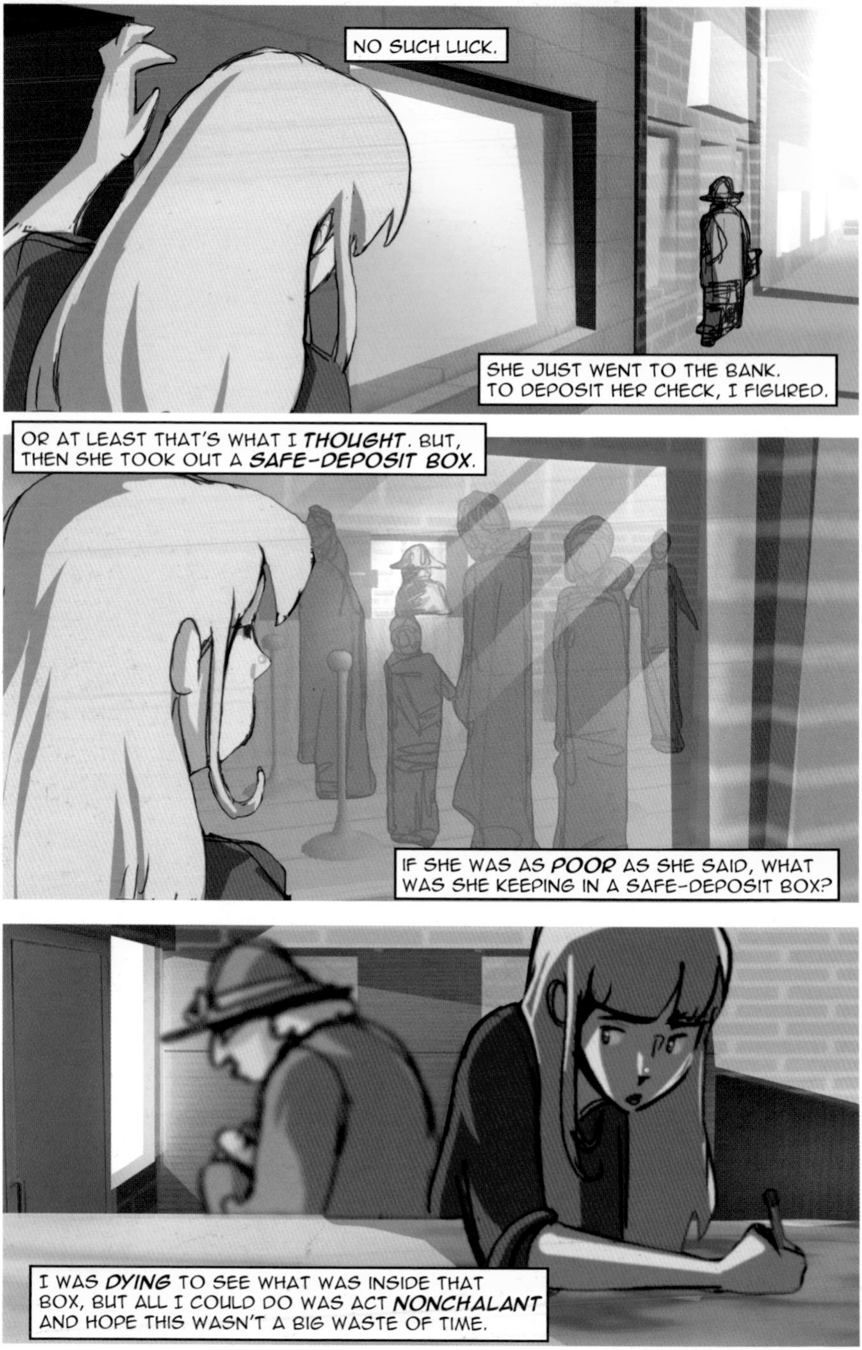
NO SUCH LUCK.
SHE JUST WENT TO THE BANK. TO DEPOSIT HER CHECK, I FIGURED.
OR AT LEAST THAT'S WHAT I THOUGHT. BUT, THEN SHE TOOK OUT A SAFE-DEPOSIT BOX.
IF SHE WAS AS POOR AS SHE SAID, WHAT WAS SHE KEEPING IN A SAFE-DEPOSIT BOX?
I WAS DYING TO SEE WHAT WAS INSIDE THAT BOX, BUT ALL I COULD DO WAS ACT NONCHALANT AND HOPE THIS WASN'T A BIG WASTE OF TIME.

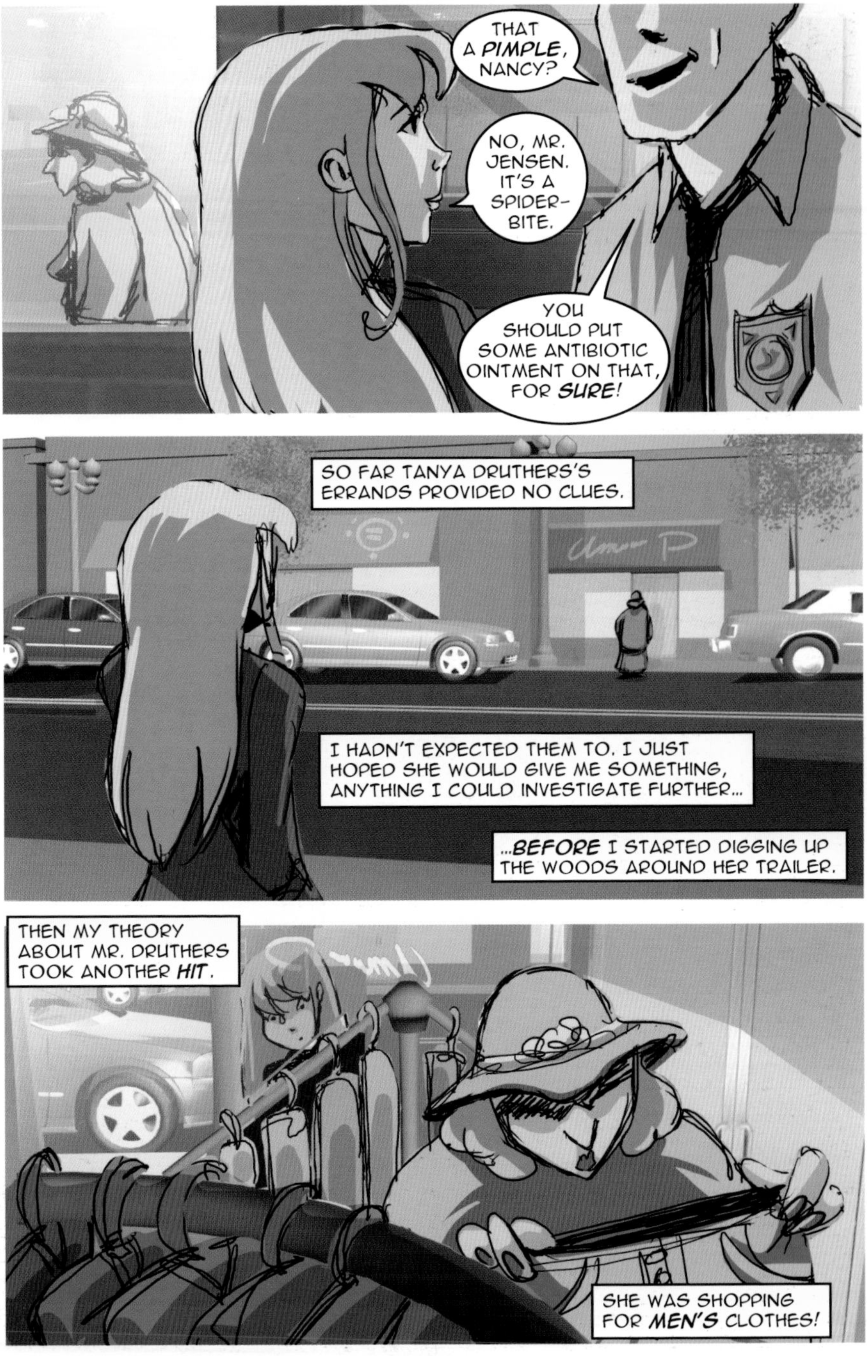
THAT A *PIMPLE*, NANCY?
NO, MR. JENSEN. IT'S A SPIDER-BITE.
YOU SHOULD PUT SOME ANTIBIOTIC OINTMENT ON THAT, FOR *SURE*!
SO FAR TANYA DRUTHERS'S ERRANDS PROVIDED NO CLUES.
I HADN'T EXPECTED THEM TO. I JUST HOPED SHE WOULD GIVE ME SOMETHING, ANYTHING I COULD INVESTIGATE FURTHER...
...*BEFORE* I STARTED DIGGING UP THE WOODS AROUND HER TRAILER.
THEN MY THEORY ABOUT MR. DRUTHERS TOOK ANOTHER *HIT*.
SHE WAS SHOPPING FOR *MEN'S* CLOTHES!

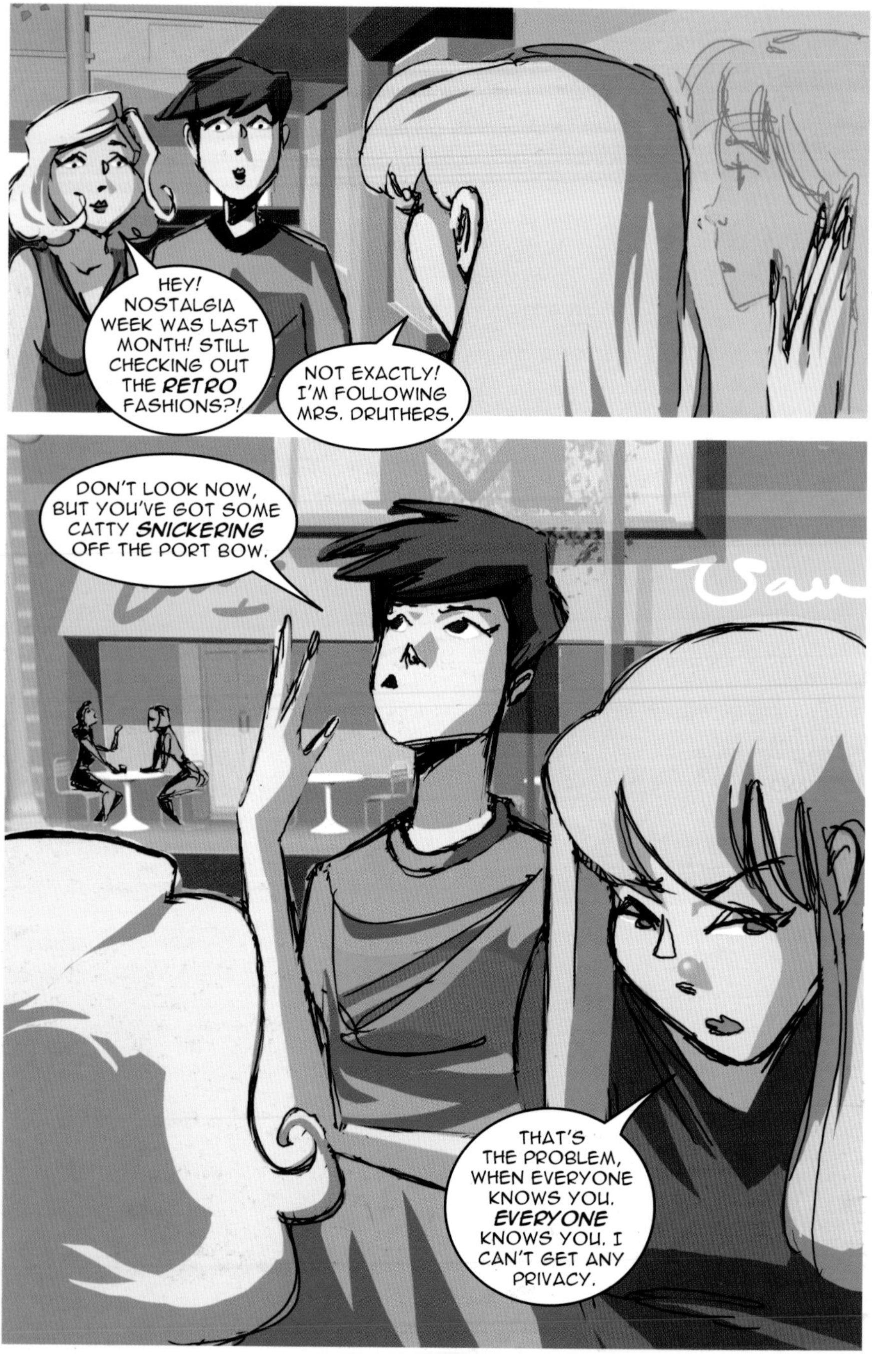
HEY! NOSTALGIA WEEK WAS LAST MONTH! STILL CHECKING OUT THE *RETRO* FASHIONS?!
NOT EXACTLY! I'M FOLLOWING MRS. DRUTHERS.
DON'T LOOK NOW, BUT YOU'VE GOT SOME CATTY *SNICKERING* OFF THE PORT BOW.
THAT'S THE PROBLEM, WHEN EVERYONE KNOWS YOU. *EVERYONE* KNOWS YOU. I CAN'T GET ANY PRIVACY.

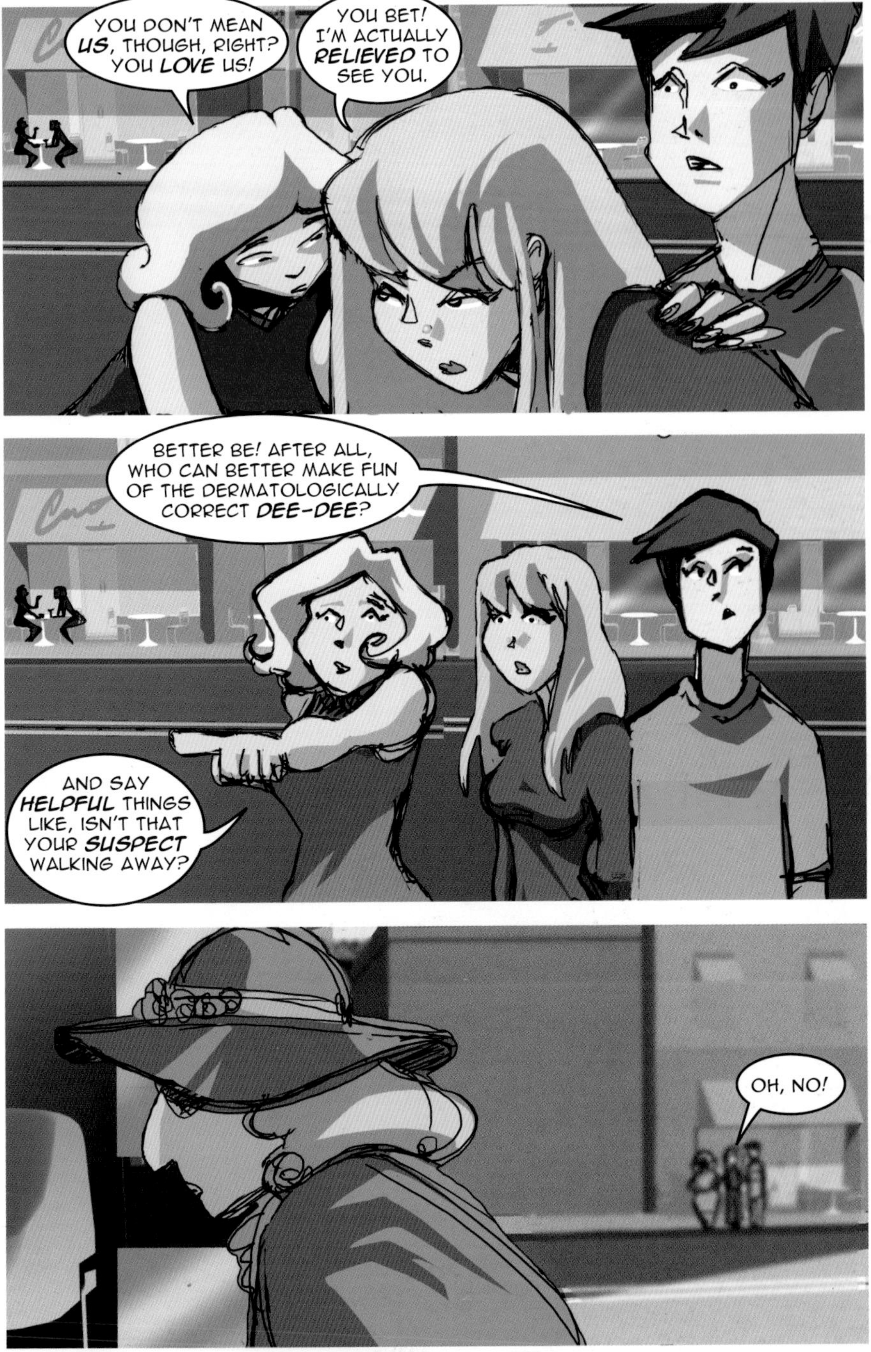
YOU DON'T MEAN US, THOUGH, RIGHT? YOU LOVE US!
YOU BET! I'M ACTUALLY RELIEVED TO SEE YOU.
BETTER BE! AFTER ALL, WHO CAN BETTER MAKE FUN OF THE DERMATOLOGICALLY CORRECT DEE-DEE?
AND SAY HELPFUL THINGS LIKE, ISN'T THAT YOUR SUSPECT WALKING AWAY?
OH, NO!

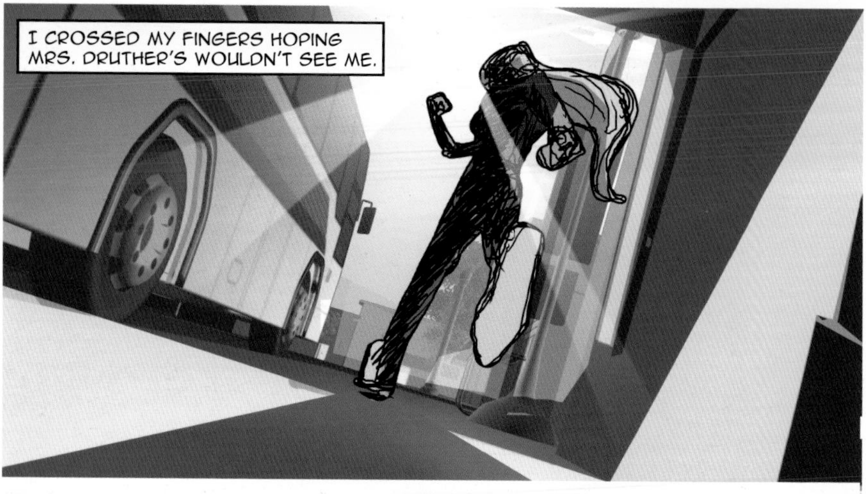
I CROSSED MY FINGERS HOPING MRS. DRUTHER'S WOULDN'T SEE ME.

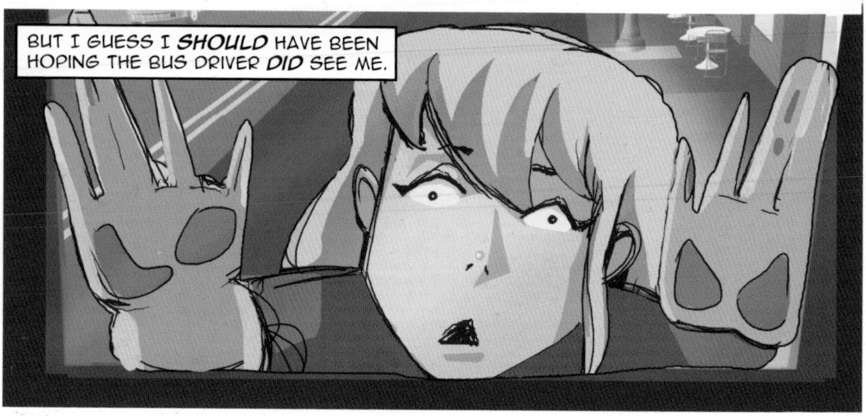
BUT I GUESS I **SHOULD** HAVE BEEN HOPING THE BUS DRIVER **DID** SEE ME.

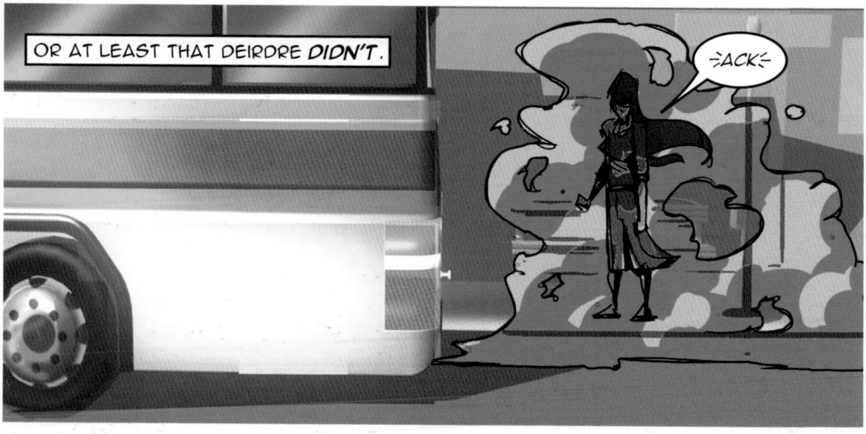
OR AT LEAST THAT DEIRDRE **DIDN'T**.
ACK

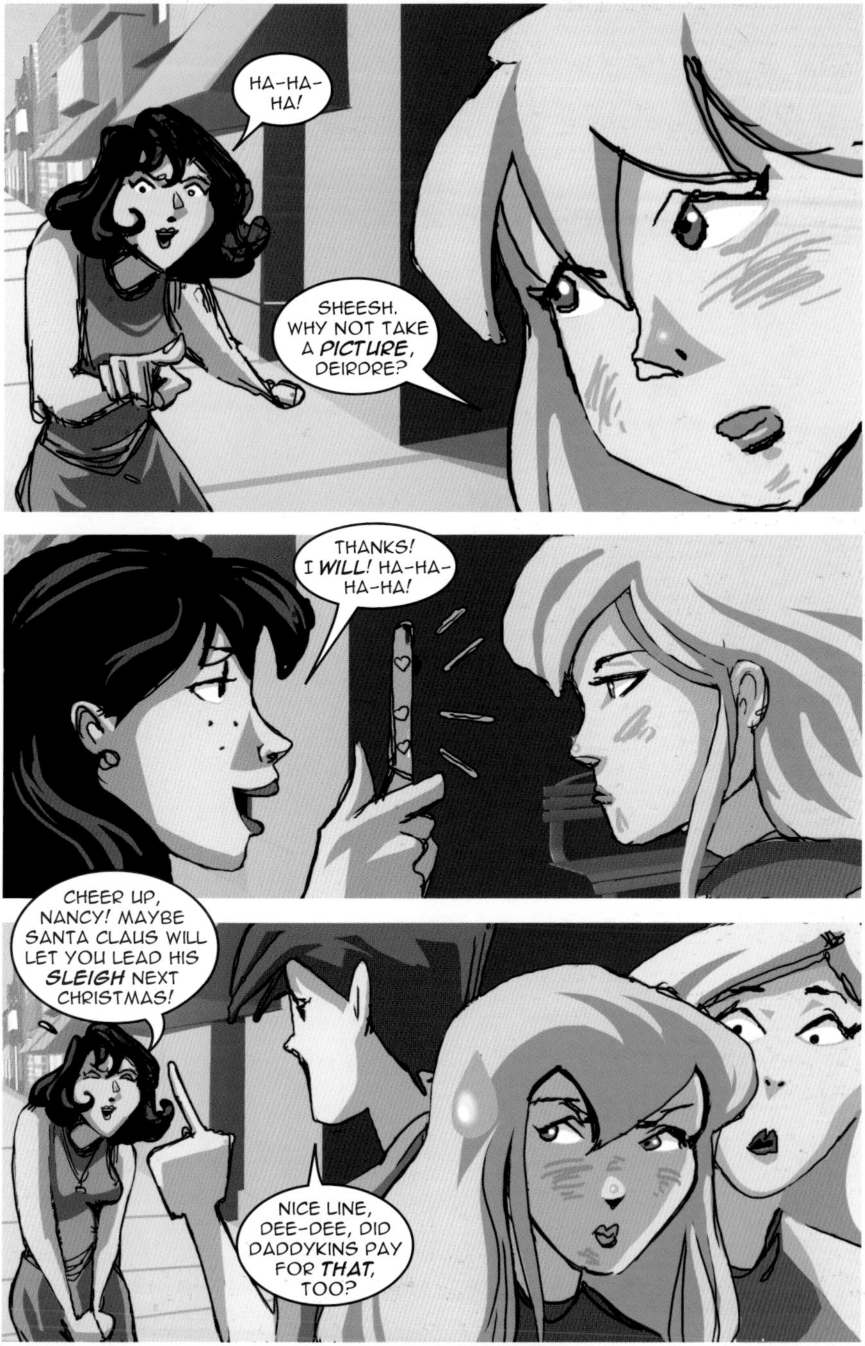
HA-HA-HA!
SHEESH. WHY NOT TAKE A *PICTURE*, DEIRDRE?
THANKS! I *WILL*! HA-HA-HA-HA!
CHEER UP, NANCY! MAYBE SANTA CLAUS WILL LET YOU LEAD HIS *SLEIGH* NEXT CHRISTMAS!
NICE LINE, DEE-DEE, DID DADDYKINS PAY FOR *THAT*, TOO?

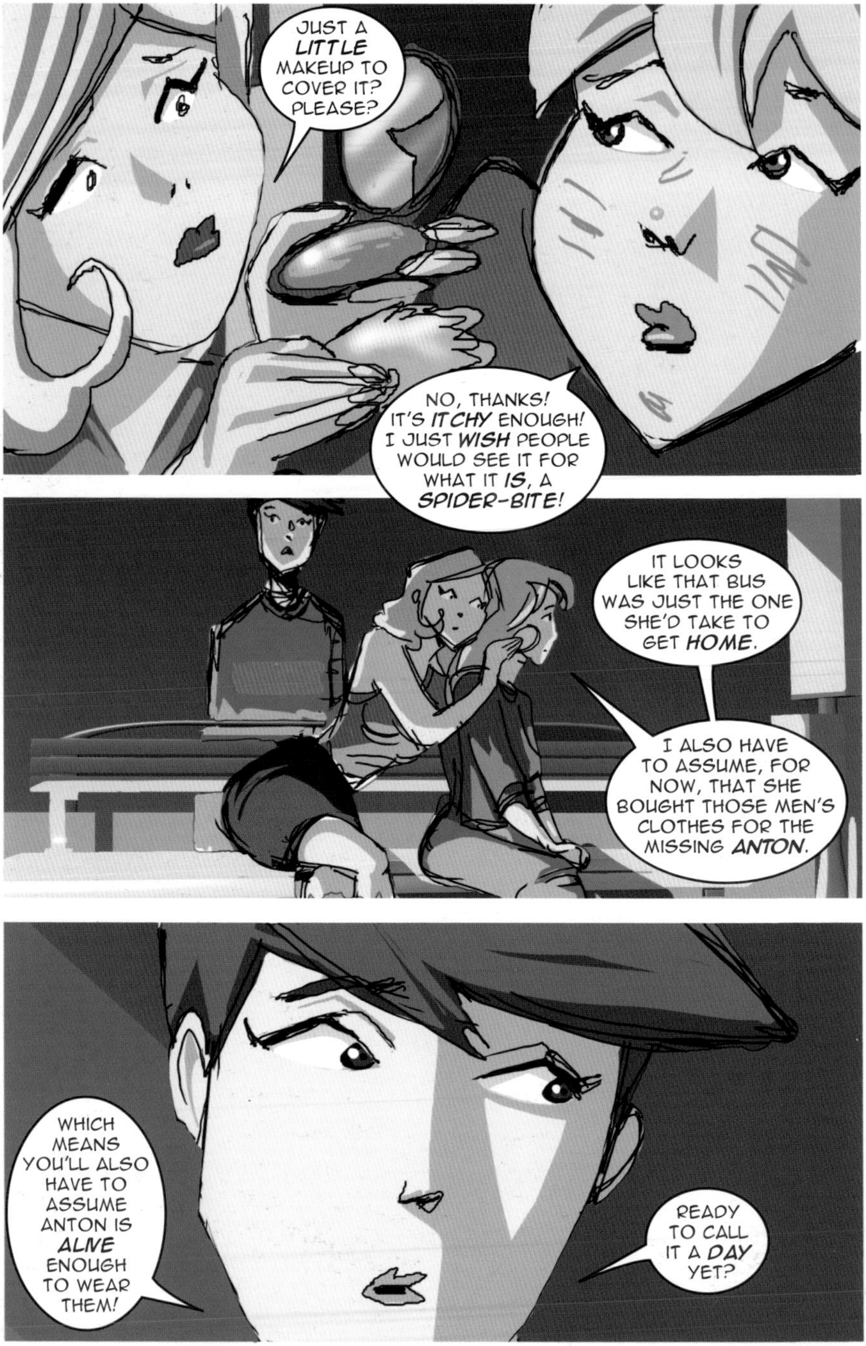
JUST A LITTLE MAKEUP TO COVER IT? PLEASE?
NO, THANKS! IT'S ITCHY ENOUGH! I JUST WISH PEOPLE WOULD SEE IT FOR WHAT IT IS, A SPIDER-BITE!
IT LOOKS LIKE THAT BUS WAS JUST THE ONE SHE'D TAKE TO GET HOME.
I ALSO HAVE TO ASSUME, FOR NOW, THAT SHE BOUGHT THOSE MEN'S CLOTHES FOR THE MISSING ANTON.
WHICH MEANS YOU'LL ALSO HAVE TO ASSUME ANTON IS ALIVE ENOUGH TO WEAR THEM!
READY TO CALL IT A DAY YET?

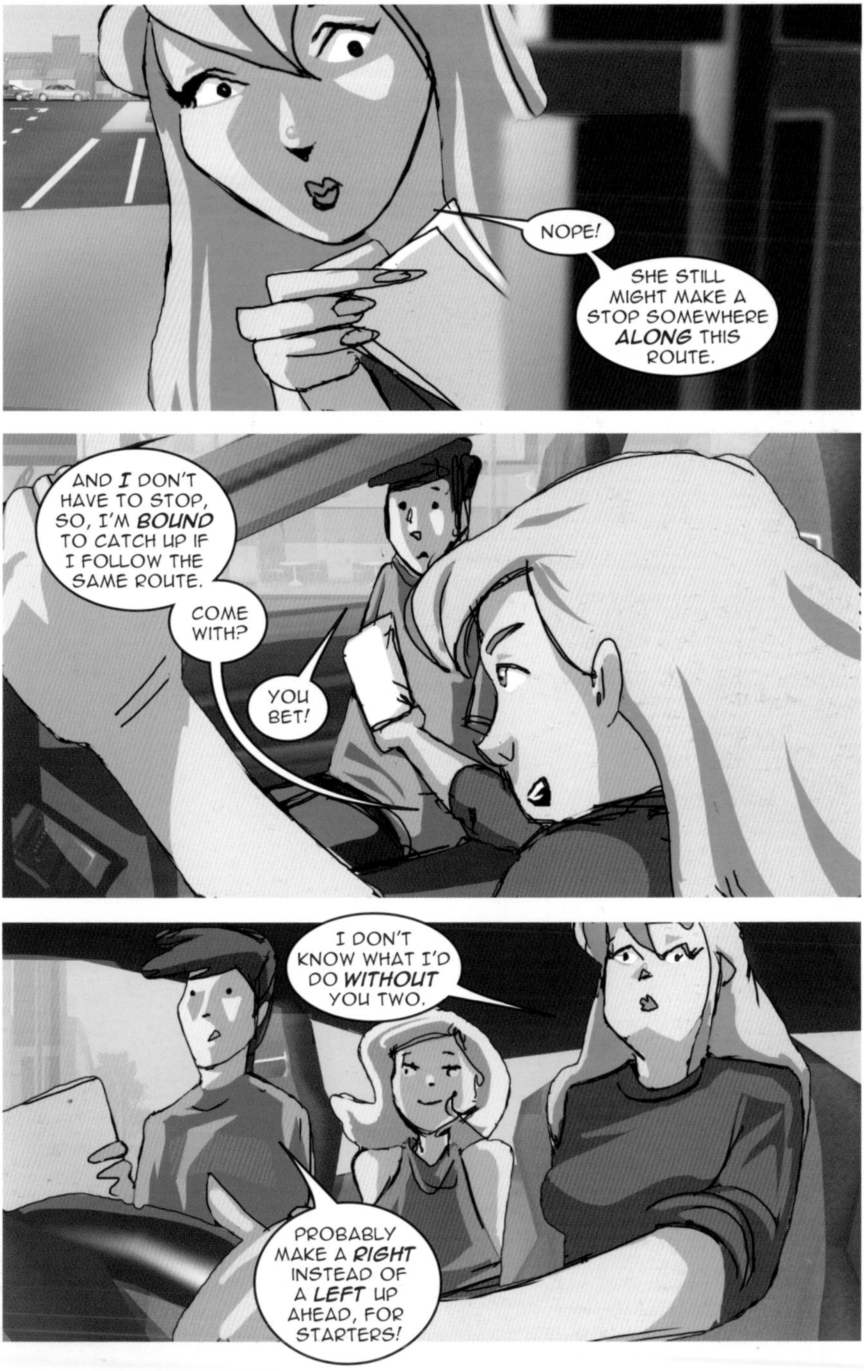
NOPE!
SHE STILL MIGHT MAKE A STOP SOMEWHERE ALONG THIS ROUTE.
AND I DON'T HAVE TO STOP, SO, I'M BOUND TO CATCH UP IF I FOLLOW THE SAME ROUTE.
COME WITH?
YOU BET!
I DON'T KNOW WHAT I'D DO WITHOUT YOU TWO.
PROBABLY MAKE A RIGHT INSTEAD OF A LEFT UP AHEAD, FOR STARTERS!

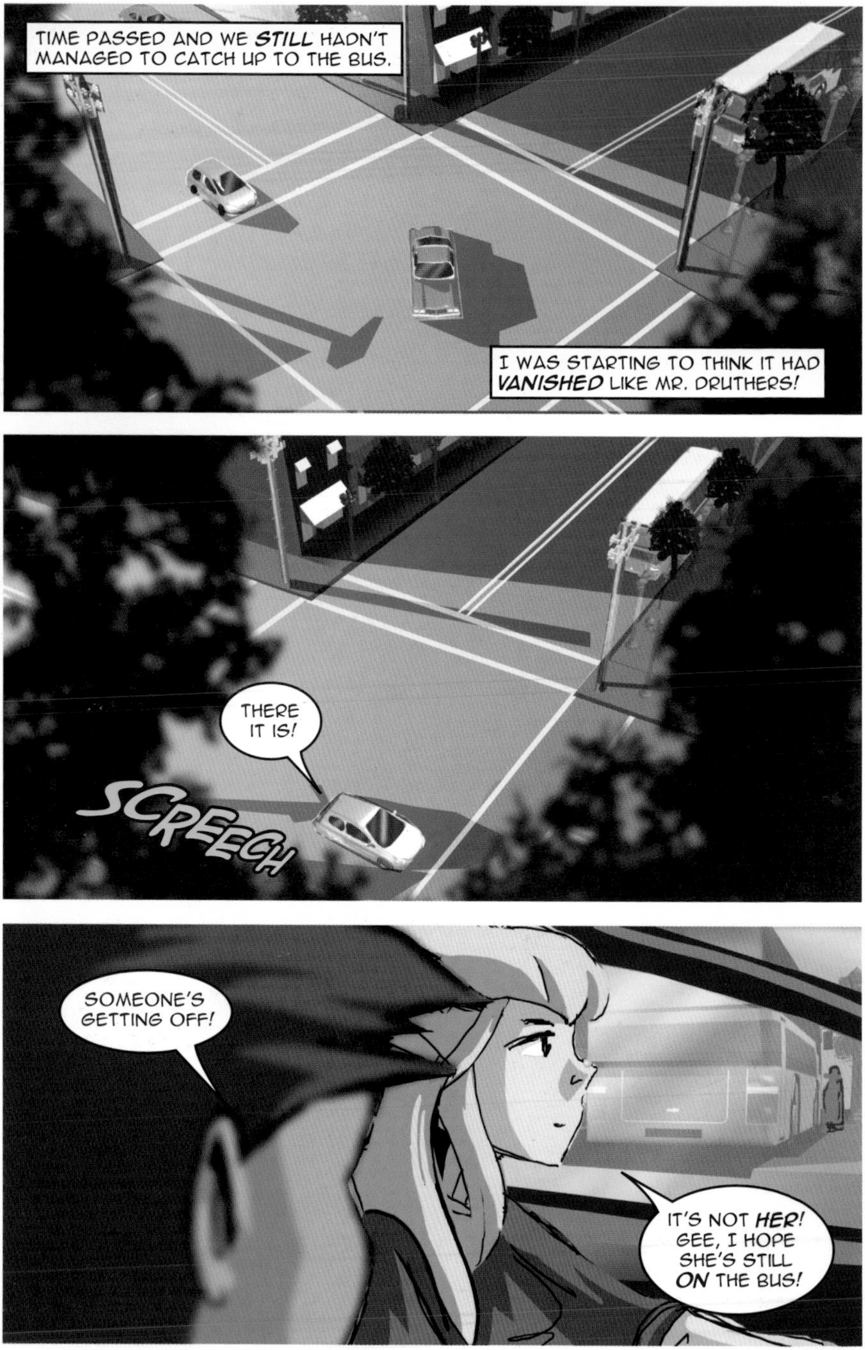
TIME PASSED AND WE STILL HADN'T MANAGED TO CATCH UP TO THE BUS.
I WAS STARTING TO THINK IT HAD VANISHED LIKE MR. DRUTHERS!
THERE IT IS!
SCREECH
SOMEONE'S GETTING OFF!
IT'S NOT HER! GEE, I HOPE SHE'S STILL ON THE BUS!

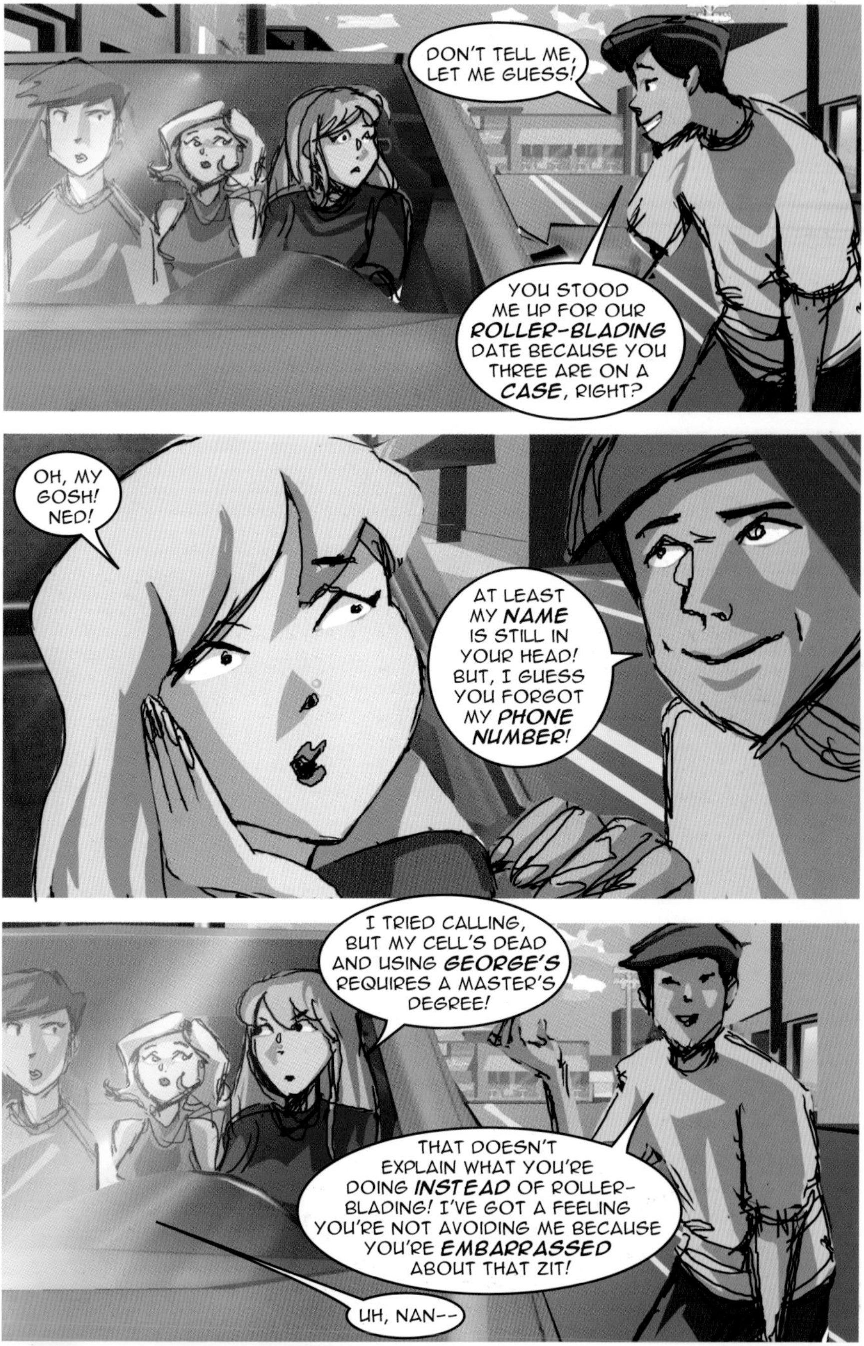
DON'T TELL ME, LET ME GUESS!
YOU STOOD ME UP FOR OUR ***ROLLER-BLADING*** DATE BECAUSE YOU THREE ARE ON A ***CASE***, RIGHT?
OH, MY GOSH! NED!
AT LEAST MY ***NAME*** IS STILL IN YOUR HEAD! BUT, I GUESS YOU FORGOT MY ***PHONE NUMBER***!
I TRIED CALLING, BUT MY CELL'S DEAD AND USING ***GEORGE'S*** REQUIRES A MASTER'S DEGREE!
THAT DOESN'T EXPLAIN WHAT YOU'RE DOING ***INSTEAD*** OF ROLLER-BLADING! I'VE GOT A FEELING YOU'RE NOT AVOIDING ME BECAUSE YOU'RE ***EMBARRASSED*** ABOUT THAT ZIT!
UH, NAN--

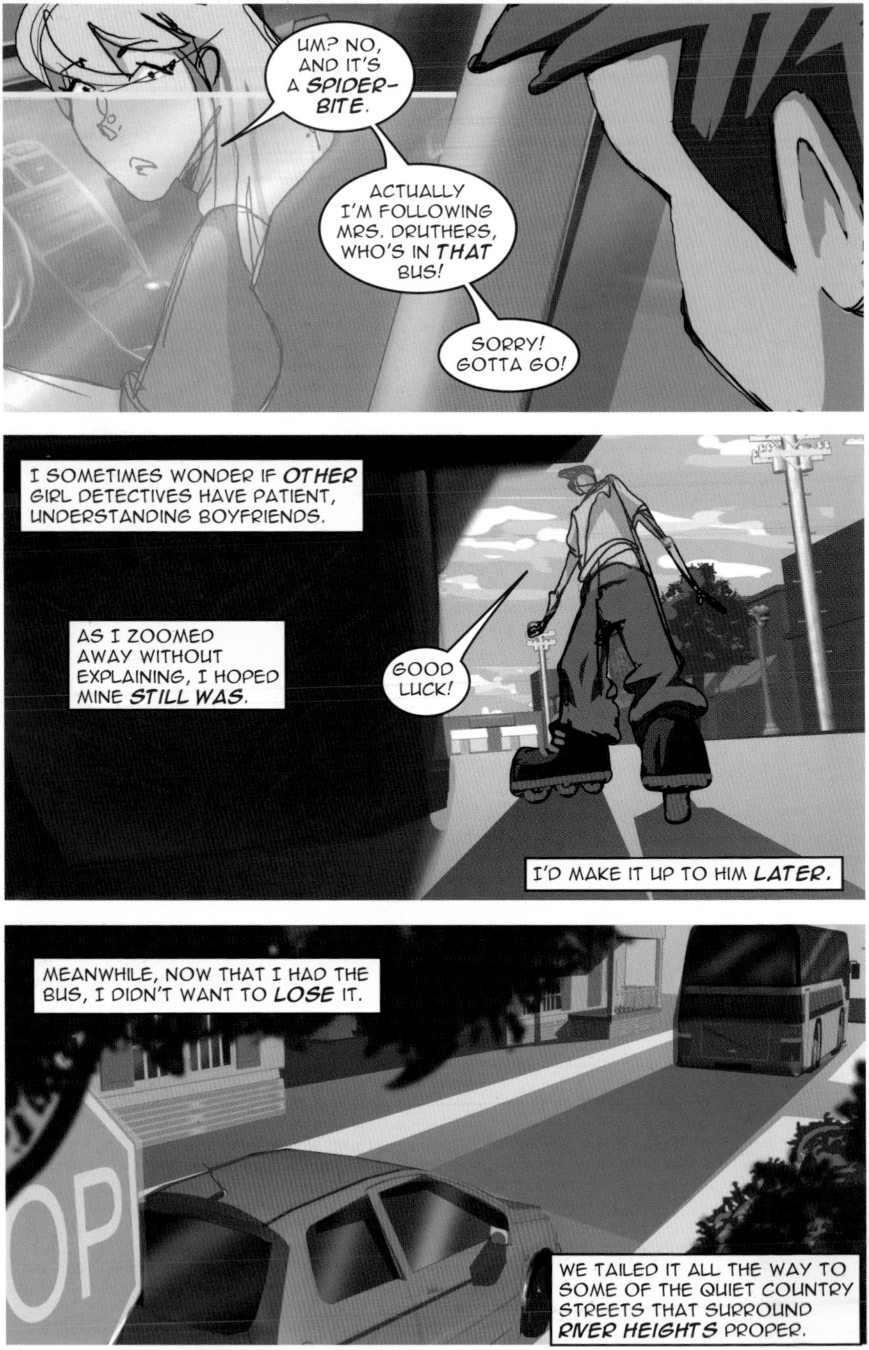
UM? NO, AND IT'S A SPIDER-BITE.
ACTUALLY I'M FOLLOWING MRS. DRUTHERS, WHO'S IN THAT BUS!
SORRY! GOTTA GO!
I SOMETIMES WONDER IF OTHER GIRL DETECTIVES HAVE PATIENT, UNDERSTANDING BOYFRIENDS.
AS I ZOOMED AWAY WITHOUT EXPLAINING, I HOPED MINE STILL WAS.
GOOD LUCK!
I'D MAKE IT UP TO HIM LATER.
MEANWHILE, NOW THAT I HAD THE BUS, I DIDN'T WANT TO LOSE IT.
OP
WE TAILED IT ALL THE WAY TO SOME OF THE QUIET COUNTRY STREETS THAT SURROUND RIVER HEIGHTS PROPER.

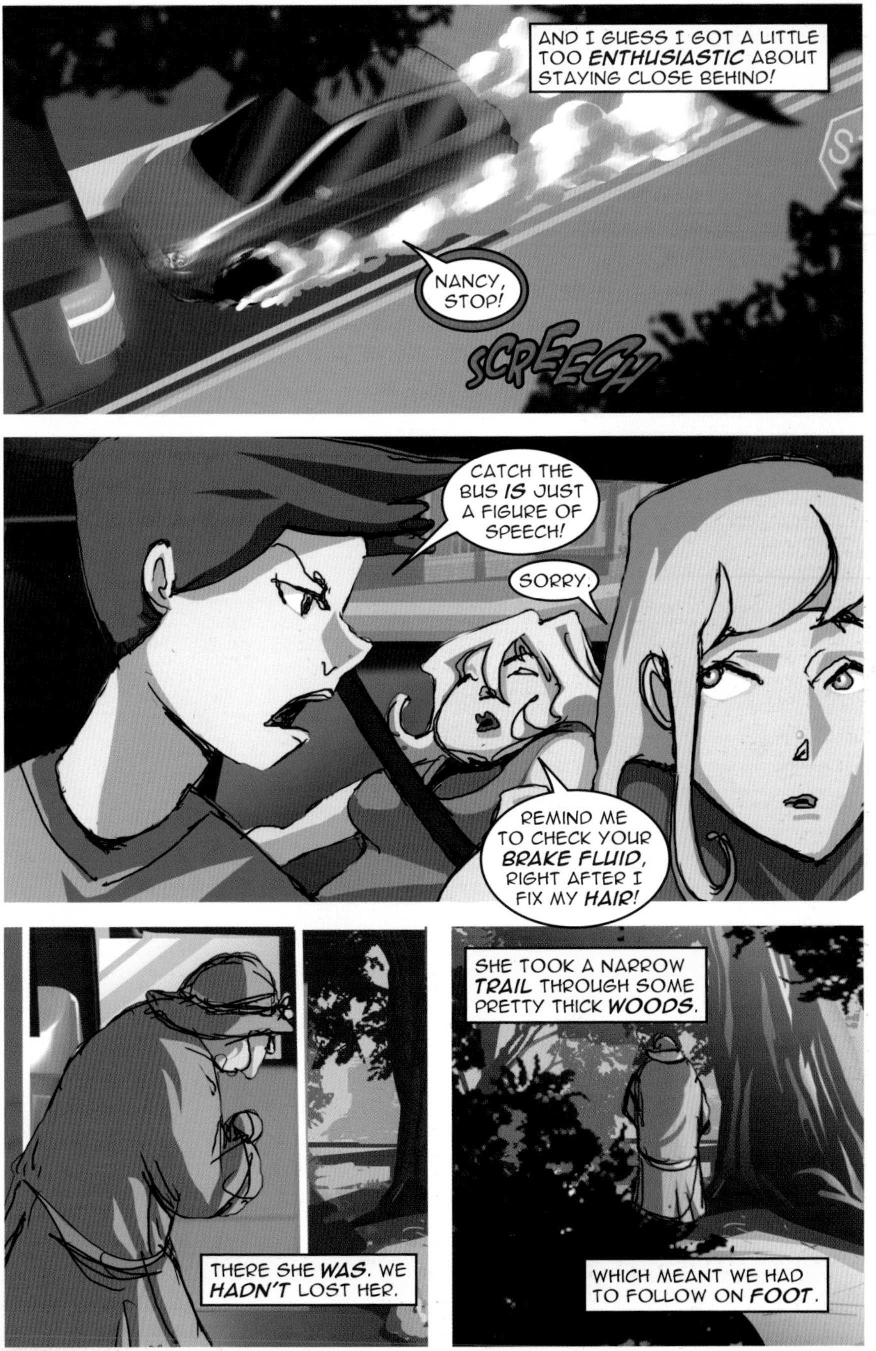
AND I GUESS I GOT A LITTLE TOO ENTHUSIASTIC ABOUT STAYING CLOSE BEHIND!
NANCY, STOP!
SCREECH
CATCH THE BUS IS JUST A FIGURE OF SPEECH!
SORRY.
REMIND ME TO CHECK YOUR BRAKE FLUID, RIGHT AFTER I FIX MY HAIR!
THERE SHE WAS. WE HADN'T LOST HER.
SHE TOOK A NARROW TRAIL THROUGH SOME PRETTY THICK WOODS.
WHICH MEANT WE HAD TO FOLLOW ON FOOT.

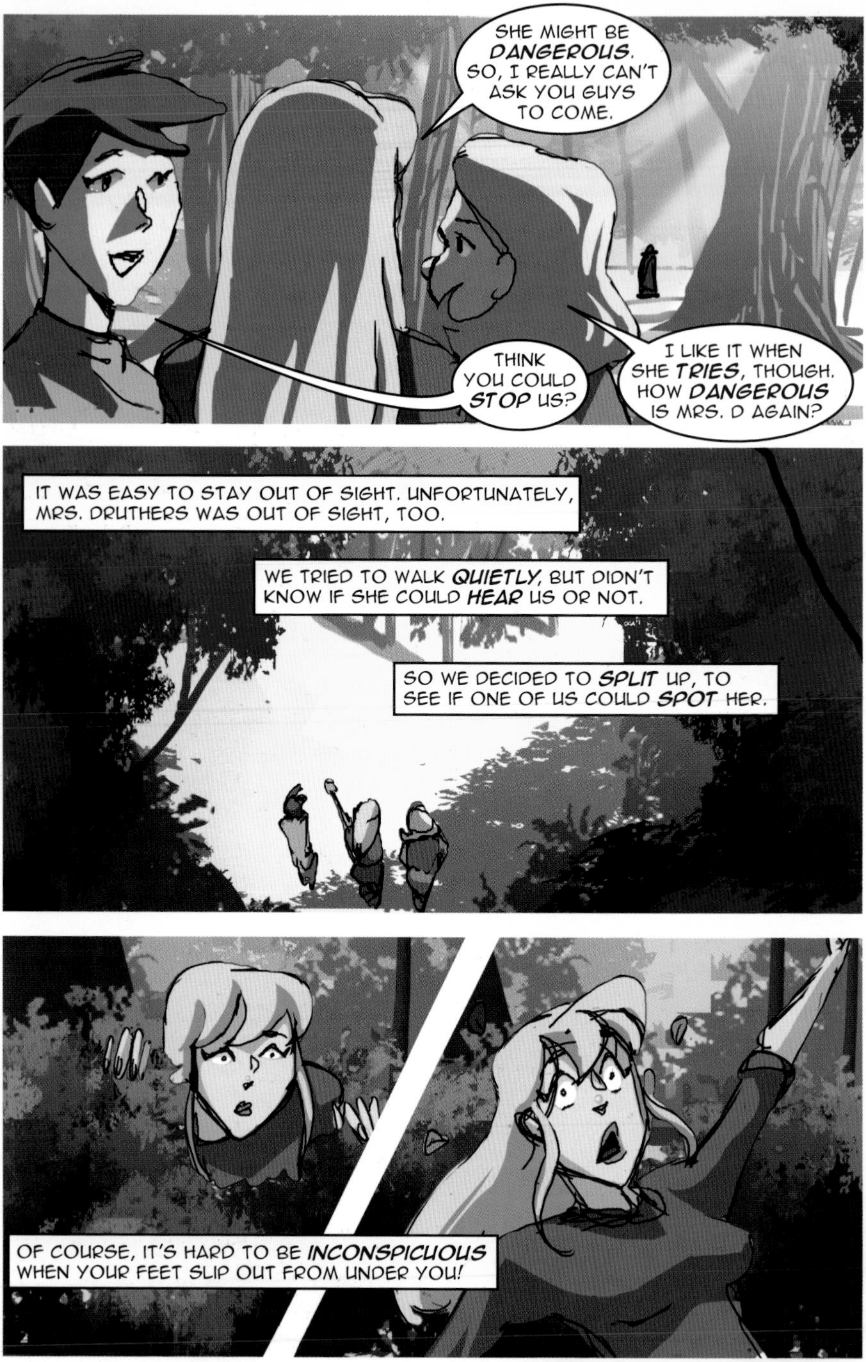
SHE MIGHT BE DANGEROUS. SO, I REALLY CAN'T ASK YOU GUYS TO COME.
THINK YOU COULD STOP US?
I LIKE IT WHEN SHE TRIES, THOUGH. HOW DANGEROUS IS MRS. D AGAIN?
IT WAS EASY TO STAY OUT OF SIGHT. UNFORTUNATELY, MRS. DRUTHERS WAS OUT OF SIGHT, TOO.
WE TRIED TO WALK QUIETLY, BUT DIDN'T KNOW IF SHE COULD HEAR US OR NOT.
SO WE DECIDED TO SPLIT UP, TO SEE IF ONE OF US COULD SPOT HER.
OF COURSE, IT'S HARD TO BE INCONSPICUOUS WHEN YOUR FEET SLIP OUT FROM UNDER YOU!

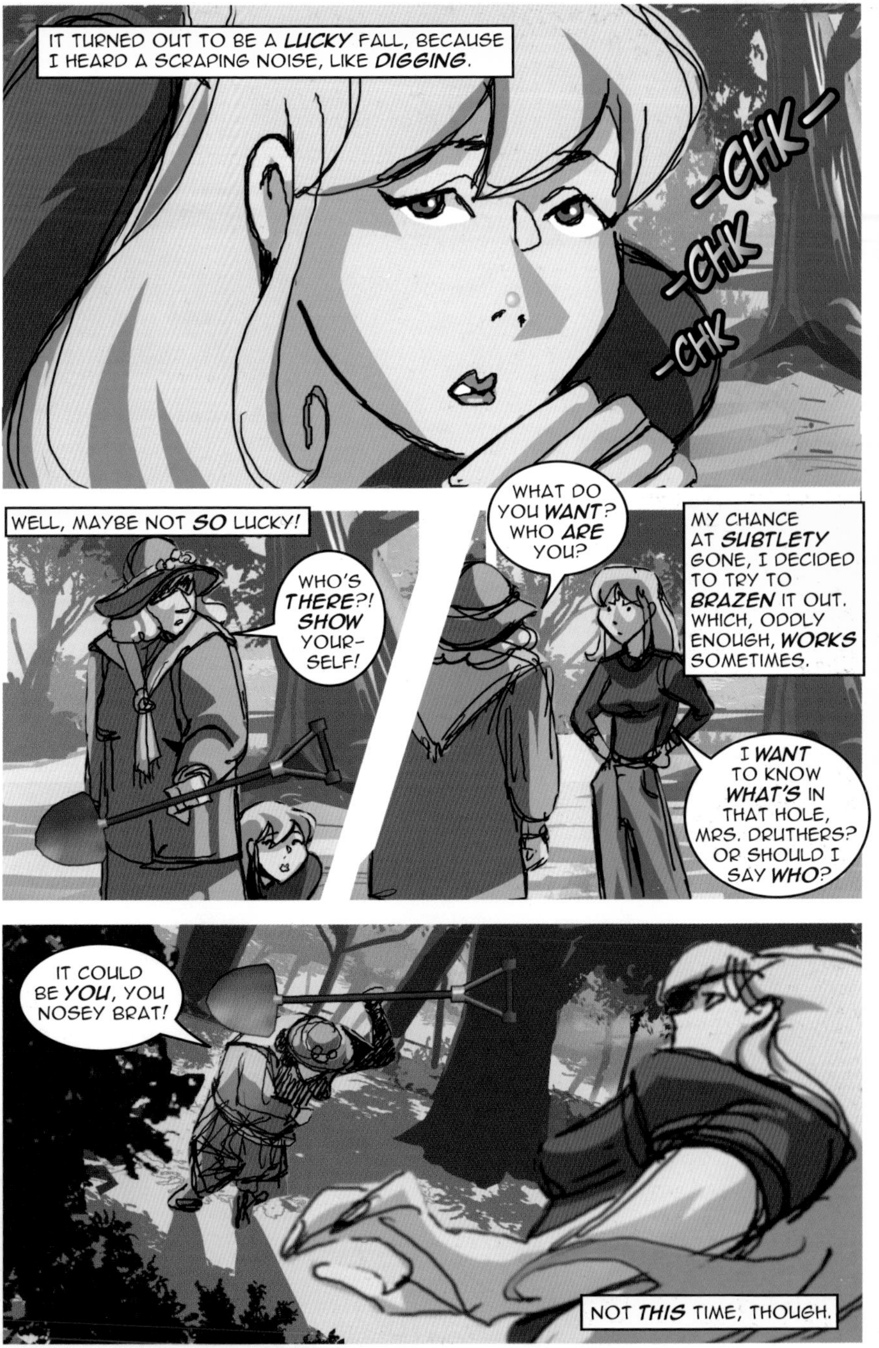
IT TURNED OUT TO BE A LUCKY FALL, BECAUSE I HEARD A SCRAPING NOISE, LIKE DIGGING.
-CHK-
-CHK
-CHK
WELL, MAYBE NOT SO LUCKY!
WHO'S THERE?! SHOW YOURSELF!
WHAT DO YOU WANT? WHO ARE YOU?
MY CHANCE AT SUBTLETY GONE, I DECIDED TO TRY TO BRAZEN IT OUT. WHICH, ODDLY ENOUGH, WORKS SOMETIMES.
I WANT TO KNOW WHAT'S IN THAT HOLE, MRS. DRUTHERS? OR SHOULD I SAY WHO?
IT COULD BE YOU, YOU NOSEY BRAT!
NOT THIS TIME, THOUGH.

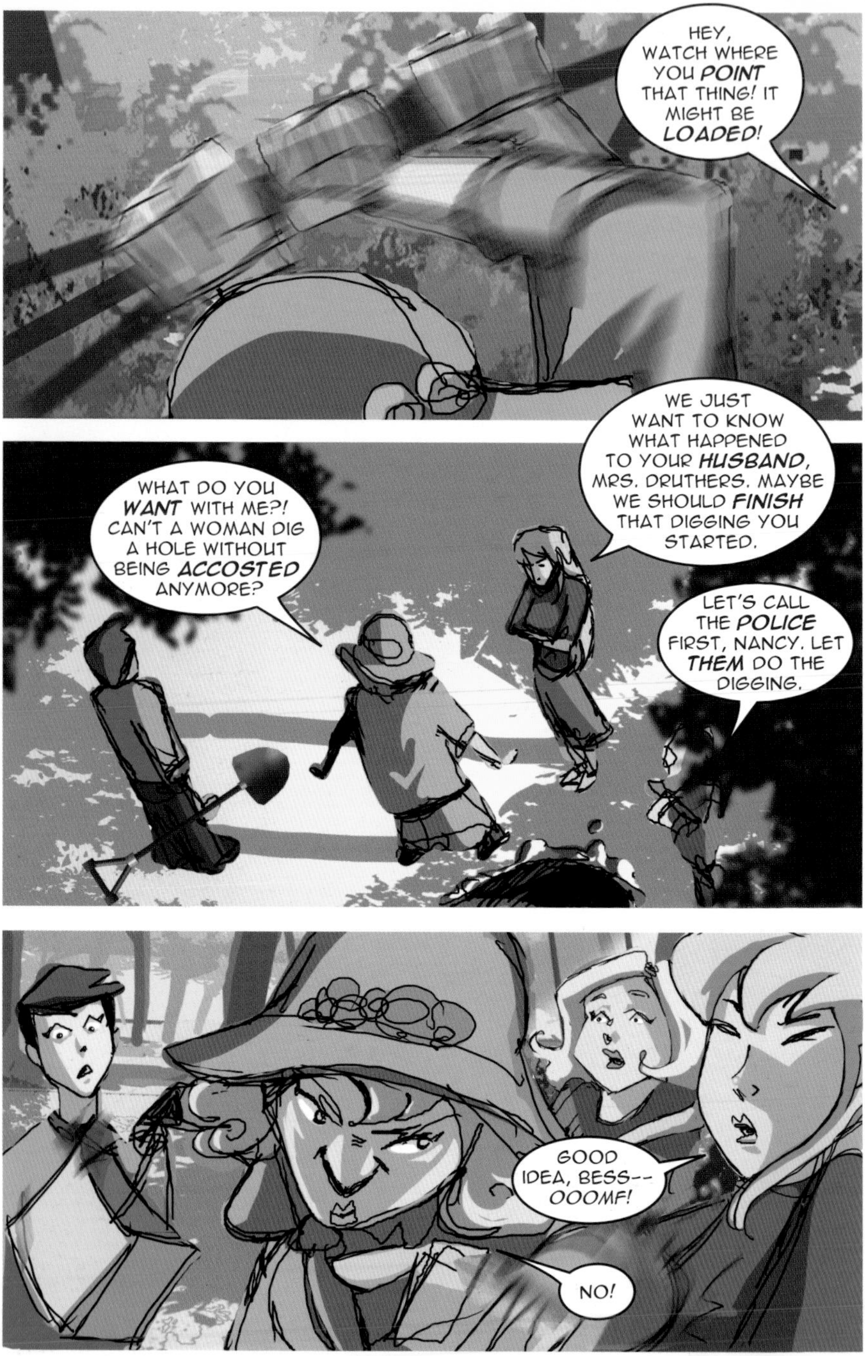
HEY, WATCH WHERE YOU POINT THAT THING! IT MIGHT BE LOADED!
WHAT DO YOU WANT WITH ME?! CAN'T A WOMAN DIG A HOLE WITHOUT BEING ACCOSTED ANYMORE?
WE JUST WANT TO KNOW WHAT HAPPENED TO YOUR HUSBAND, MRS. DRUTHERS. MAYBE WE SHOULD FINISH THAT DIGGING YOU STARTED.
LET'S CALL THE POLICE FIRST, NANCY. LET THEM DO THE DIGGING.
GOOD IDEA, BESS-- OOOMF!
NO!

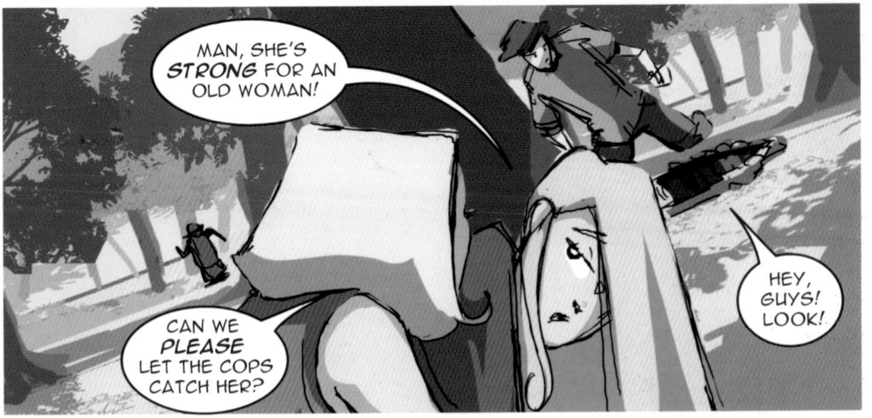
MAN, SHE'S STRONG FOR AN OLD WOMAN!
CAN WE PLEASE LET THE COPS CATCH HER?
HEY, GUYS! LOOK!

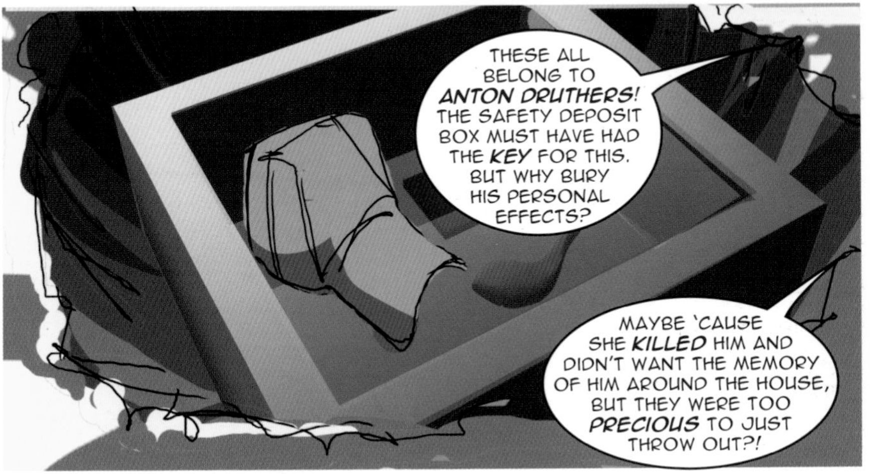
THESE ALL BELONG TO ANTON DRUTHERS! THE SAFETY DEPOSIT BOX MUST HAVE HAD THE KEY FOR THIS. BUT WHY BURY HIS PERSONAL EFFECTS?
MAYBE 'CAUSE SHE KILLED HIM AND DIDN'T WANT THE MEMORY OF HIM AROUND THE HOUSE, BUT THEY WERE TOO PRECIOUS TO JUST THROW OUT?!

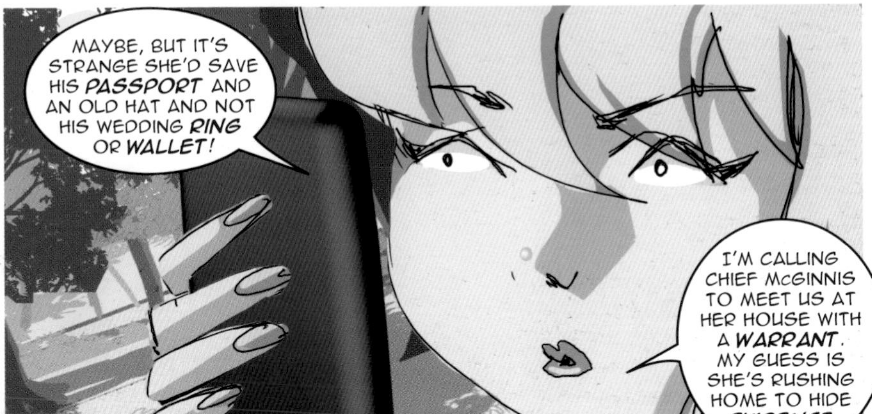
MAYBE, BUT IT'S STRANGE SHE'D SAVE HIS PASSPORT AND AN OLD HAT AND NOT HIS WEDDING RING OR WALLET!
I'M CALLING CHIEF McGINNIS TO MEET US AT HER HOUSE WITH A WARRANT. MY GUESS IS SHE'S RUSHING HOME TO HIDE EVIDENCE.

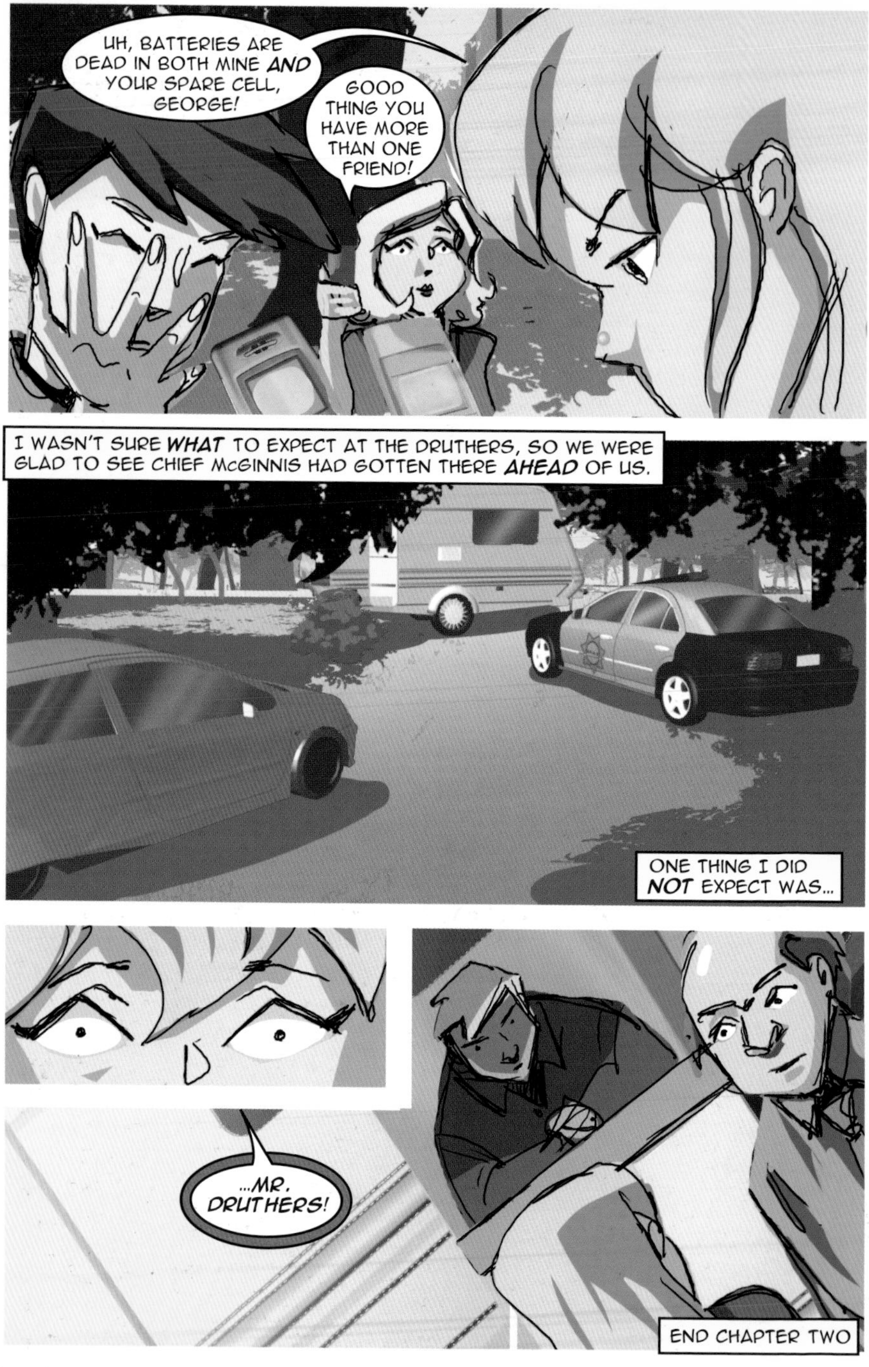
UH, BATTERIES ARE DEAD IN BOTH MINE AND YOUR SPARE CELL, GEORGE!
GOOD THING YOU HAVE MORE THAN ONE FRIEND!
I WASN'T SURE WHAT TO EXPECT AT THE DRUTHERS, SO WE WERE GLAD TO SEE CHIEF McGINNIS HAD GOTTEN THERE AHEAD OF US.
ONE THING I DID NOT EXPECT WAS...
...MR. DRUTHERS!
END CHAPTER TWO

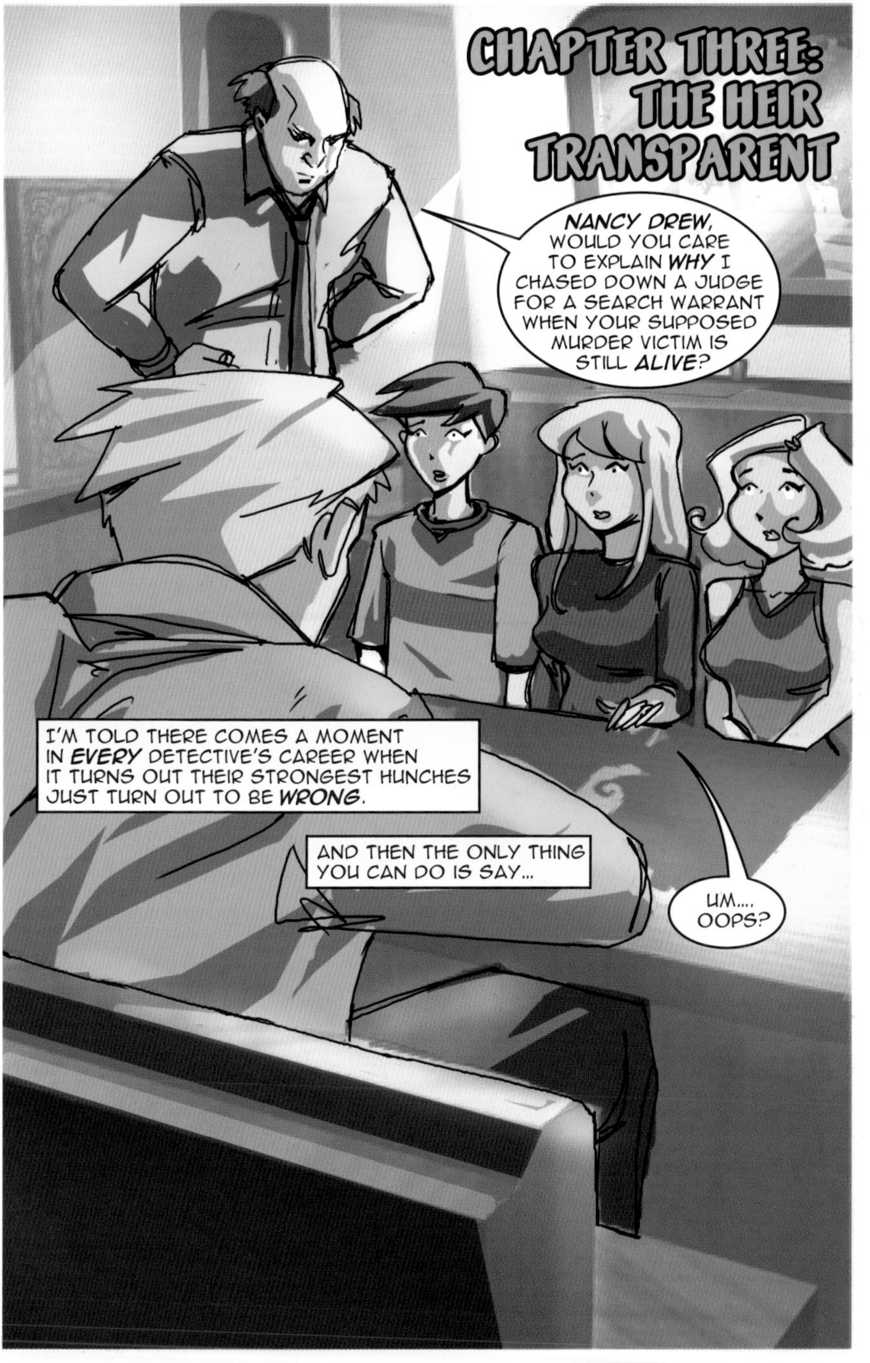
CHAPTER THREE: THE HEIR TRANSPARENT
NANCY DREW, WOULD YOU CARE TO EXPLAIN WHY I CHASED DOWN A JUDGE FOR A SEARCH WARRANT WHEN YOUR SUPPOSED MURDER VICTIM IS STILL ALIVE?
I'M TOLD THERE COMES A MOMENT IN EVERY DETECTIVE'S CAREER WHEN IT TURNS OUT THEIR STRONGEST HUNCHES JUST TURN OUT TO BE WRONG.
AND THEN THE ONLY THING YOU CAN DO IS SAY...
UM.... OOPS?

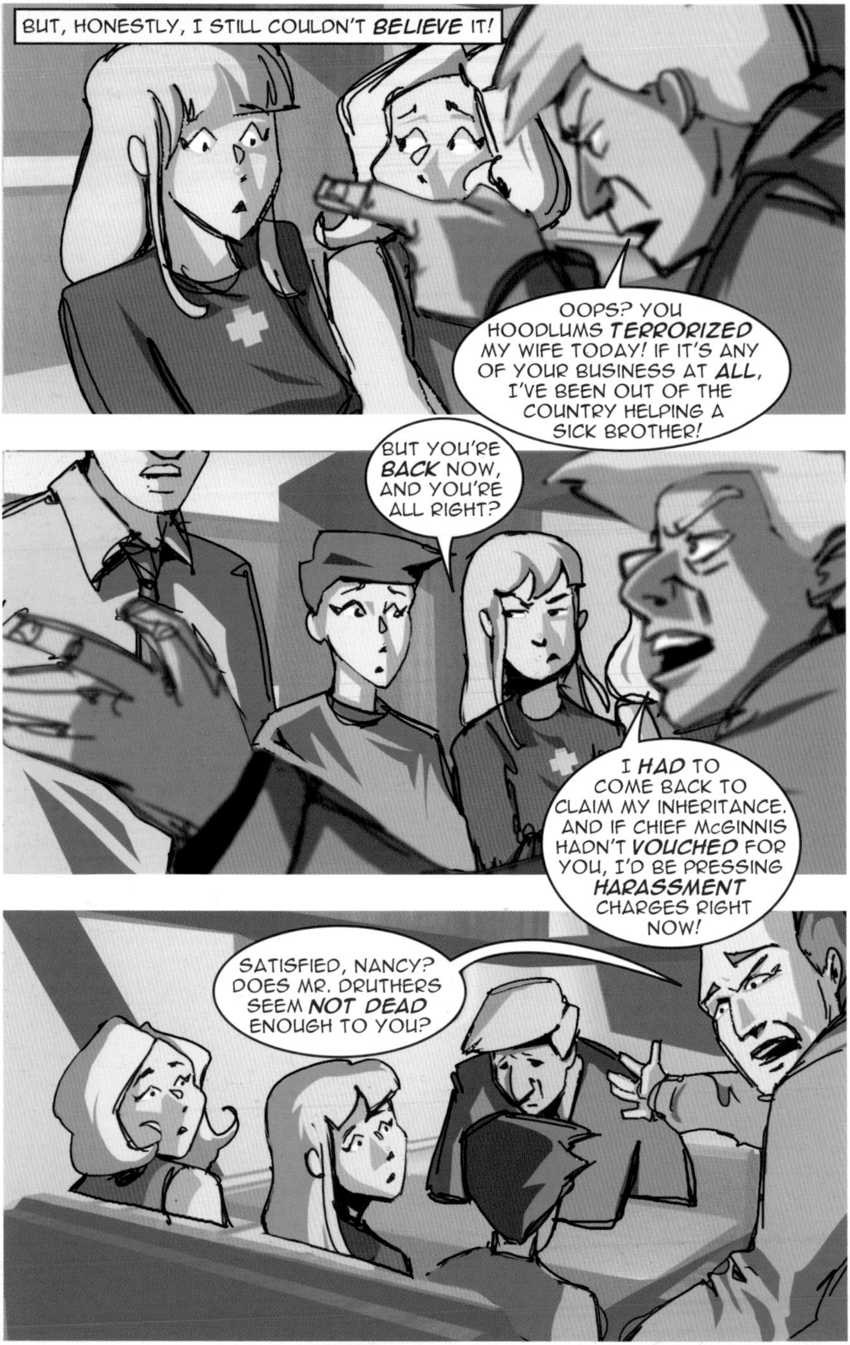
BUT, HONESTLY, I STILL COULDN'T BELIEVE IT!
OOPS? YOU HOODLUMS TERRORIZED MY WIFE TODAY! IF IT'S ANY OF YOUR BUSINESS AT ALL, I'VE BEEN OUT OF THE COUNTRY HELPING A SICK BROTHER!
BUT YOU'RE BACK NOW, AND YOU'RE ALL RIGHT?
I HAD TO COME BACK TO CLAIM MY INHERITANCE. AND IF CHIEF McGINNIS HADN'T VOUCHED FOR YOU, I'D BE PRESSING HARASSMENT CHARGES RIGHT NOW!
SATISFIED, NANCY? DOES MR. DRUTHERS SEEM NOT DEAD ENOUGH TO YOU?

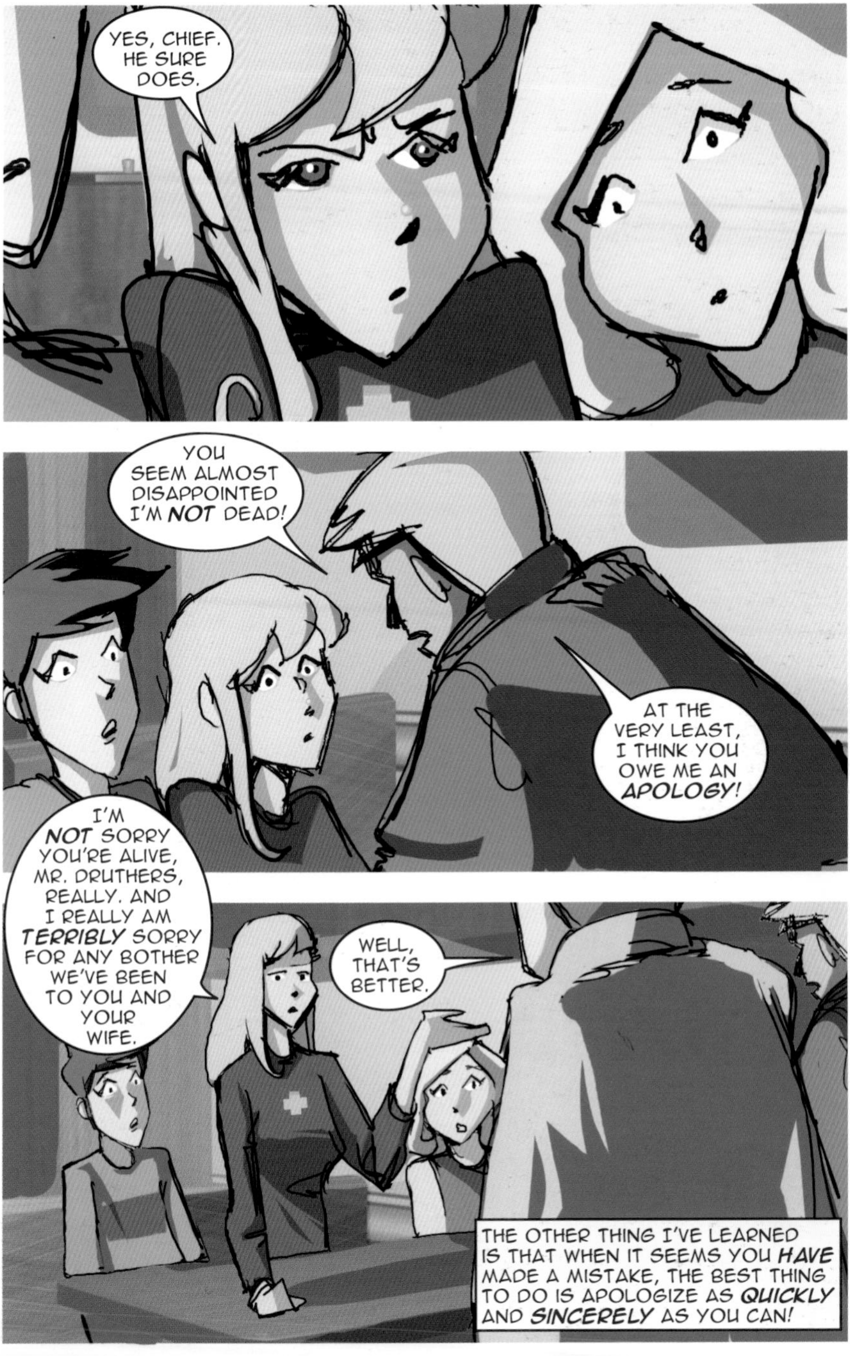
YES, CHIEF. HE SURE DOES.
YOU SEEM ALMOST DISAPPOINTED I'M **NOT** DEAD!
AT THE VERY LEAST, I THINK YOU OWE ME AN ***APOLOGY***!
I'M **NOT** SORRY YOU'RE ALIVE, MR. DRUTHERS, REALLY. AND I REALLY AM ***TERRIBLY*** SORRY FOR ANY BOTHER WE'VE BEEN TO YOU AND YOUR WIFE.
WELL, THAT'S BETTER.
THE OTHER THING I'VE LEARNED IS THAT WHEN IT SEEMS YOU ***HAVE*** MADE A MISTAKE, THE BEST THING TO DO IS APOLOGIZE AS ***QUICKLY*** AND ***SINCERELY*** AS YOU CAN!

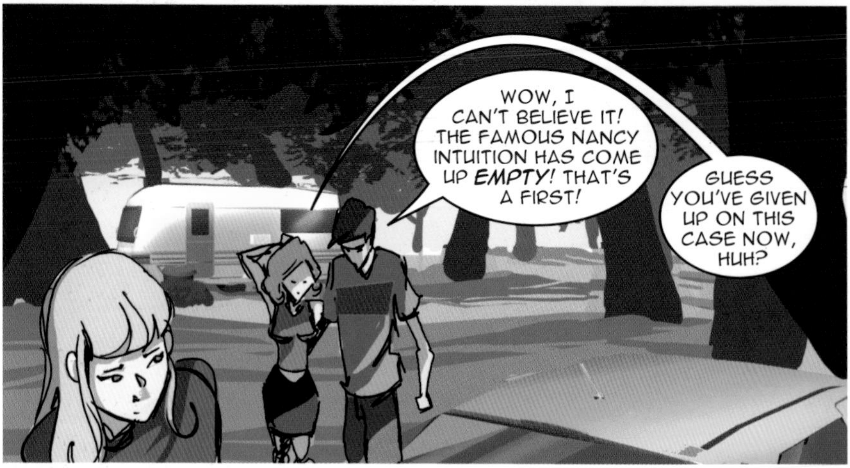
WOW, I CAN'T BELIEVE IT! THE FAMOUS NANCY INTUITION HAS COME UP EMPTY! THAT'S A FIRST!
GUESS YOU'VE GIVEN UP ON THIS CASE NOW, HUH?

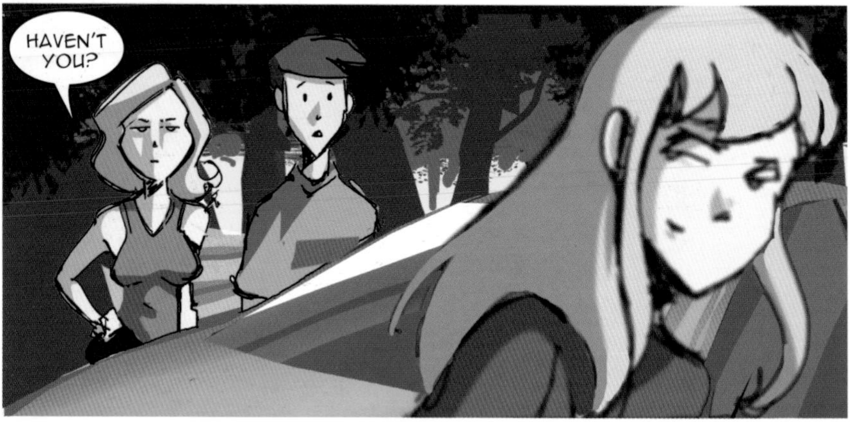
HAVEN'T YOU?

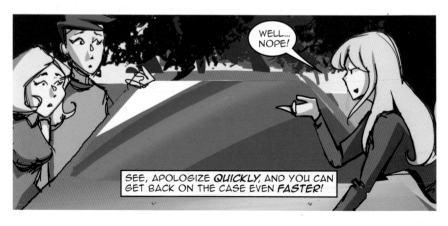

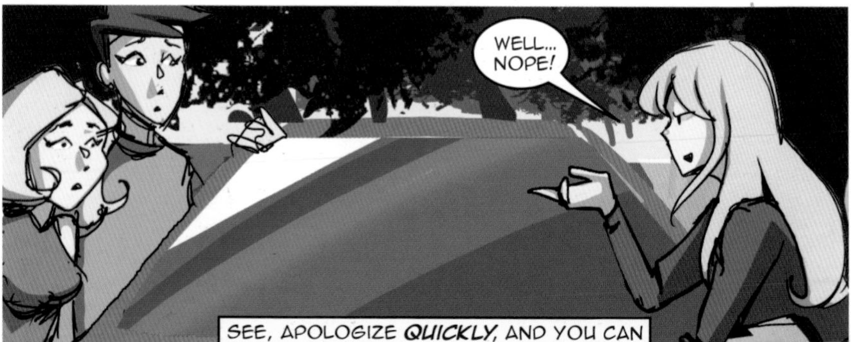
WELL... NOPE!
SEE, APOLOGIZE QUICKLY, AND YOU CAN GET BACK ON THE CASE EVEN FASTER!

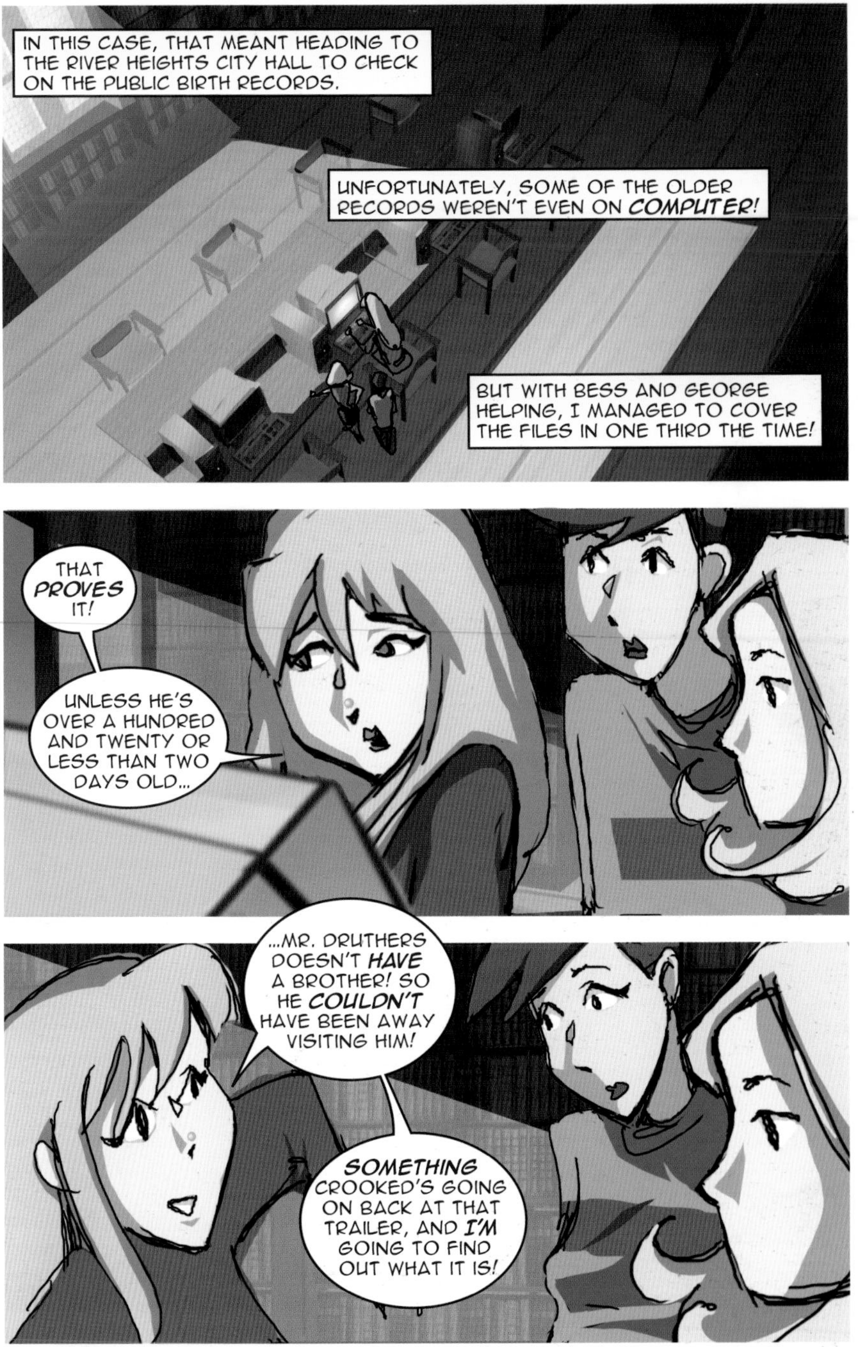
IN THIS CASE, THAT MEANT HEADING TO THE RIVER HEIGHTS CITY HALL TO CHECK ON THE PUBLIC BIRTH RECORDS.
UNFORTUNATELY, SOME OF THE OLDER RECORDS WEREN'T EVEN ON COMPUTER!
BUT WITH BESS AND GEORGE HELPING, I MANAGED TO COVER THE FILES IN ONE THIRD THE TIME!
THAT PROVES IT!
UNLESS HE'S OVER A HUNDRED AND TWENTY OR LESS THAN TWO DAYS OLD...
...MR. DRUTHERS DOESN'T HAVE A BROTHER! SO HE COULDN'T HAVE BEEN AWAY VISITING HIM!
SOMETHING CROOKED'S GOING ON BACK AT THAT TRAILER, AND I'M GOING TO FIND OUT WHAT IT IS!

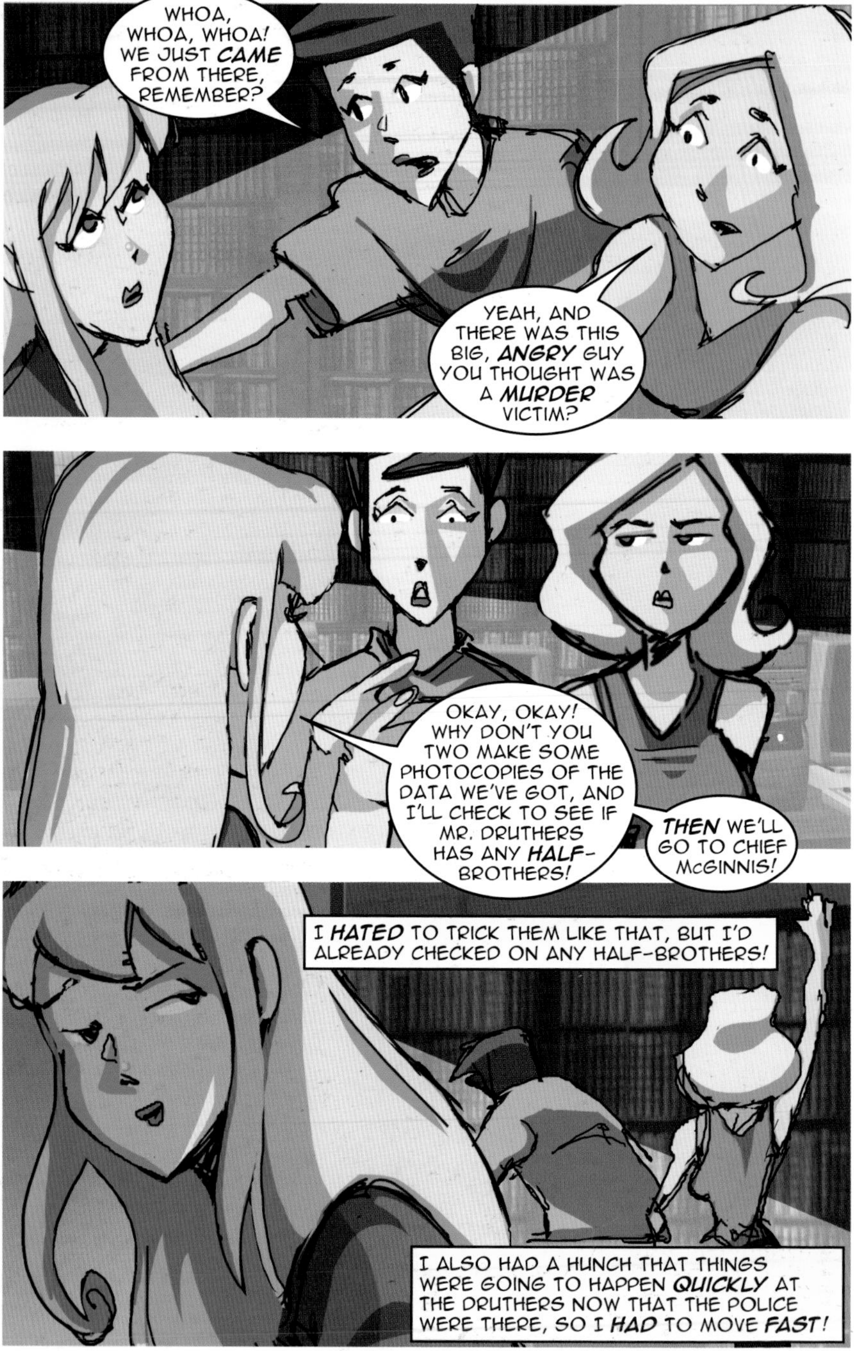
WHOA, WHOA, WHOA! WE JUST CAME FROM THERE, REMEMBER?
YEAH, AND THERE WAS THIS BIG, ANGRY GUY YOU THOUGHT WAS A MURDER VICTIM?
OKAY, OKAY! WHY DON'T YOU TWO MAKE SOME PHOTOCOPIES OF THE DATA WE'VE GOT, AND I'LL CHECK TO SEE IF MR. DRUTHERS HAS ANY HALF-BROTHERS!
THEN WE'LL GO TO CHIEF McGINNIS!
I HATED TO TRICK THEM LIKE THAT, BUT I'D ALREADY CHECKED ON ANY HALF-BROTHERS!
I ALSO HAD A HUNCH THAT THINGS WERE GOING TO HAPPEN QUICKLY AT THE DRUTHERS NOW THAT THE POLICE WERE THERE, SO I HAD TO MOVE FAST!

I PARKED MY CAR A HALF MILE AWAY, AND *HID* IT UNDER SOME BRUSH.

THE PLACE SEEMED EMPTY WHEN I ARRIVED, SO IT WAS A *PERFECT* CHANCE TO SEARCH FOR CLUES.

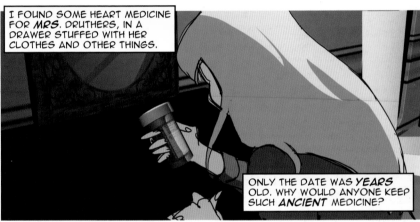

I FOUND SOME HEART MEDICINE FOR *MRS.* DRUTHERS, IN A DRAWER STUFFED WITH HER CLOTHES AND OTHER THINGS.

ONLY THE DATE WAS *YEARS* OLD. WHY WOULD ANYONE KEEP SUCH *ANCIENT* MEDICINE?

THEN, WHEN I SAW MY SPIDER-BITTEN NOSE IN A MIRROR, THE ONE THAT LOOKED JUST LIKE A *PIMPLE*, I REALIZED *EXACTLY* WHAT HAD BEEN GOING ON.

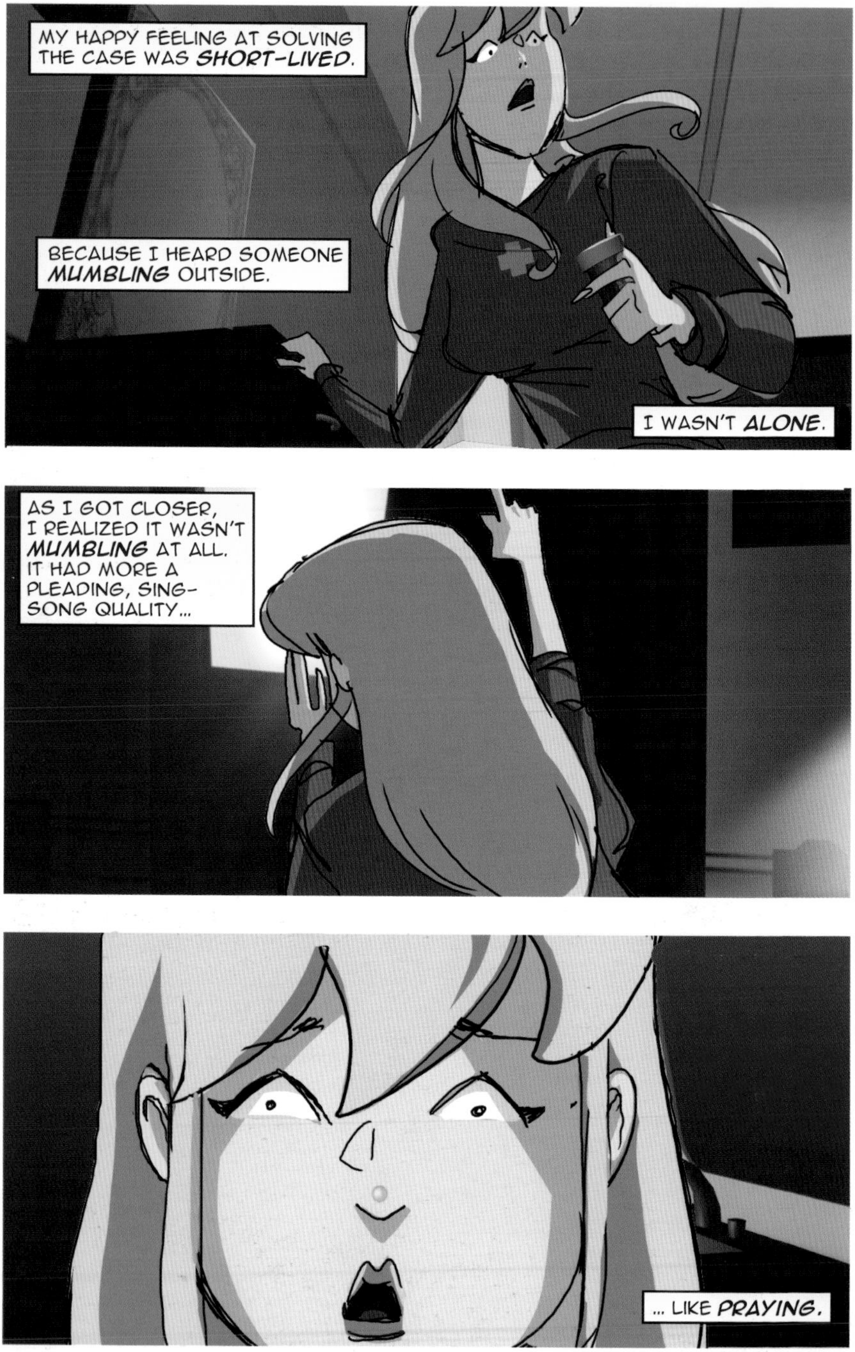
MY HAPPY FEELING AT SOLVING THE CASE WAS SHORT-LIVED.
BECAUSE I HEARD SOMEONE MUMBLING OUTSIDE.
I WASN'T ALONE.
AS I GOT CLOSER, I REALIZED IT WASN'T MUMBLING AT ALL. IT HAD MORE A PLEADING, SING-SONG QUALITY...
... LIKE PRAYING.

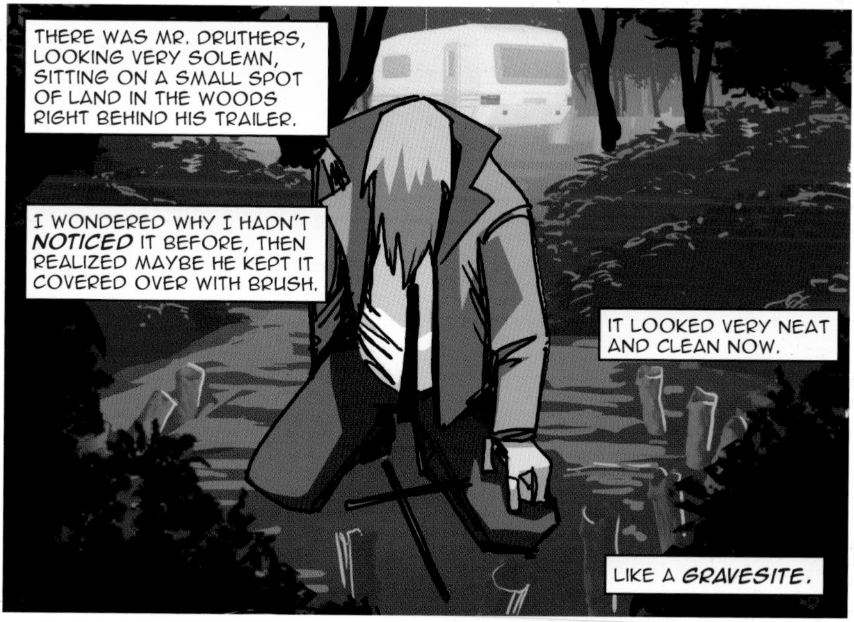
THERE WAS MR. DRUTHERS, LOOKING VERY SOLEMN, SITTING ON A SMALL SPOT OF LAND IN THE WOODS RIGHT BEHIND HIS TRAILER.
I WONDERED WHY I HADN'T NOTICED IT BEFORE, THEN REALIZED MAYBE HE KEPT IT COVERED OVER WITH BRUSH.
IT LOOKED VERY NEAT AND CLEAN NOW.
LIKE A GRAVESITE.

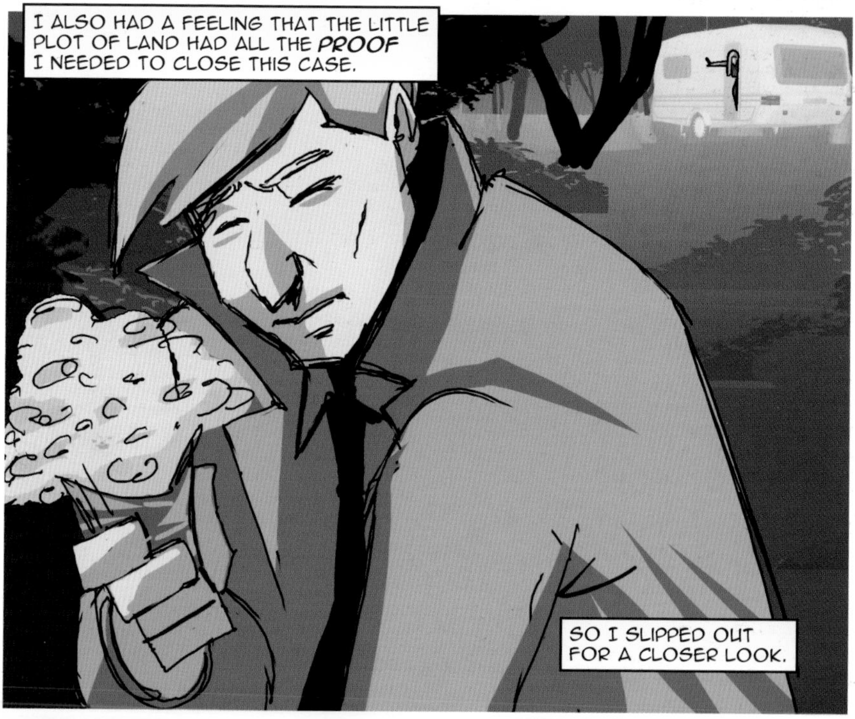
I ALSO HAD A FEELING THAT THE LITTLE PLOT OF LAND HAD ALL THE PROOF I NEEDED TO CLOSE THIS CASE.
SO I SLIPPED OUT FOR A CLOSER LOOK.

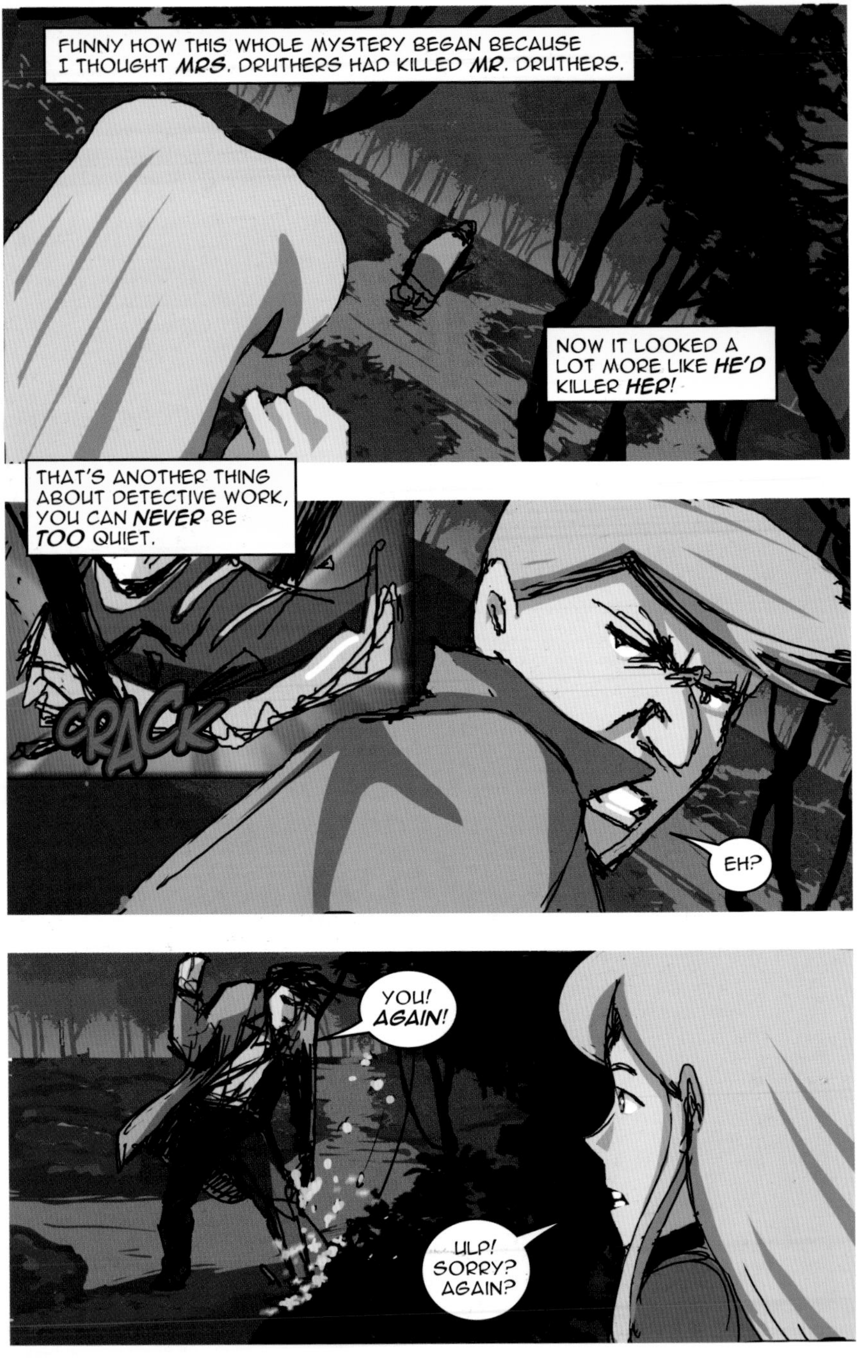

FUNNY HOW THIS WHOLE MYSTERY BEGAN BECAUSE I THOUGHT MRS. DRUTHERS HAD KILLED MR. DRUTHERS.
NOW IT LOOKED A LOT MORE LIKE HE'D KILLER HER!
THAT'S ANOTHER THING ABOUT DETECTIVE WORK, YOU CAN NEVER BE TOO QUIET.
CRACK
EH?
YOU! AGAIN!
ULP! SORRY? AGAIN?

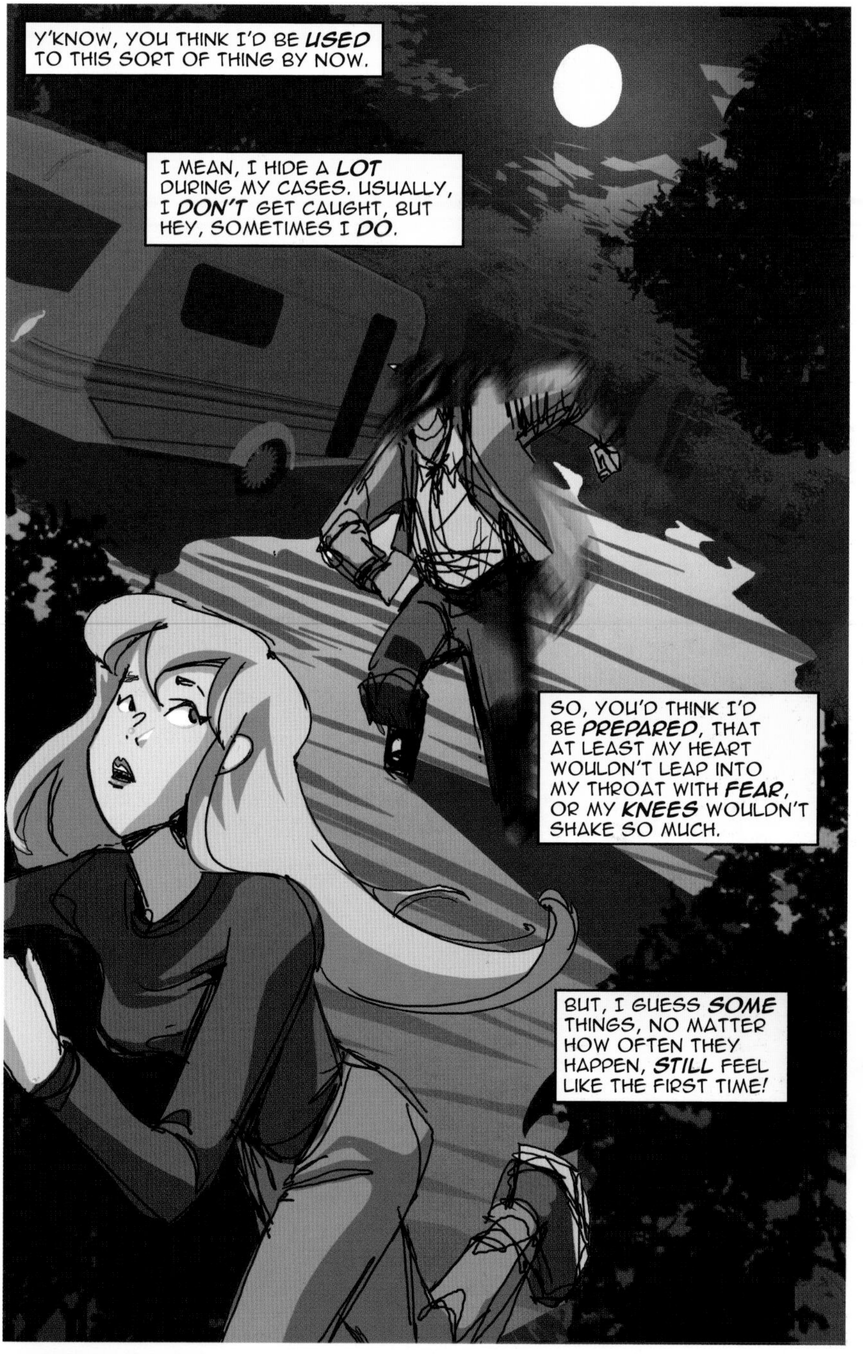
Y'KNOW, YOU THINK I'D BE USED TO THIS SORT OF THING BY NOW.
I MEAN, I HIDE A LOT DURING MY CASES. USUALLY, I DON'T GET CAUGHT, BUT HEY, SOMETIMES I DO.
SO, YOU'D THINK I'D BE PREPARED, THAT AT LEAST MY HEART WOULDN'T LEAP INTO MY THROAT WITH FEAR, OR MY KNEES WOULDN'T SHAKE SO MUCH.
BUT, I GUESS SOME THINGS, NO MATTER HOW OFTEN THEY HAPPEN, STILL FEEL LIKE THE FIRST TIME!

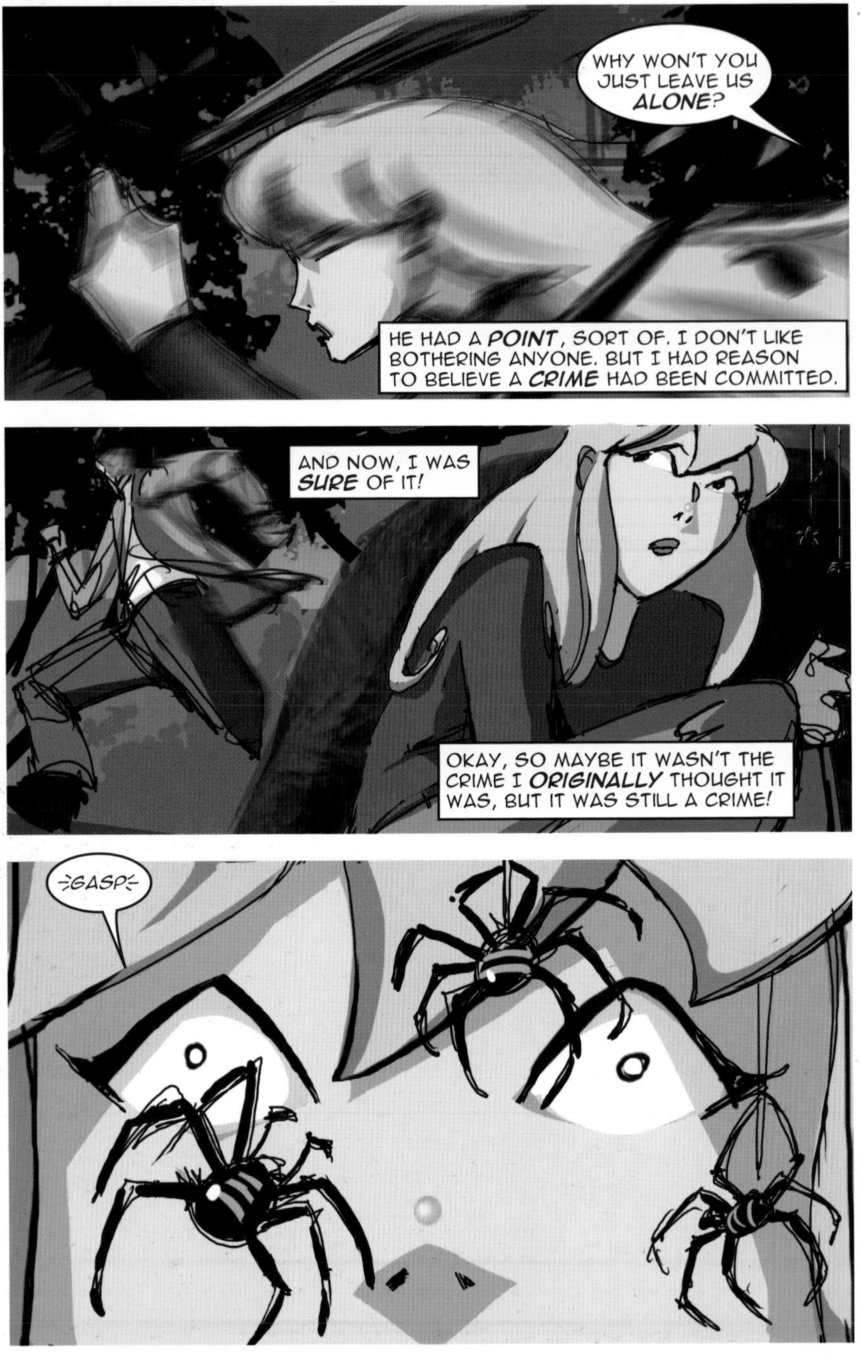
WHY WON'T YOU JUST LEAVE US ALONE?
HE HAD A POINT, SORT OF. I DON'T LIKE BOTHERING ANYONE. BUT I HAD REASON TO BELIEVE A CRIME HAD BEEN COMMITTED.
AND NOW, I WAS SURE OF IT!
OKAY, SO MAYBE IT WASN'T THE CRIME I ORIGINALLY THOUGHT IT WAS, BUT IT WAS STILL A CRIME!
GASP

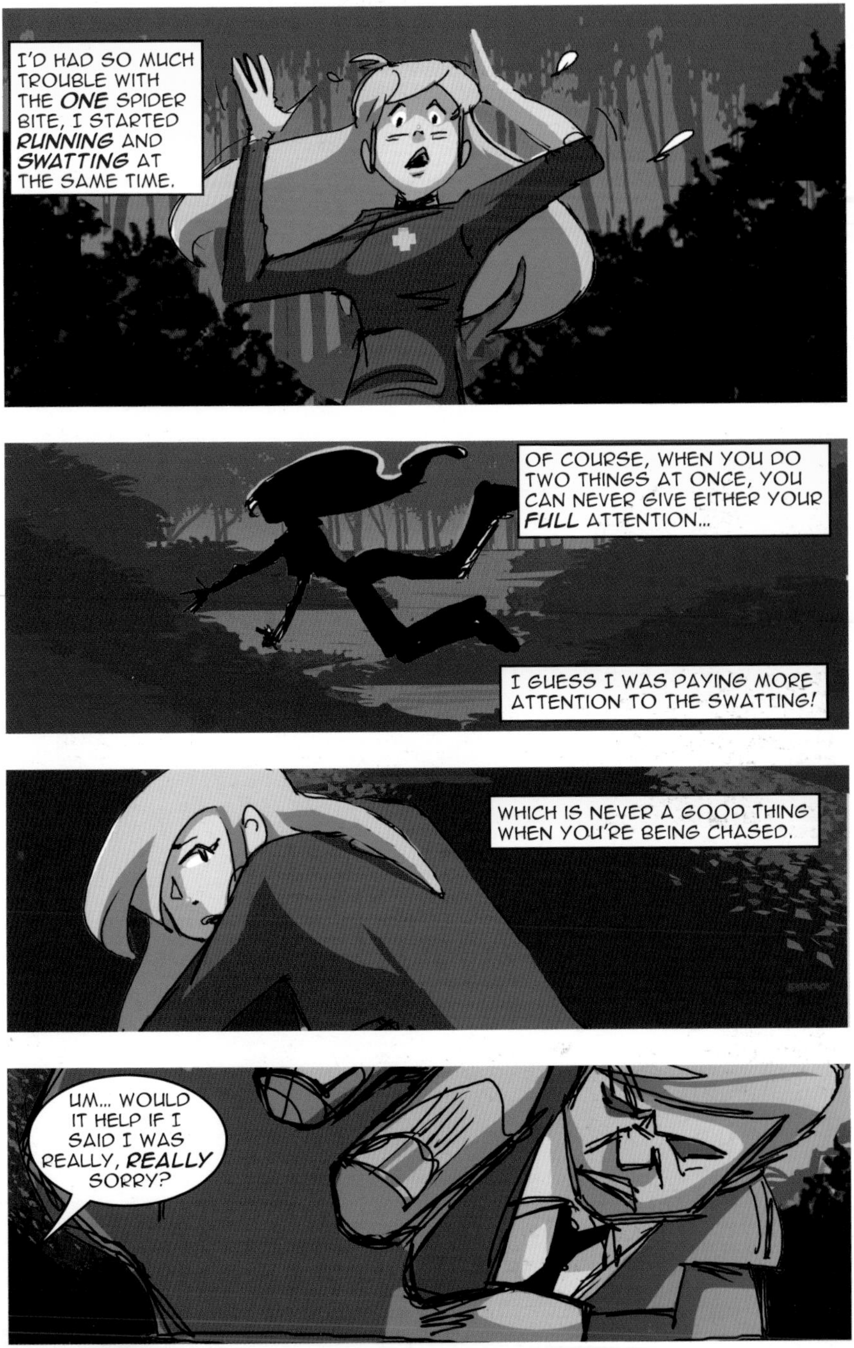
I'D HAD SO MUCH TROUBLE WITH THE ONE SPIDER BITE, I STARTED RUNNING AND SWATTING AT THE SAME TIME.
OF COURSE, WHEN YOU DO TWO THINGS AT ONCE, YOU CAN NEVER GIVE EITHER YOUR FULL ATTENTION...
I GUESS I WAS PAYING MORE ATTENTION TO THE SWATTING!
WHICH IS NEVER A GOOD THING WHEN YOU'RE BEING CHASED.
UM... WOULD IT HELP IF I SAID I WAS REALLY, REALLY SORRY?

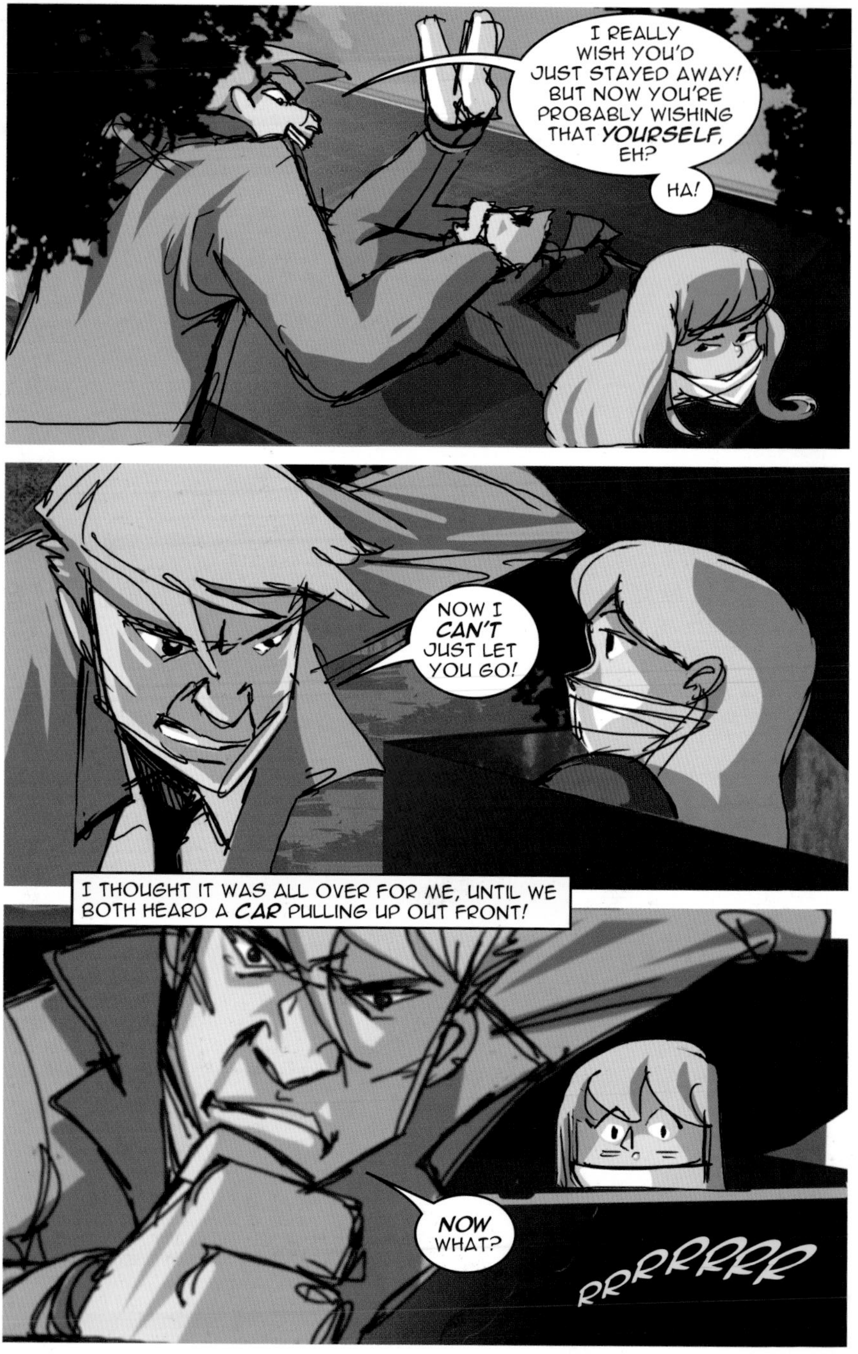
I REALLY WISH YOU'D JUST STAYED AWAY! BUT NOW YOU'RE PROBABLY WISHING THAT YOURSELF, EH?
HA!
NOW I CAN'T JUST LET YOU GO!
I THOUGHT IT WAS ALL OVER FOR ME, UNTIL WE BOTH HEARD A CAR PULLING UP OUT FRONT!
NOW WHAT?
RRRRRRRR

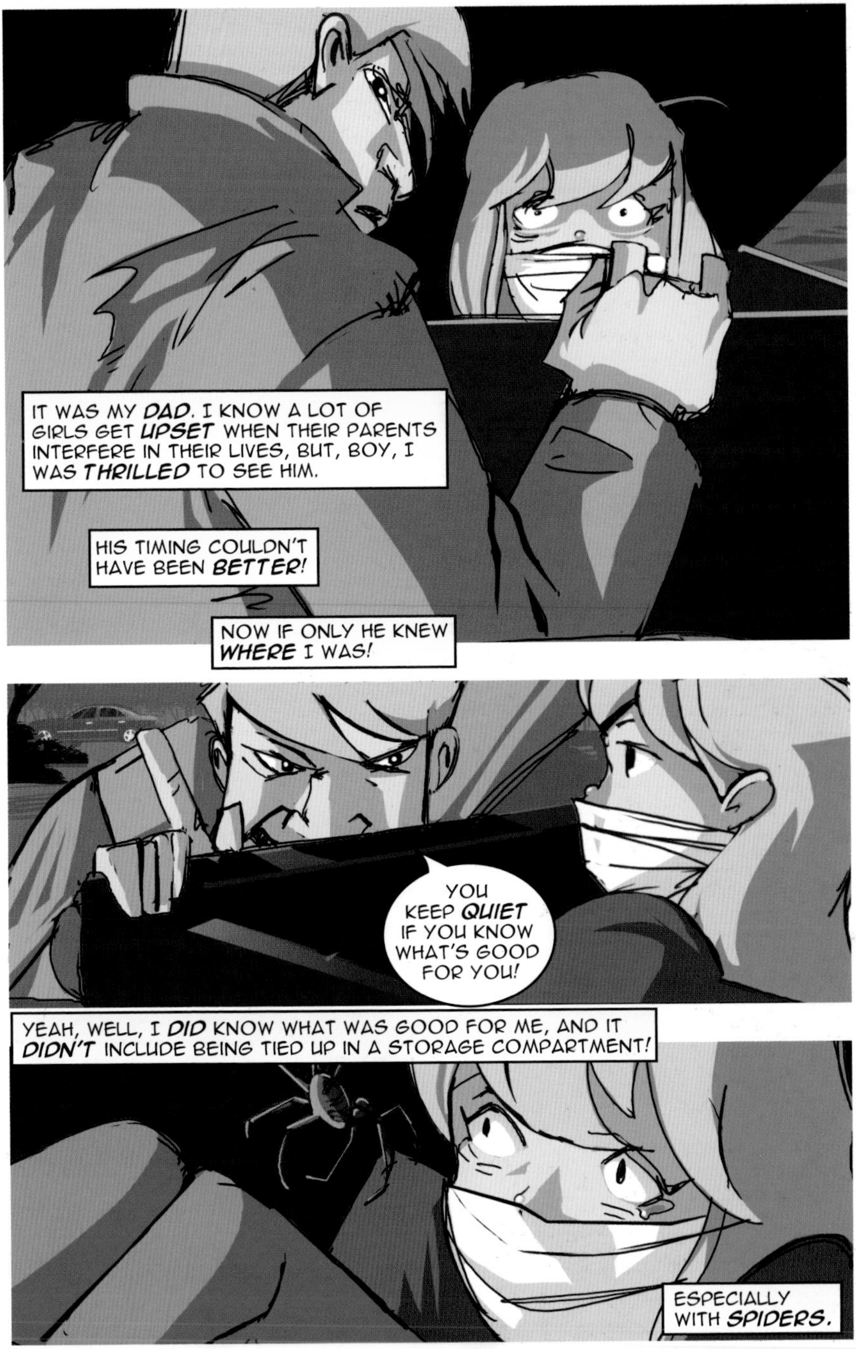
IT WAS MY DAD. I KNOW A LOT OF GIRLS GET UPSET WHEN THEIR PARENTS INTERFERE IN THEIR LIVES, BUT, BOY, I WAS THRILLED TO SEE HIM.
HIS TIMING COULDN'T HAVE BEEN BETTER!
NOW IF ONLY HE KNEW WHERE I WAS!
YOU KEEP QUIET IF YOU KNOW WHAT'S GOOD FOR YOU!
YEAH, WELL, I DID KNOW WHAT WAS GOOD FOR ME, AND IT DIDN'T INCLUDE BEING TIED UP IN A STORAGE COMPARTMENT!
ESPECIALLY WITH SPIDERS.

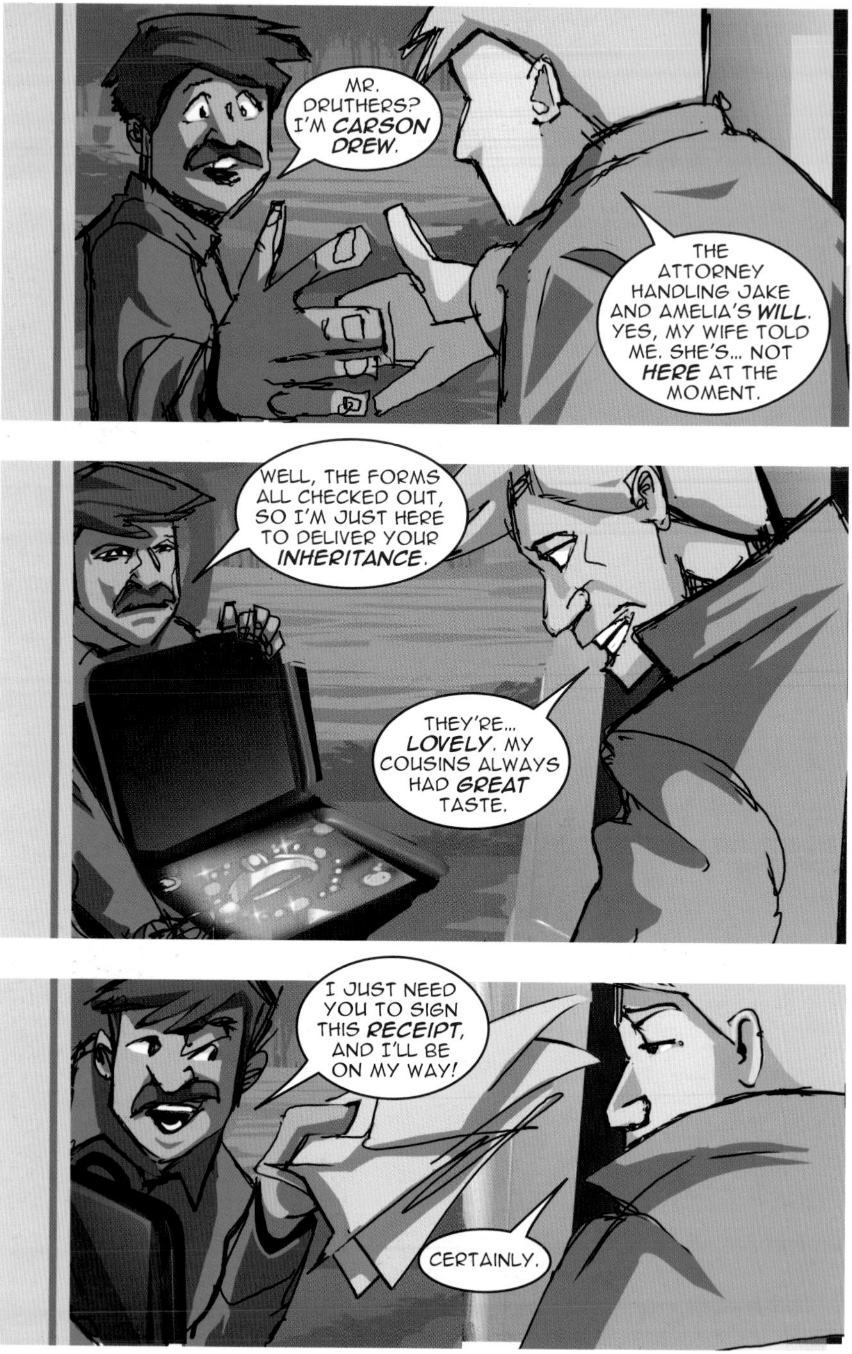
MR. DRUTHERS? I'M CARSON DREW.
THE ATTORNEY HANDLING JAKE AND AMELIA'S WILL. YES, MY WIFE TOLD ME. SHE'S... NOT HERE AT THE MOMENT.
WELL, THE FORMS ALL CHECKED OUT, SO I'M JUST HERE TO DELIVER YOUR INHERITANCE.
THEY'RE... LOVELY. MY COUSINS ALWAYS HAD GREAT TASTE.
I JUST NEED YOU TO SIGN THIS RECEIPT, AND I'LL BE ON MY WAY!
CERTAINLY.

FUNNY ABOUT THAT LAKE JUST *VANISHING*, EH?

BY LEANING AGAINST THE TRAILER, I COULD HEAR EVERY WORD. JUDGING FROM THE *PLEASANT* CONVERSATION, MY DAD HAD NO *CLUE* WHERE I WAS.

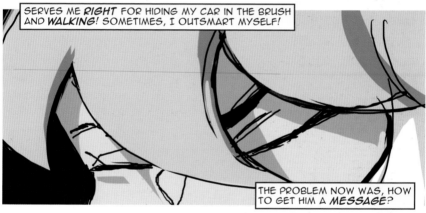

SERVES ME *RIGHT* FOR HIDING MY CAR IN THE BRUSH AND *WALKING*! SOMETIMES, I OUTSMART MYSELF!

THE PROBLEM NOW WAS, HOW TO GET HIM A *MESSAGE*?

WHEN I WAS JUST A LITTLE GIRL, MY FATHER TAUGHT ME *MORSE CODE*.

THE SIMPLEST MESSAGE YOU CAN SEND IS A CALL FOR HELP, SOS, WHICH IS THREE SHORT TAPS, THREE LONG TAPS, THEN THREE SHORT ONES AGAIN.

TAP-TAP-TAP
TAP- TAP- T AP-
TAP-TAP-TAP

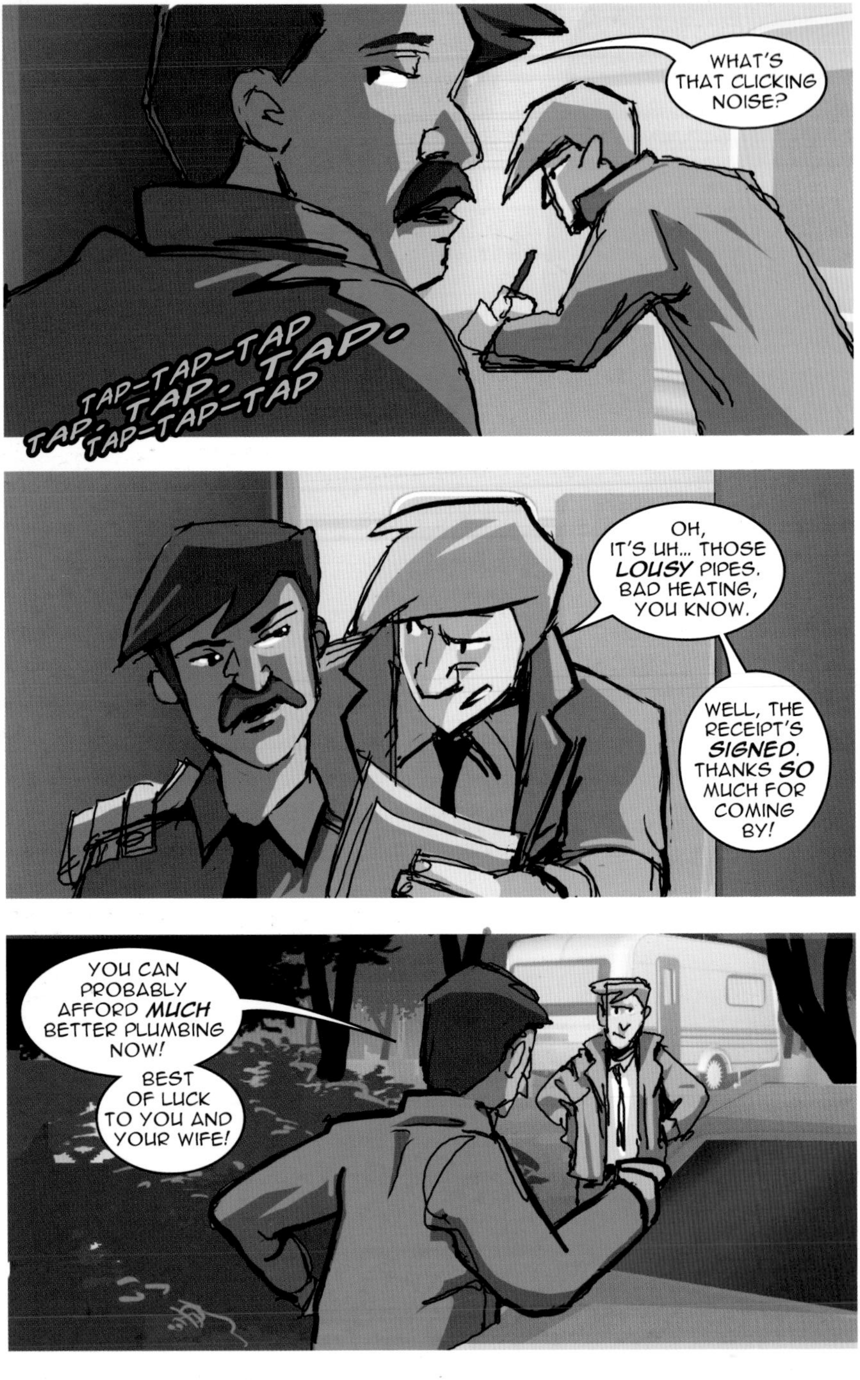
WHAT'S THAT CLICKING NOISE?
TAP-TAP-TAP TAP. TAP. TAP. TAP-TAP-TAP
OH, IT'S UH... THOSE LOUSY PIPES. BAD HEATING, YOU KNOW.
WELL, THE RECEIPT'S SIGNED. THANKS SO MUCH FOR COMING BY!
YOU CAN PROBABLY AFFORD MUCH BETTER PLUMBING NOW!
BEST OF LUCK TO YOU AND YOUR WIFE!

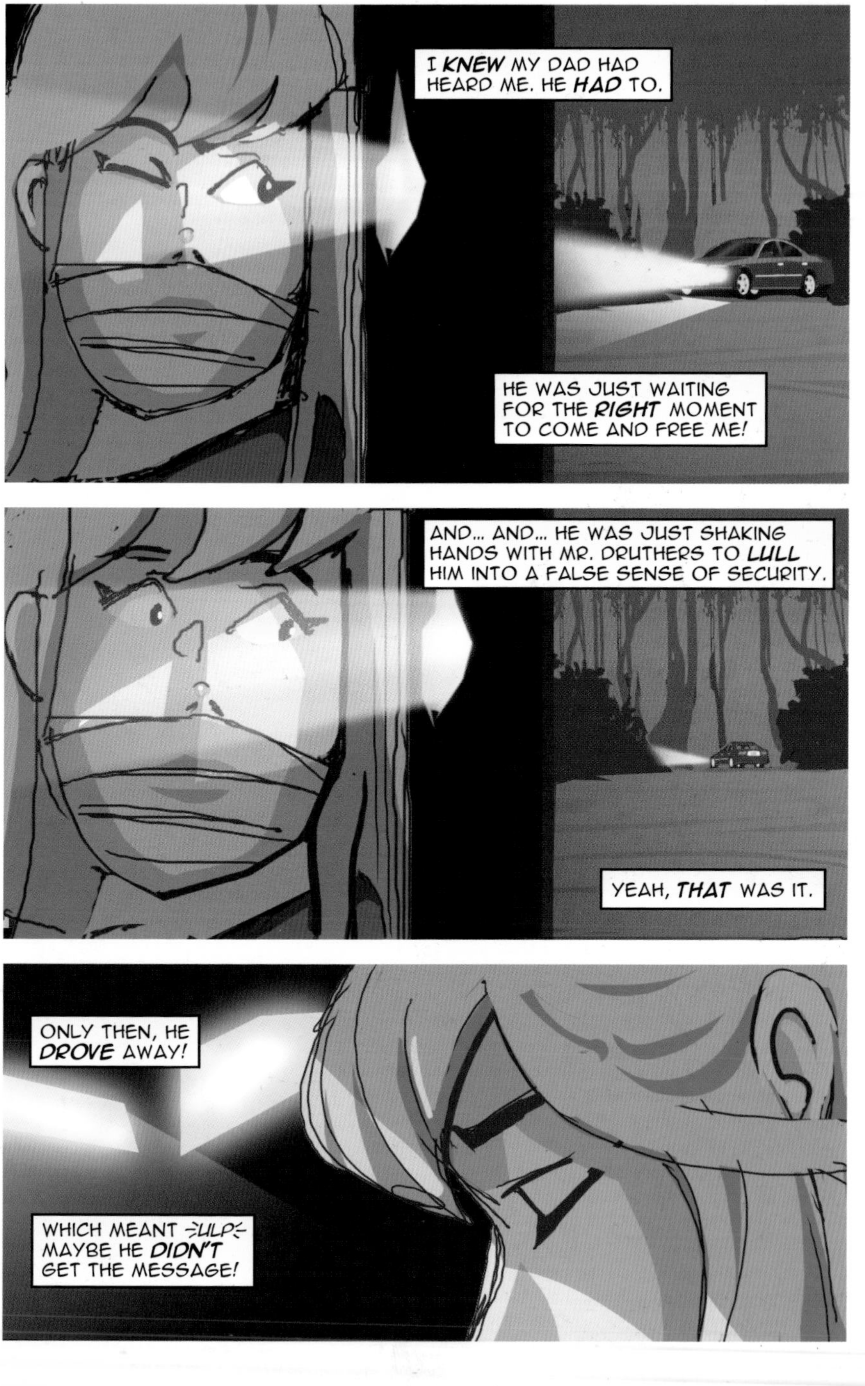
I KNEW MY DAD HAD HEARD ME. HE HAD TO.
HE WAS JUST WAITING FOR THE RIGHT MOMENT TO COME AND FREE ME!
AND... AND... HE WAS JUST SHAKING HANDS WITH MR. DRUTHERS TO LULL HIM INTO A FALSE SENSE OF SECURITY.
YEAH, THAT WAS IT.
ONLY THEN, HE DROVE AWAY!
WHICH MEANT ULP MAYBE HE DIDN'T GET THE MESSAGE!

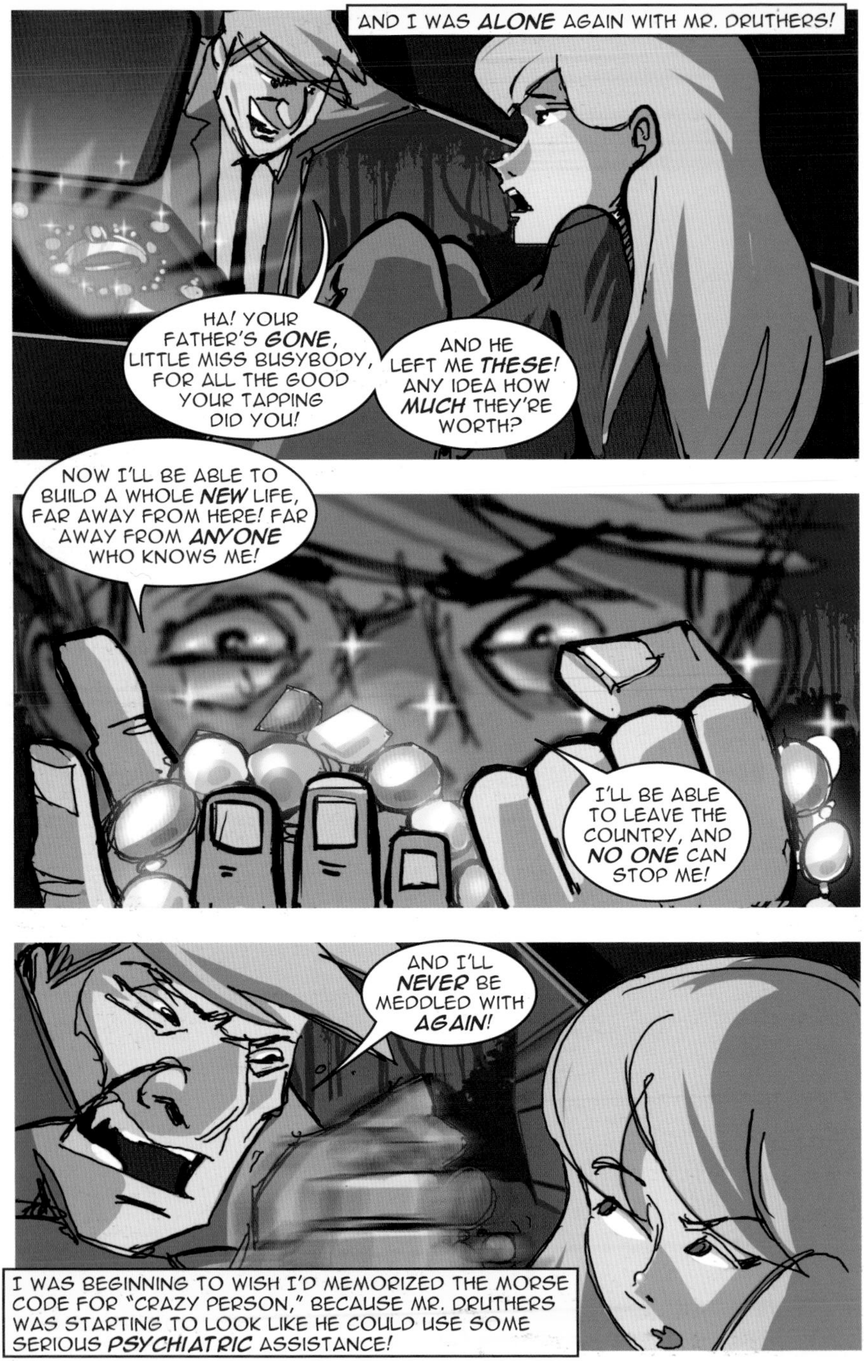

AND I WAS ALONE AGAIN WITH MR. DRUTHERS!
HA! YOUR FATHER'S GONE, LITTLE MISS BUSYBODY, FOR ALL THE GOOD YOUR TAPPING DID YOU!
AND HE LEFT ME THESE! ANY IDEA HOW MUCH THEY'RE WORTH?
NOW I'LL BE ABLE TO BUILD A WHOLE NEW LIFE, FAR AWAY FROM HERE! FAR AWAY FROM ANYONE WHO KNOWS ME!
I'LL BE ABLE TO LEAVE THE COUNTRY, AND NO ONE CAN STOP ME!
AND I'LL NEVER BE MEDDLED WITH AGAIN!
I WAS BEGINNING TO WISH I'D MEMORIZED THE MORSE CODE FOR "CRAZY PERSON," BECAUSE MR. DRUTHERS WAS STARTING TO LOOK LIKE HE COULD USE SOME SERIOUS PSYCHIATRIC ASSISTANCE!

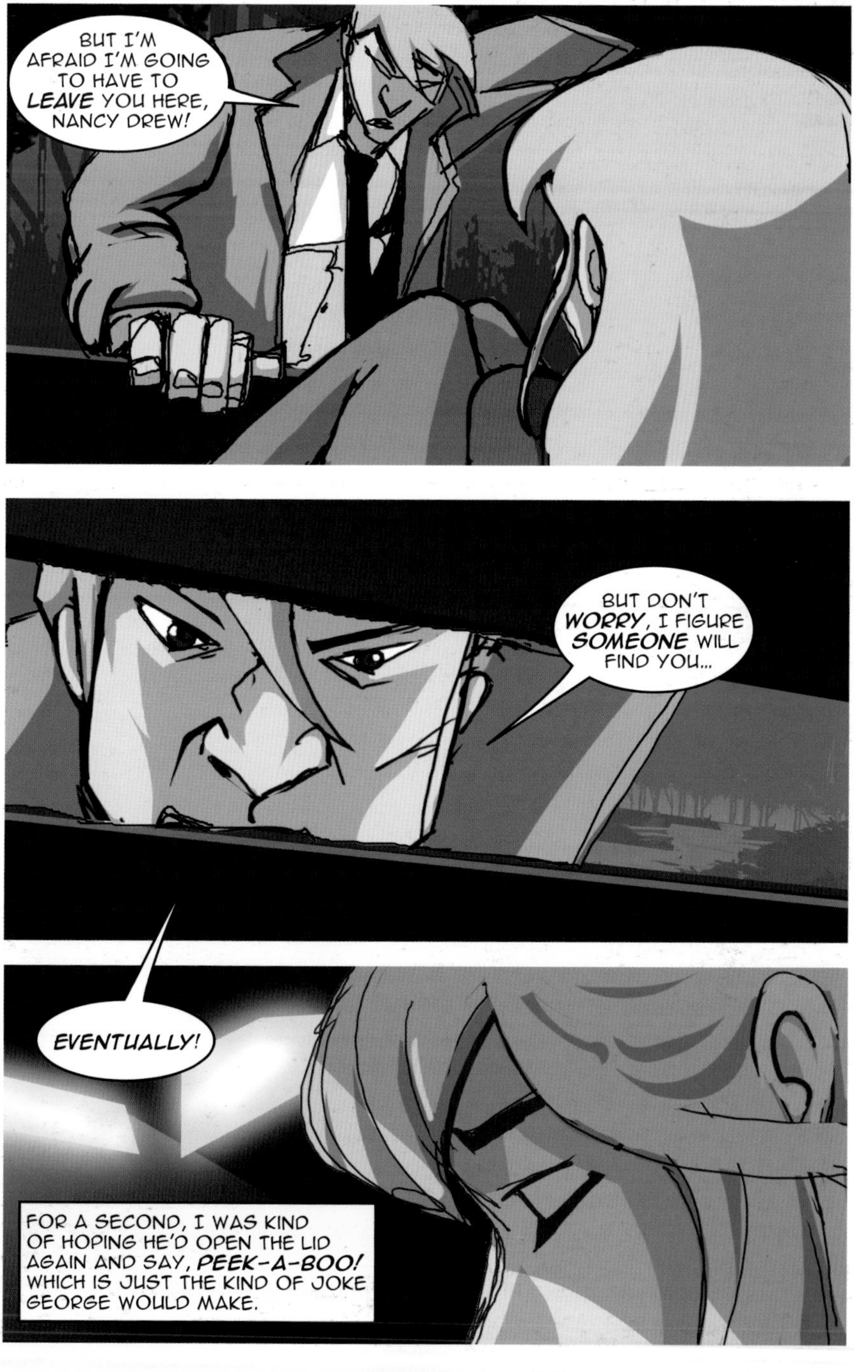
BUT I'M AFRAID I'M GOING TO HAVE TO *LEAVE* YOU HERE, NANCY DREW!
BUT DON'T *WORRY*, I FIGURE *SOMEONE* WILL FIND YOU...
EVENTUALLY!
FOR A SECOND, I WAS KIND OF HOPING HE'D OPEN THE LID AGAIN AND SAY, *PEEK-A-BOO!* WHICH IS JUST THE KIND OF JOKE GEORGE WOULD MAKE.

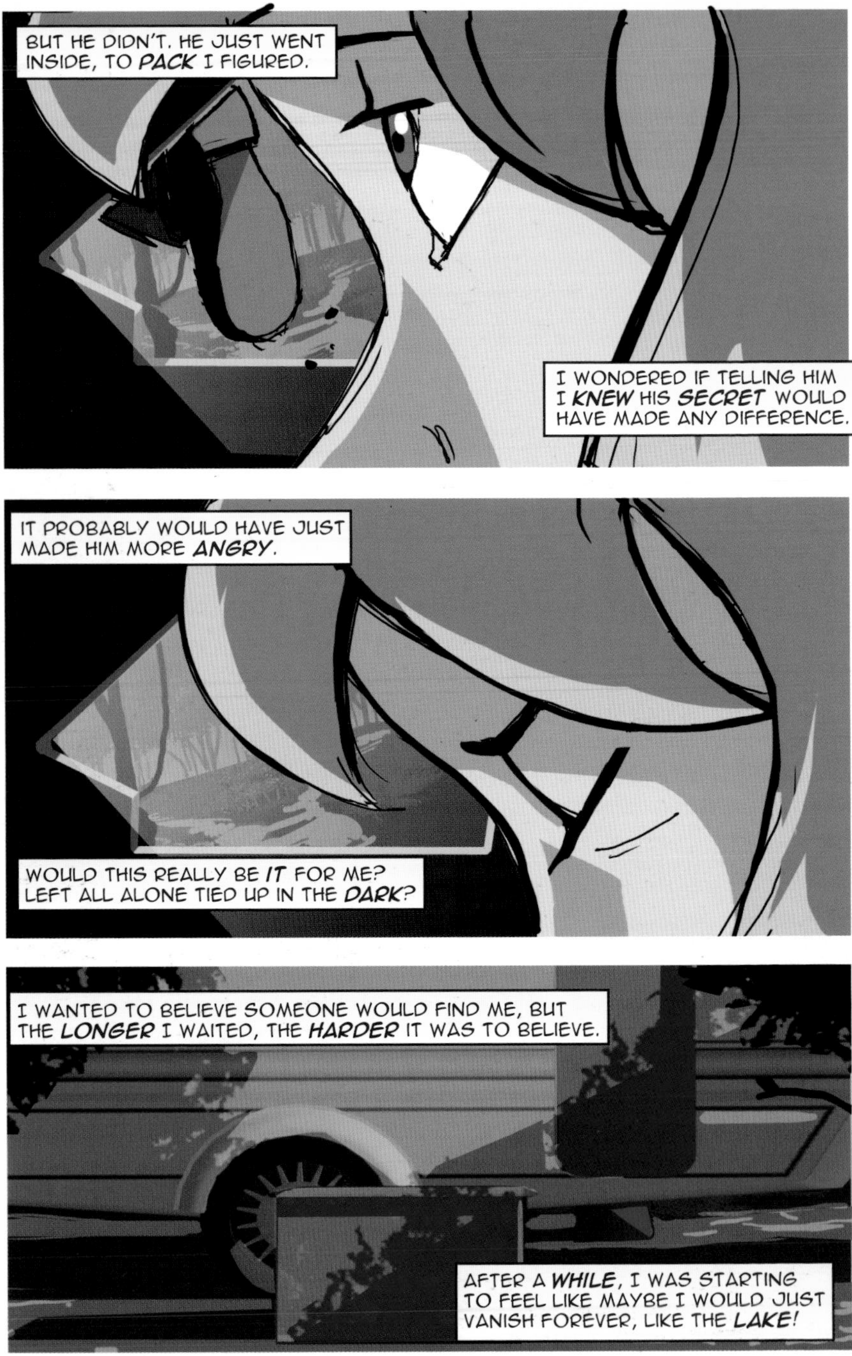
BUT HE DIDN'T. HE JUST WENT INSIDE, TO PACK I FIGURED.
I WONDERED IF TELLING HIM I KNEW HIS SECRET WOULD HAVE MADE ANY DIFFERENCE.
IT PROBABLY WOULD HAVE JUST MADE HIM MORE ANGRY.
WOULD THIS REALLY BE IT FOR ME? LEFT ALL ALONE TIED UP IN THE DARK?
I WANTED TO BELIEVE SOMEONE WOULD FIND ME, BUT THE LONGER I WAITED, THE HARDER IT WAS TO BELIEVE.
AFTER A WHILE, I WAS STARTING TO FEEL LIKE MAYBE I WOULD JUST VANISH FOREVER, LIKE THE LAKE!

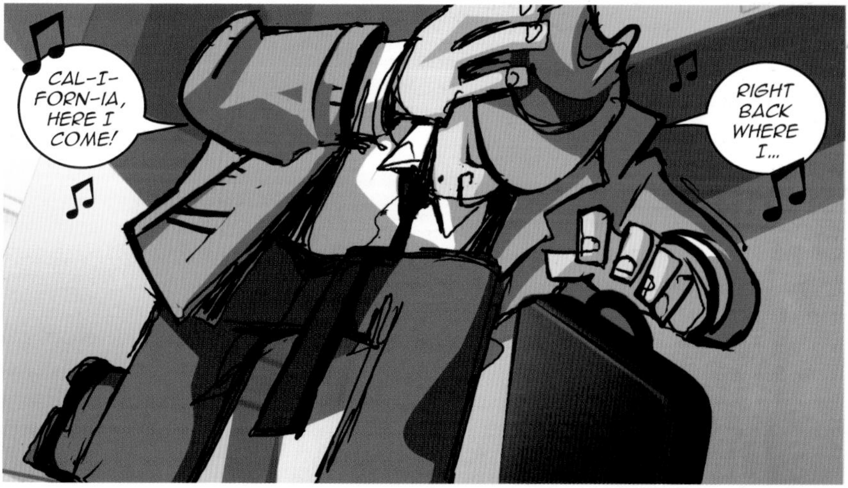
CAL-I-FORN-IA, HERE I COME!
RIGHT BACK WHERE I...

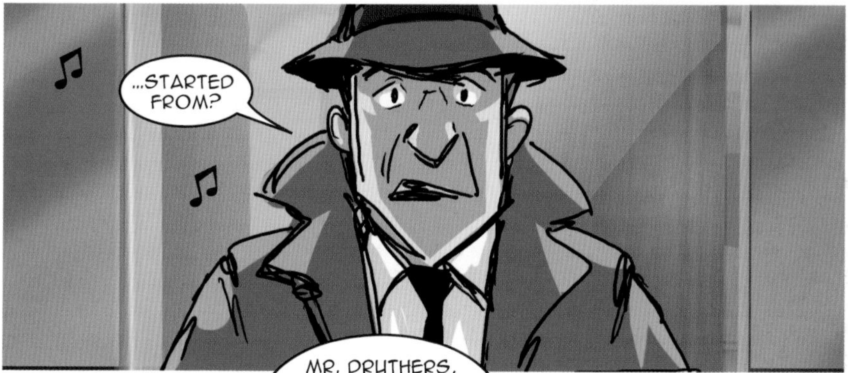
...STARTED FROM?

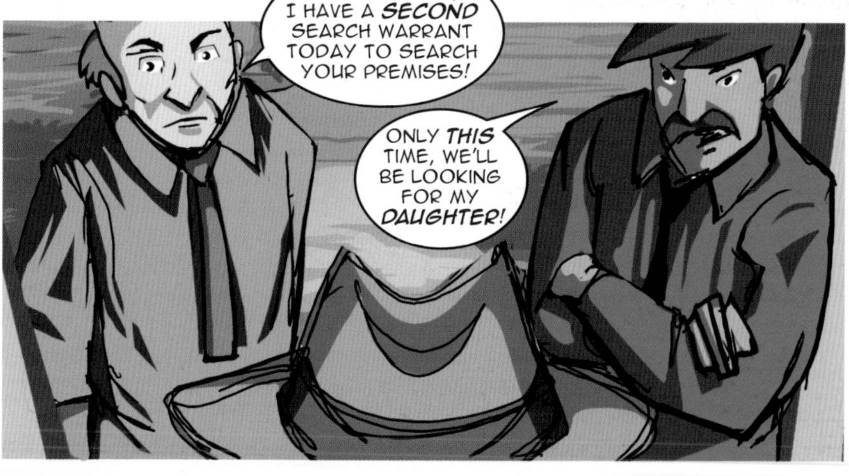
MR. DRUTHERS, I HAVE A SECOND SEARCH WARRANT TODAY TO SEARCH YOUR PREMISES!
ONLY THIS TIME, WE'LL BE LOOKING FOR MY DAUGHTER!

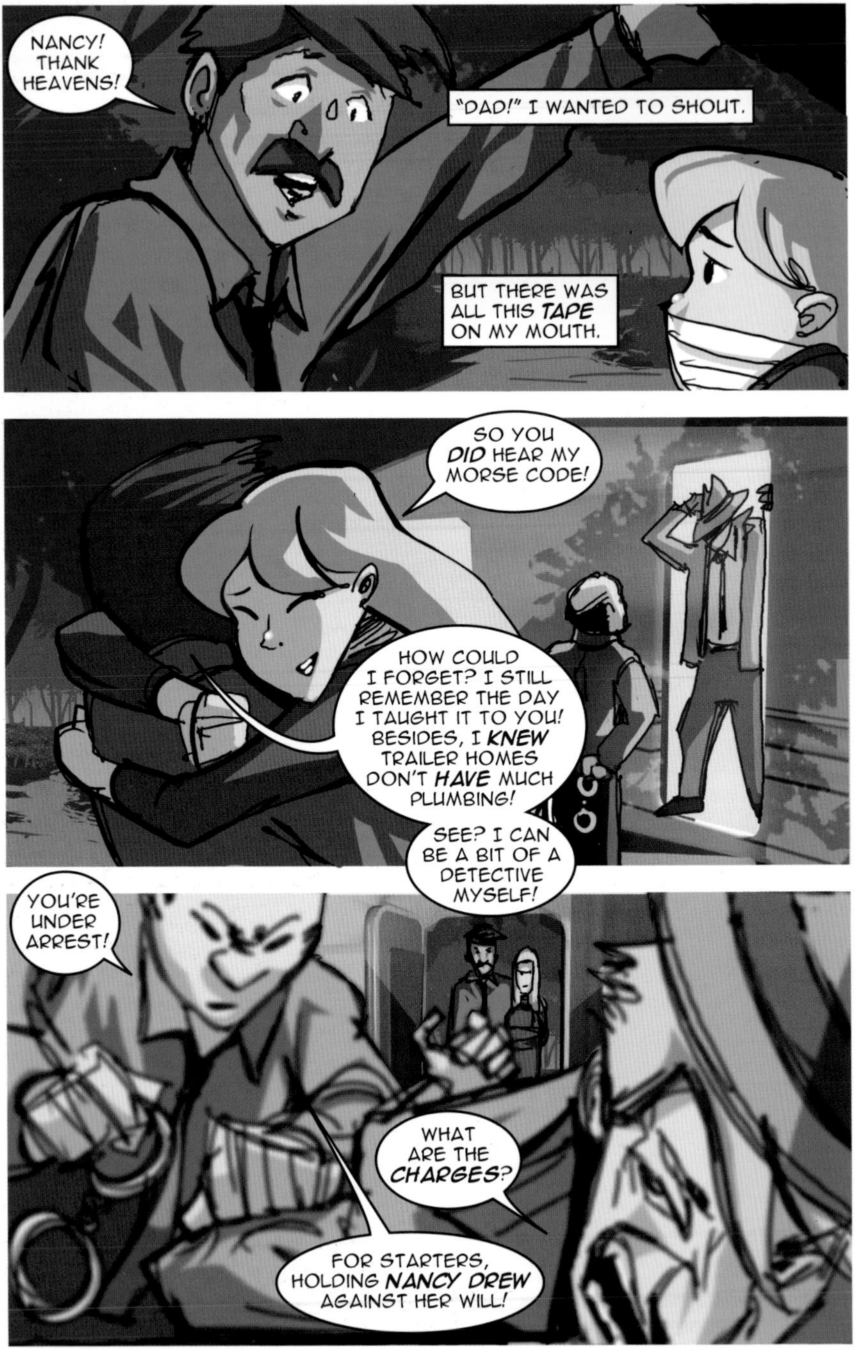
NANCY! THANK HEAVENS!
"DAD!" I WANTED TO SHOUT.
BUT THERE WAS ALL THIS TAPE ON MY MOUTH.
SO YOU DID HEAR MY MORSE CODE!
HOW COULD I FORGET? I STILL REMEMBER THE DAY I TAUGHT IT TO YOU! BESIDES, I KNEW TRAILER HOMES DON'T HAVE MUCH PLUMBING!
SEE? I CAN BE A BIT OF A DETECTIVE MYSELF!
YOU'RE UNDER ARREST!
WHAT ARE THE CHARGES?
FOR STARTERS, HOLDING NANCY DREW AGAINST HER WILL!

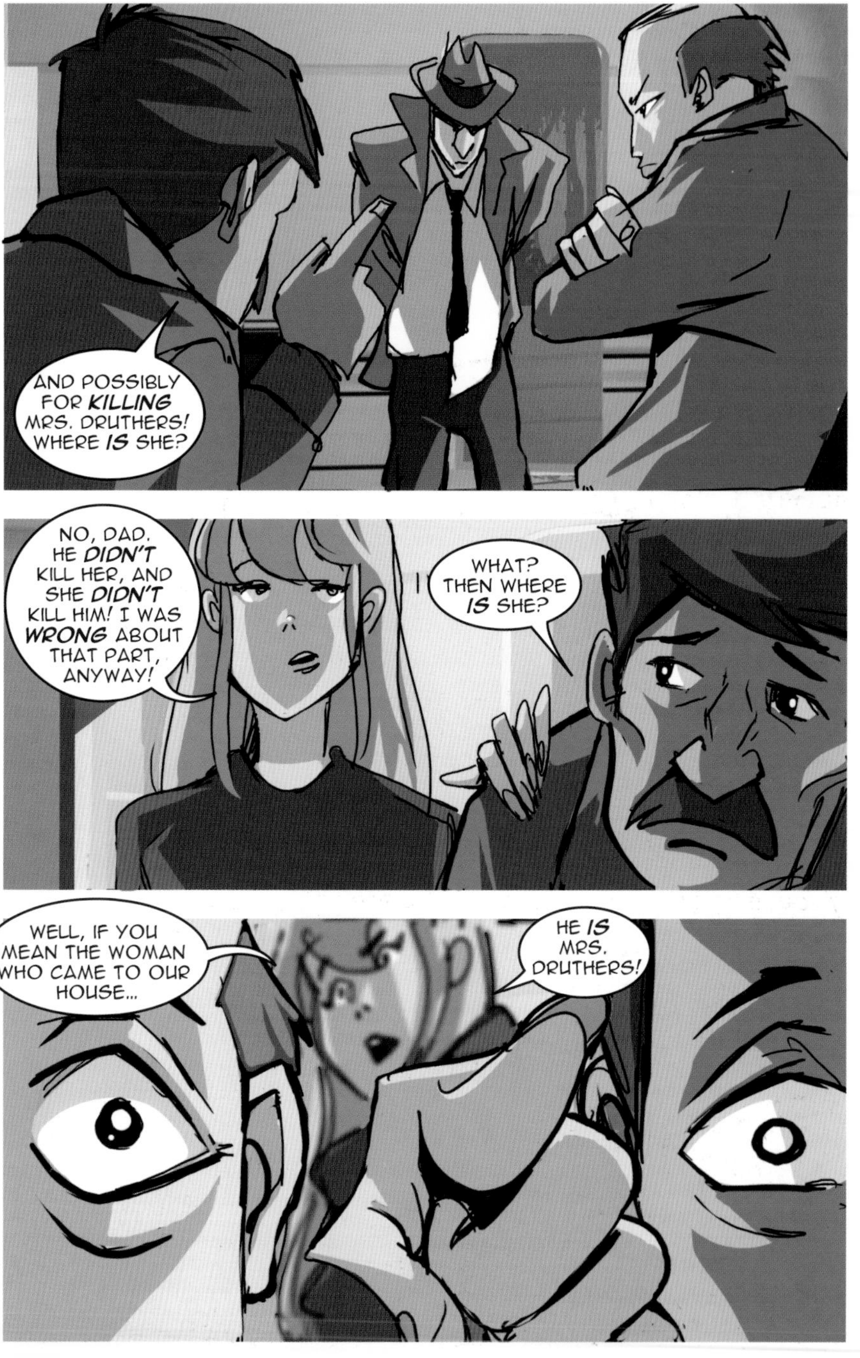
AND POSSIBLY FOR *KILLING* MRS. DRUTHERS! WHERE *IS* SHE?
NO, DAD. HE *DIDN'T* KILL HER, AND SHE *DIDN'T* KILL HIM! I WAS *WRONG* ABOUT THAT PART, ANYWAY!
WHAT? THEN WHERE *IS* SHE?
WELL, IF YOU MEAN THE WOMAN WHO CAME TO OUR HOUSE...
HE *IS* MRS. DRUTHERS!

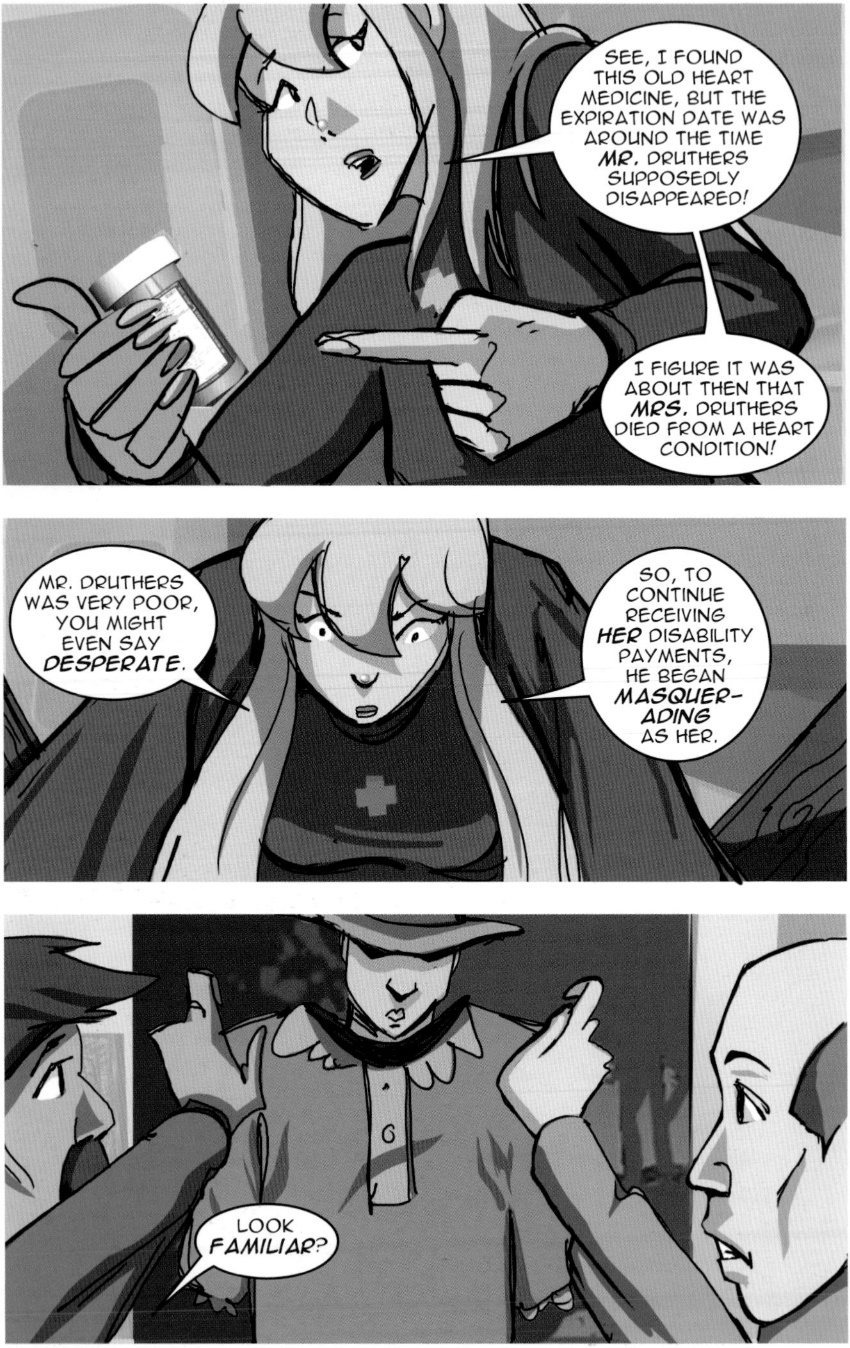
SEE, I FOUND THIS OLD HEART MEDICINE, BUT THE EXPIRATION DATE WAS AROUND THE TIME MR. DRUTHERS SUPPOSEDLY DISAPPEARED!
I FIGURE IT WAS ABOUT THEN THAT MRS. DRUTHERS DIED FROM A HEART CONDITION!
MR. DRUTHERS WAS VERY POOR, YOU MIGHT EVEN SAY DESPERATE.
SO, TO CONTINUE RECEIVING HER DISABILITY PAYMENTS, HE BEGAN MASQUER-ADING AS HER.
LOOK FAMILIAR?

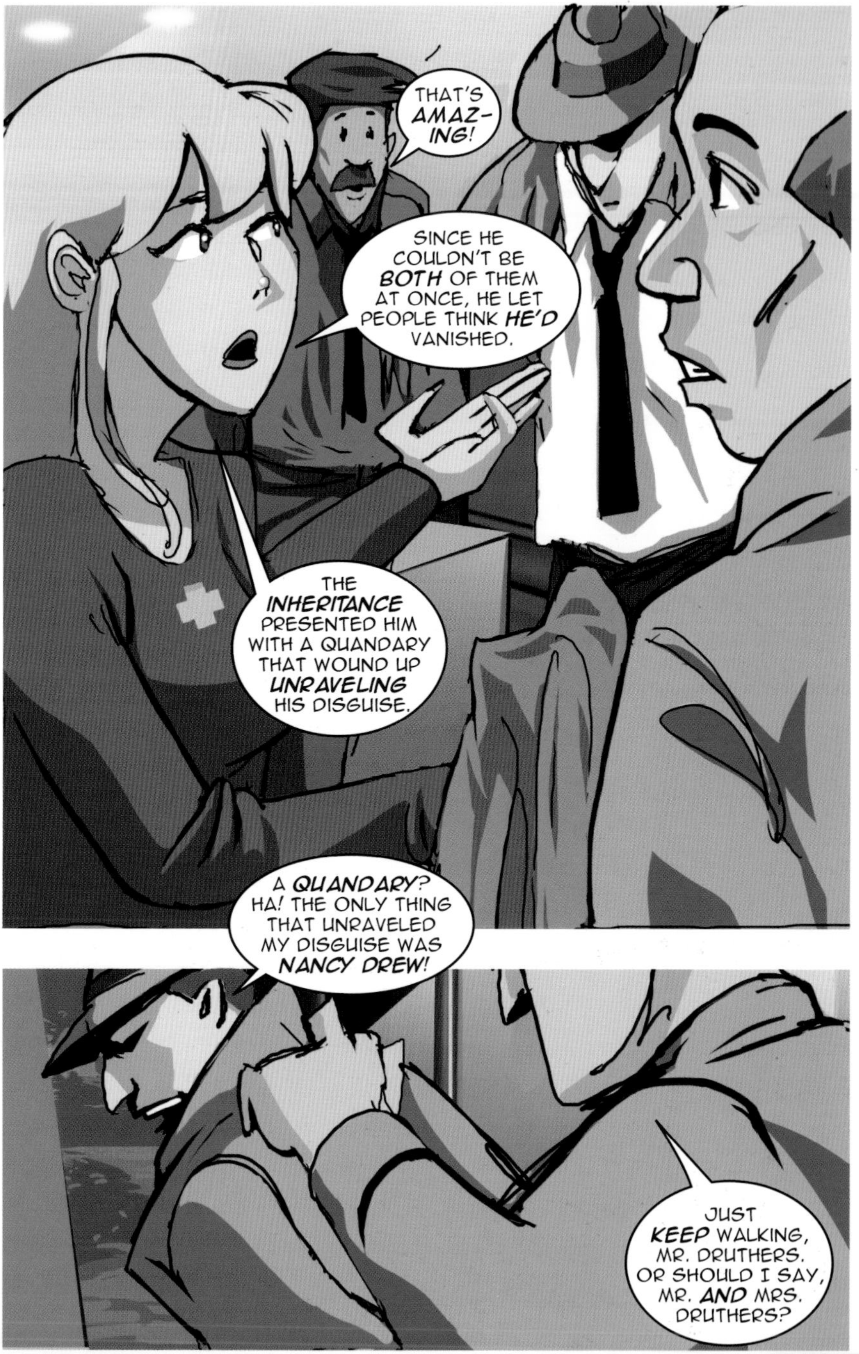
THAT'S AMAZ-ING!
SINCE HE COULDN'T BE BOTH OF THEM AT ONCE, HE LET PEOPLE THINK HE'D VANISHED.
THE INHERITANCE PRESENTED HIM WITH A QUANDARY THAT WOUND UP UNRAVELING HIS DISGUISE.
A QUANDARY? HA! THE ONLY THING THAT UNRAVELED MY DISGUISE WAS NANCY DREW!
JUST KEEP WALKING, MR. DRUTHERS. OR SHOULD I SAY, MR. AND MRS. DRUTHERS?

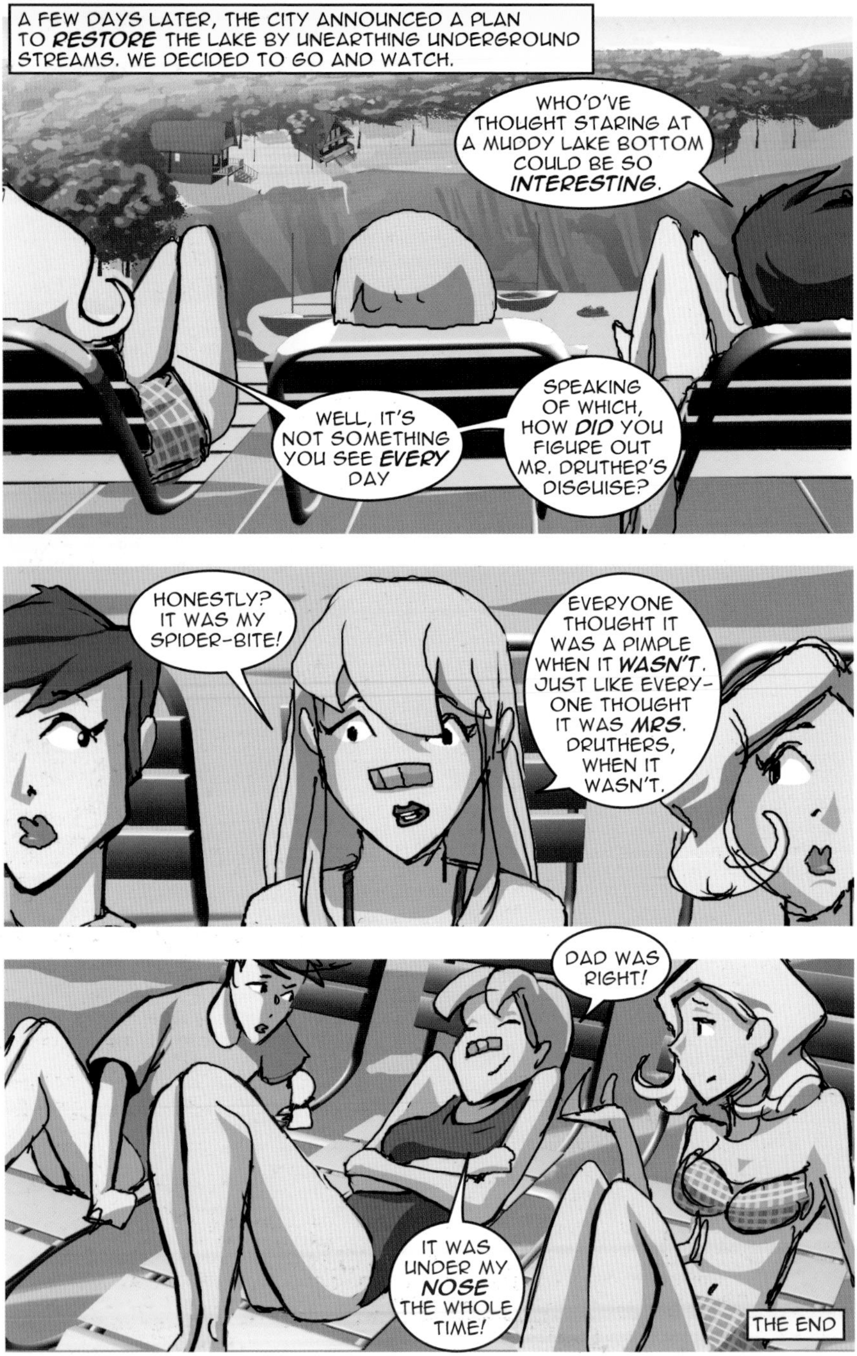
A FEW DAYS LATER, THE CITY ANNOUNCED A PLAN TO RESTORE THE LAKE BY UNEARTHING UNDERGROUND STREAMS. WE DECIDED TO GO AND WATCH.
WHO'D'VE THOUGHT STARING AT A MUDDY LAKE BOTTOM COULD BE SO INTERESTING.
WELL, IT'S NOT SOMETHING YOU SEE EVERY DAY
SPEAKING OF WHICH, HOW DID YOU FIGURE OUT MR. DRUTHER'S DISGUISE?
HONESTLY? IT WAS MY SPIDER-BITE!
EVERYONE THOUGHT IT WAS A PIMPLE WHEN IT WASN'T. JUST LIKE EVERY-ONE THOUGHT IT WAS MRS. DRUTHERS, WHEN IT WASN'T.
DAD WAS RIGHT!
IT WAS UNDER MY NOSE THE WHOLE TIME!
THE END

Special Advance Preview of NANCY DREW Graphic Novel #6 – "Mr. Cheeters Is Missing"

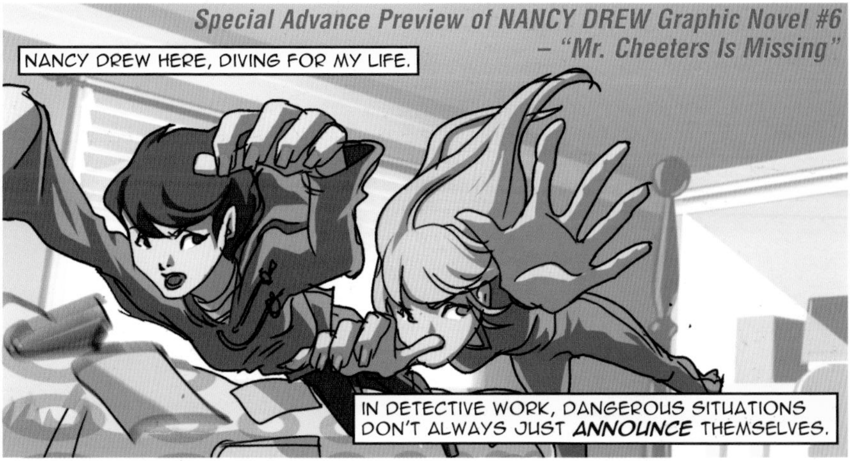
NANCY DREW HERE, DIVING FOR MY LIFE.
IN DETECTIVE WORK, DANGEROUS SITUATIONS DON'T ALWAYS JUST ANNOUNCE THEMSELVES.

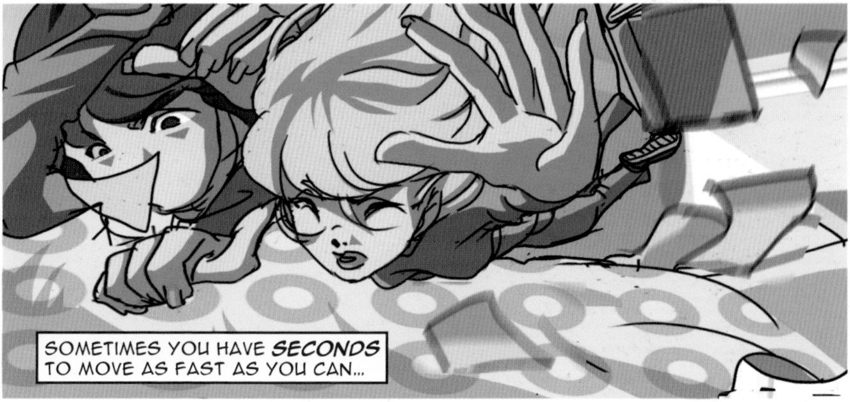
SOMETIMES YOU HAVE SECONDS TO MOVE AS FAST AS YOU CAN...

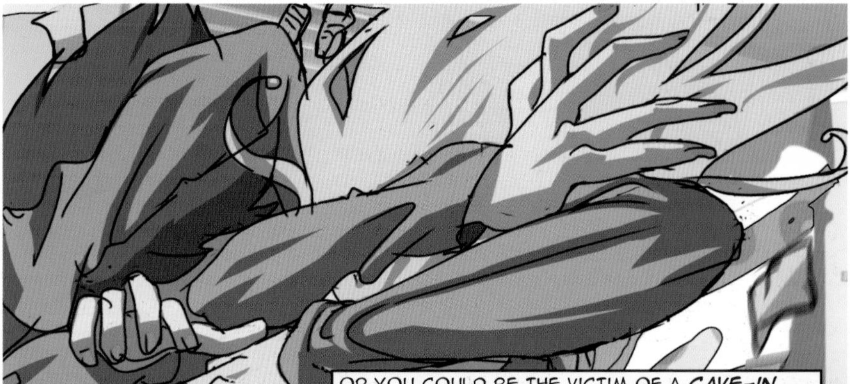
OR YOU COULD BE THE VICTIM OF A CAVE-IN, A TIME BOMB, A HOUSE COLLAPSING, OR EVEN...

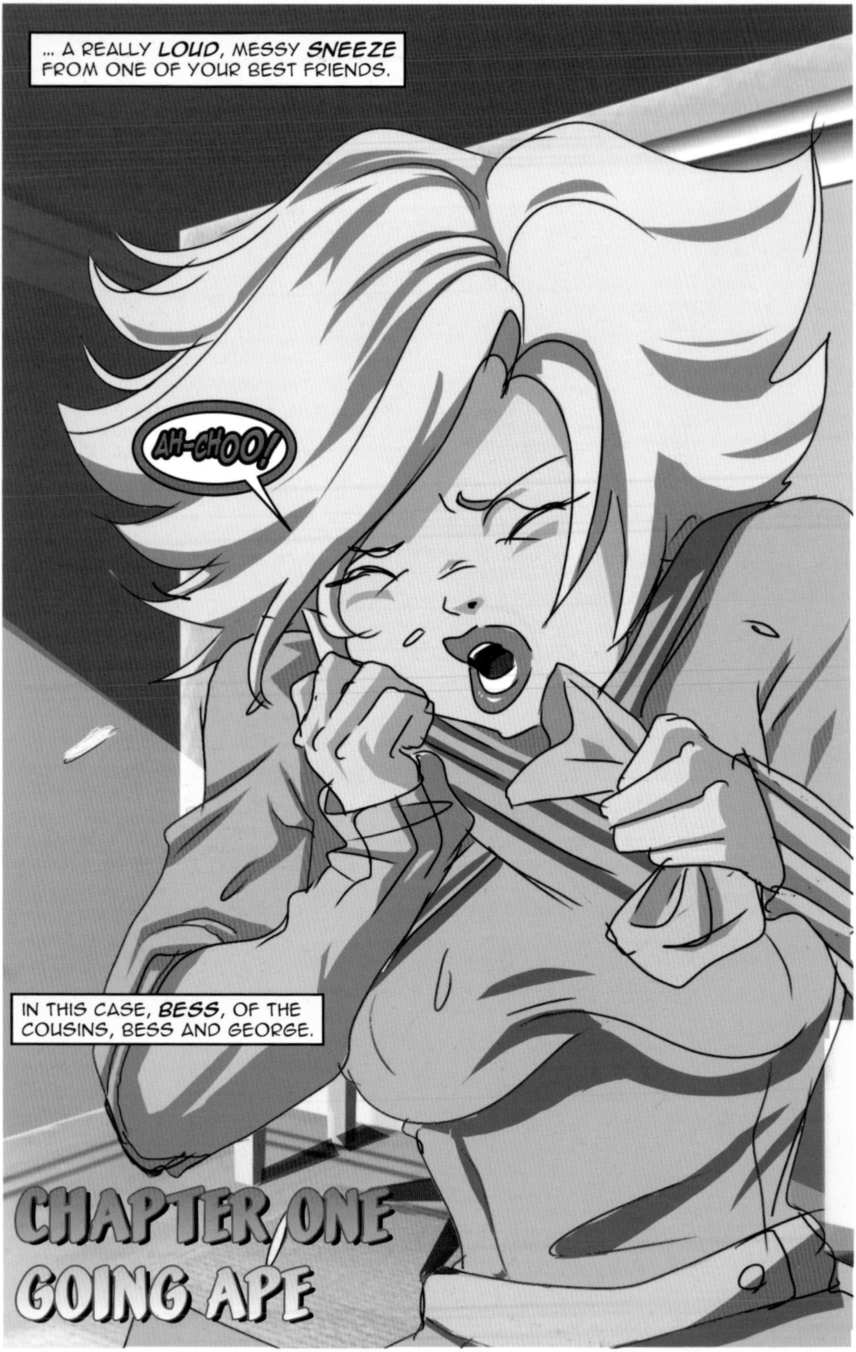
... A REALLY **LOUD**, MESSY **SNEEZE** FROM ONE OF YOUR BEST FRIENDS.
AH-CHOO!
IN THIS CASE, **BESS**, OF THE COUSINS, BESS AND GEORGE.
CHAPTER ONE
GOING APE

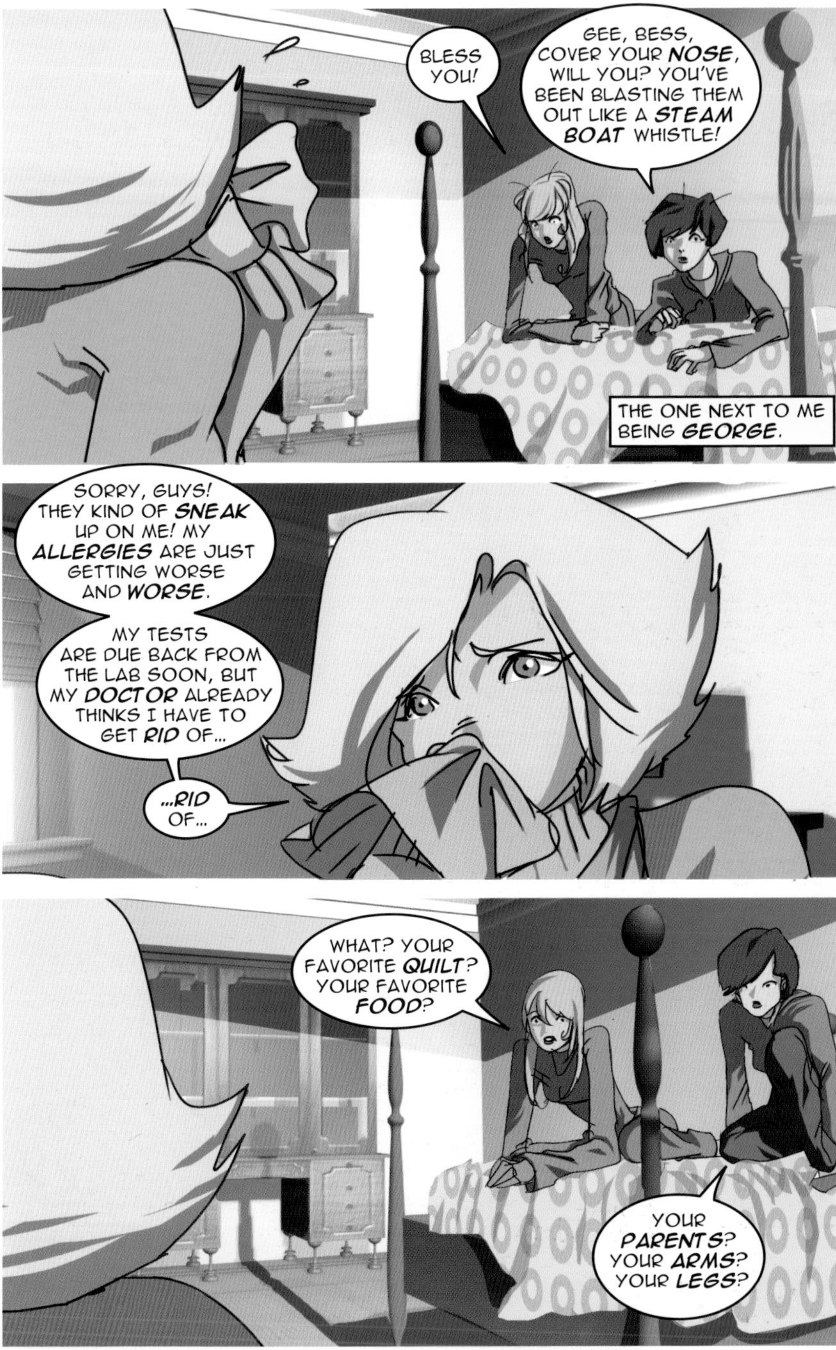
BLESS YOU!
GEE, BESS, COVER YOUR NOSE, WILL YOU? YOU'VE BEEN BLASTING THEM OUT LIKE A STEAM BOAT WHISTLE!
THE ONE NEXT TO ME BEING GEORGE.
SORRY, GUYS! THEY KIND OF SNEAK UP ON ME! MY ALLERGIES ARE JUST GETTING WORSE AND WORSE.
MY TESTS ARE DUE BACK FROM THE LAB SOON, BUT MY DOCTOR ALREADY THINKS I HAVE TO GET RID OF...
...RID OF...
WHAT? YOUR FAVORITE QUILT? YOUR FAVORITE FOOD?
YOUR PARENTS? YOUR ARMS? YOUR LEGS?

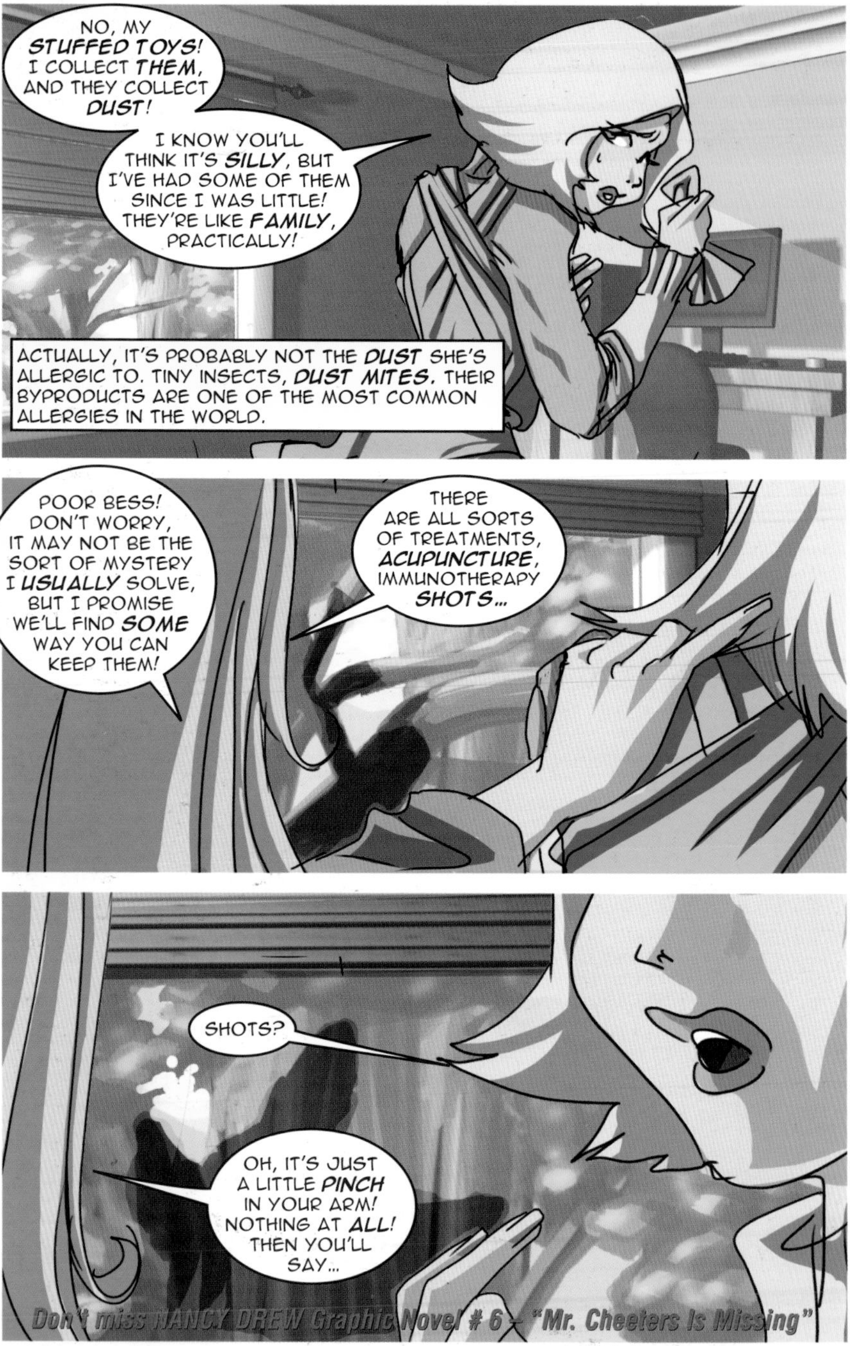
NO, MY STUFFED TOYS! I COLLECT THEM, AND THEY COLLECT DUST!
I KNOW YOU'LL THINK IT'S SILLY, BUT I'VE HAD SOME OF THEM SINCE I WAS LITTLE! THEY'RE LIKE FAMILY, PRACTICALLY!
ACTUALLY, IT'S PROBABLY NOT THE DUST SHE'S ALLERGIC TO. TINY INSECTS, DUST MITES. THEIR BYPRODUCTS ARE ONE OF THE MOST COMMON ALLERGIES IN THE WORLD.
POOR BESS! DON'T WORRY, IT MAY NOT BE THE SORT OF MYSTERY I USUALLY SOLVE, BUT I PROMISE WE'LL FIND SOME WAY YOU CAN KEEP THEM!
THERE ARE ALL SORTS OF TREATMENTS, ACUPUNCTURE, IMMUNOTHERAPY SHOTS...
SHOTS?
OH, IT'S JUST A LITTLE PINCH IN YOUR ARM! NOTHING AT ALL! THEN YOU'LL SAY...
Don't miss NANCY DREW Graphic Novel # 6 – "Mr. Cheeters Is Missing"

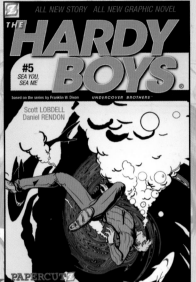

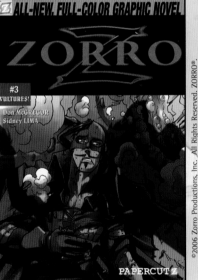